A CLOSED EYE

Anita Brookner

A CLOSED EYE

Anita Brookner has written twelve novels, including *Fraud, Brief Lives, Lewis Percy, Latecomers,* and *The Debut.* Winner of the Booker Prize, she is also an international authority on eighteenth-century painting.

Anita Brookner

A
CLOSED
EYE

VINTAGE CONTEMPORARIES
Vintage Books
A Division of Random House, Inc.
New York · Toronto

First Vintage Contemporaries Edition, January 1993

Library of Congress Cataloging-in-Publication Data
Brookner, Anita.
A closed eye / Anita Brookner. — 1st Vintage contemporaries ed.
p.   cm. — (Vintage contemporaries)
ISBN 0-679-74340-5
I. Title.
[PR6052.R5816C56   1993]
823'.914—dc20   92-56358
CIP

Canadian Cataloguing in Publication Data
Brookner, Anita.
A closed eye
ISBN 0-679-74340-5
I. Title.
PR6052.R5875C5   1993
823'.914   C92-095493-6

Book design by Carole Lowenstein

Author photograph © Jerry Bauer

Manufactured in the United States of America
10 9 8 7 6 5 4 3 2 1

She strikes me as a person who is begging off from full knowledge,—who has struck a truce with painful truth, and is trying awhile the experiment of living with closed eyes.

—HENRY JAMES, *Madame de Mauves*

A CLOSED EYE

1

'Résidence Cécil,
Rue du Château,
La Tour de Peilz (Vaud),
Suisse.

'20 August.

'My dear Lizzie,' (she wrote),

'No doubt you will be surprised to hear from me after all this time, and from such a strange place. Not that it is so very strange: indeed, it is extremely civilized, but you probably think of us still, if you think of us at all, in that house in Wellington Square which you once knew so well, though not perhaps in the happiest of circumstances. However, those days are now to be consigned to the past. I have had a great deal of time since then in which to reflect, and although I have reached no very firm conclusions I do know what courage is needed to see one through a life. You, my dear Lizzie, have always had that sort of courage. I was always impressed by you, even when you were a tiny child. But of course one does not say these things to a child.

'The point of this letter is to ask you whether you would like to spend a little holiday here. I know how hard you work —my own short working life was frivolous in comparison—

and the air of this place would do you so much good. There
are not many distractions for a girl of your age, but if you like
to walk, the countryside is beautiful, and if you like to read,
as I remember you always did, there is an excellent bookshop.
Come at any time; there is snow in the winter, and the
flowers are quite beautiful in the spring. And it is very pretty.
I have grown quite fond of the place. I doubt if I shall ever
go home now.

'You see, we came to Switzerland when my husband's
health began to fail. He had enormous faith in the clinic here;
one of his colleagues had benefited from similar treatment,
swore he was a new man after a month's stay. There was
nothing really wrong with Freddie, but he was old and tired,
and of course his heart was broken. In the first instance we
only came for advice, but the moment he left Professor
Lecoudray's consulting room he said he felt better. He was
not better, but it seemed only decent to help him to maintain
that illusion. His final illness lasted six months; we found it
convenient to take this rather nice flat, which Freddie liked,
on a long lease. We both hated hotels. And there was room
in the flat for Freddie's nurse, Madame Irène. She stayed with
me until he died, and still looks in from time to time. A nice
woman, a good woman. And I have a very charming neighbour, Monsieur Papineau, so I am not at all lonely.'

(Such lies, she thought.)

'Dear Lizzie, I am rather rich. There is no inoffensive way
of saying this, but your holiday would be entirely at my
expense. In addition to getting you away from London, I
should like to spoil you a little. When we last met I thought
you were looking very pale and thin (but you were always
thin, even as a baby), and yet you seemed hardy. You singu-
larly failed to take after your father, and you did not even look
very much like your mother, although of course she was also
fair, much fairer as a girl, when I knew her, than after you

were born. Her hair seemed to darken then; it often happens. She was my dearest friend. My more serious purpose in wanting to see you is to tell you what I remember of her. You were only a child when she died. How long ago it seems! We were dear, dear friends. I still miss her.

'You would be entirely free to come and go as you pleased here. If you wanted to spend an evening at home with me I could tell you about those early days, when your mother and I were girls. It is important that you should think of her as a strong healthy woman, and not as you remember her. You see, I know you a little. I know the shock you had, and I don't want it to have had a permanent effect.

'You are young, and you have your future before you. Dear Lizzie, don't let an impression of sadness dim your love of life, which is too precious to be wasted. I have always felt that you had it in you to be something remarkable, and I should like, if I may, to help you towards whatever you see as your goal.

'So, all I need is a telephone call or a postcard to say when you are coming. I will send your air ticket (Geneva, terribly quick) and await you here with the most eager anticipation. Forgive this long letter: letter-writing is the exile's main occupation. Dear Lizzie, do come soon.

'There is just one thing I ought to say before we meet. One name must never be mentioned. I know that you, who were always so sensitive, will understand.

'With love, as always,

'Your old friend Harriet (Lytton).'

2

SHE ADDRESSED her letter to Miss Elizabeth Peckham, 59 Judd Street Mansions, Judd Street, London WC1, Grande Bretagne, and thought about Lizzie finding it when she returned home in the evening from her job at the Staveley Press, where she worked as a picture researcher. She thought about the flat, which she had visited twice. The first occasion had been entirely memorable; the second, inevitably, less so. She had been oddly anxious about the girl, who seemed so cold, so self-contained. The pretext for that second visit (but was it already four years ago?) was the return of a cardigan, which had somehow found its way to the house in Wellington Square; it had been kept in a carrier bag, until, in the great clearing up that had taken place, she had made her way to Judd Street in the darkening evening, through the rush-hour crowds, in the chance of finding Lizzie at home.

The building, Lizzie's home now, had been gloomy, badly lit, with a black and white tiled floor and a huge caged lift. Once inside the flat she had had an impression of dimness, although lamps were lit, one with its shade turned up to give a better light. Lizzie must have got up from her desk to open the door; on the blotter was an empty carton of low-fat yoghourt. An open volume of Vuillard reproductions lay on a depressing brown sofa. The girl had been polite, as if not really surprised at seeing her, although she could not have been expected. She was always polite, or rather patient, as if waiting to get on with her own thoughts, willing to put up with distractions, but not willing to prolong them. Everyone knew that Lizzie was clever. 'Have you thought of what you want to do later?' Freddie had asked her when she was a silent adolescent. 'I'm going to write,' said the girl unhesitatingly. 'But not straight away, not until I'm old.' 'How old?' Harriet had persisted. 'Forty,' was the answer. Freddie, behind a newspaper, had laughed; he was already over seventy. But Harriet had taken her seriously. 'You will have to travel, I suppose, and have lots of interesting experiences.' 'Oh, no,' Lizzie had said. 'It will all come out of my head.' That was all that she would say. Prudently, she would divulge no more of her plans. In any case she seemed to be guarding her self-imposed designs, was already wedded to austerity and self-management. She gave the impression that no one would understand what she already understood so well herself.

Helpless, and not helped by any normal social noises, Harriet had glanced round the pitiless room, large, cold, dominated by the desk. A very small electric fire remained unlit. Lizzie had been wearing a sweater and jeans: Harriet had supposed that she changed into them when she came home, but in fact Lizzie had worn them to work like everyone else.

'Is there anything you need, Lizzie?' she had asked. 'You see, we are going away for a while. I thought I should let you know.'

'Oh, yes,' said Lizzie politely.

'I don't like to think of you so much on your own. Of course, you have your work, I do see that. And you must have many friends.'

'Friends? Yes, I suppose so. But my work keeps me quite busy.'

'And you are still in touch with Elspeth, of course?'

'I see her sometimes,' said the girl indifferently.

'And your father is still in America? Washington, isn't it?'

'Yes.'

'Well then, dear.' She paused. She had the feeling that Lizzie was waiting for her to leave. 'I hope you are eating properly,' she said. 'Nutrition is so important at your age.'

'I have lunch,' said Lizzie. 'I don't want much in the evening.' She registered politeness, even resignation, but remained standing.

'Then I will let you get on with your work,' said Harriet, as much to let the girl out of an impasse which she had no means of negotiating, as to admit defeat to herself. Perhaps Lizzie was unused to company, she thought. But she had always been reticent.

'Goodbye then, dear. I will be in touch when we return.'

'Goodbye. Thank you for bringing the cardigan.'

'I was always Harriet to you in the old days. Do you remember?'

'Of course,' said Lizzie, turning to the door.

Out in the street Harriet had thought of the peculiar anxiety surrounding the girl, anxiety which she did nothing to disseminate, as if it were her protection, wariness her weapon. Pale, slight, she seemed as childlike now as she had done eight years earlier, when she was fourteen, when the conversation about her future profession had taken place. Harriet supposed that she had forgotten all about it, but this was not the case.

But Lizzie Peckham's decision was intact. Harriet Lytton's visit had not affected her one way or the other, apart from an underlying annoyance, although she rather wished she had got rid of the empty yoghourt carton, and made a resolution to do so in future as soon as she had finished her supper. Otherwise she felt no misgivings about herself, although she was aware that other people found her difficult. This did not upset her. She accepted herself totally.

Harriet, in the street, was thinking along similar lines. I suppose I have become difficult to get along with, she mused. Living so long with my thoughts has made me awkward, unmanageable. I may have been intrusive, asking all those questions. Politeness was her own armour, against the world, but also against what was within herself. She would be grateful, for once, to get home, and once home, to get away. This darkness usually found her standing at the window, looking out on to the dimly lit street, until she turned with a sigh to Freddie and the task of tempting him to eat. Food was always on her mind: another anxiety.

And now, in the Résidence Cécil, when all that could have happened had already happened, she turned again from the window, where, unknown to herself, she stood each evening to catch the last glimpse of animation in the little street, the room behind her warm, bright, empty, waiting for a presence which she herself could not bestow. She thought about dinner, but felt a distaste for the meal she had no wish to eat. I could walk round to the Beau Rivage, she thought, as she so often did. Yet once in the flat she found it difficult to leave— and knew that when the time came she would heat some milk and go to bed. Evenings were very long.

On an impulse she moved to the telephone.

'Joseph? Je vous dérange? Venez boire un verre.'

'En anglais, Harriet, *en anglais.'*

'Your English is perfect, as you know. It is my French that needs improving. You are quite heartless, Joseph.'

She could hear his eager steps on the stairs while she was still tidying her hair. This was quite unnecessary, she knew, for Monsieur Papineau did not find her attractive, although he seemed to delight in her company. They were indeed both past the age of romance: indeed, romance had not been much in evidence in her own life at any time. And Monsieur Papineau—Joseph—was the very antithesis of romance, although his approach to life was comprehensively amorous. Monsieur Papineau, quite simply, loved. A man of serenity, naïve, hopeful, childlike, he relished what the day brought him as only the very innocent can afford to do. His delightful rotundities spoke of the care which he devoted to his diet; Harriet saw him every morning, with his string bag, alert in the entrance, sniffing the air appreciatively, before stepping forth to begin the day's consultations with shopkeepers. Sometimes he devised a treat for himself, lunch in one of the fine restaurants in Geneva, or perhaps a day going round the shops in Lausanne. He was pleasantly wealthy, or at least she supposed he was, and passionately Anglophile. On Saturdays he would go to the station bookstall in Geneva and buy up the English magazines: *Vogue, Country Life, The Economist.* He had been at Oxford, had held a post at the Swiss Embassy in London, but remained, after a lifetime of presumably honourable activity, like a boy, pre-sexual. He dressed floridly, in coloured waistcoats, with a silk handkerchief cascading from his breast pocket. Harriet, from her window in the morning, could see the top of his tartan cap, or the voluminous beret he wore when it was damp.

He had been marvellous when Freddie was ill. *'Allons-y, avançons,'* he had joked, supporting the bent figure as it crept up the stairs. He had had more patience with Freddie than Harriet had had herself, regarded an afternoon spent in Freddie's largely wordless company as a treat in itself, just one of the many that filled his pleasant days. She remained drily grateful to him for his ministrations, yet aware that he could never share her own dark thoughts.

He beamed at her in the open doorway.

'Ah.' She sniffed. *'Monsieur Rochas?'*

'No,' he said happily. *'Gentleman, de Givenchy.'*

Never very expertly shaved—unusual, she thought, in a diplomat, although he was now long retired—he exuded *bonhomie* and waves of scent as he followed her into the salon, rubbing his hands with enjoyment.

'Such an interesting day,' he said, in his faultless English. 'I went through my photographs. All the early albums, you know. Father and I on holiday at Bembridge. We went there every year when I was a boy. Father had the yacht then, of course.'

'Your mother died young, I think you told me?' said Harriet, pouring out the Muscadet. She had heard this story before, many times, but it served as a subject for conversation in this strange place.

'I never knew her,' he said. 'She died when I was a baby. But I have photographs. A beautiful woman. Father never forgot her, never thought of marrying again.'

'And how did you grow up to be so contented? One would think you had had a great deal of love to be so, well, so happy, so satisfied . . . I don't know how to put it. You always strike me as a very fulfilled person.'

'Fulfilled!' He took a handful of peanuts, a couple of which came to rest on his canary-yellow tie. 'I am fulfilled, Harriet! But I owe that entirely to Missy.'

'Of course, Missy,' said Harriet. The beloved governess, with whom he had certainly been in love, as a child, as a boy, perhaps even as a man.

'I cannot remember life without Missy,' he went on. 'She was with me until she died, you know.' As always, at this point in his recital his eyes filled with tears. 'She kept house for me, when I was working.'

'Where did you live?' she asked.

'Hyde Park Gate. A flat, just big enough for the two of us. When she died I came back here: I couldn't have stayed on. In any event I had already retired. There was nothing to keep me.' His face fell into the pouches and folds characteristic of old age. For a moment he looked almost mature.

'So we both ended up in the Résidence Cécil.'

'But you will go home, Harriet! Once you have recovered your spirits. And what shall I do without you?'

She smiled at him. 'I shall have to go back to London at some point, I suppose. The house is still there. But that is what I cannot face—the empty house.'

His face sprang into an energetic grimace of sympathy.

'Ah, yes. The empty house. Without Freddie. I understand.'

She was silent, as always, when this matter arose, not quite knowing how to convey the fact that Freddie's death was the last link in the chain that had once bound her to her own life, that she had in more ways than one outlived him, even before he died, and that she now functioned in ghostly form, as if all the living substance had been withdrawn, and only her strong and obstinate heart, beating away imperviously, held her on this earth.

'Have you no one left?' he ventured.

'Why, yes. My parents are still alive, incredibly enough. I don't know why I say that, but they always strike me as too young to be old. They are in their late seventies now, but still very active. They've always been popular, sociable. They used to love dancing. Well, those days are past, perhaps. They have aged, recently. Since my daughter died,' she said steadily.

There was a silence. *'Ma pauvre amie,'* he said finally, stretching out a mottled hand to her. But she got up, took the bottle, and poured him another glass of wine.

'I do not like the past, Joseph,' she said. 'I am not like you. Nothing in my story appeals to me. And yet, as a girl, I was happy. Happy in a very simple sense. It goes with youth, or it did in my case. Not in yours,' she smiled at him. 'Now that I look back I see a sort of progressive darkening. Paradise lost. And yet it was a very humble paradise. I was a good but silly girl,' she said. 'And I have been a good and excessively foolish woman.'

'You are still young,' he protested.

'Young? I am fifty-three. And I feel very old.'

Her tone frightened him. He did not know how to counter such bleakness, having always to hand the consolation of easy tears. Seeing this, she smiled at him.

'But I haven't told you my news!' she said. 'I may be having a young friend to stay. I have known her since she was a child; she is my goddaughter, or as good as. Her mother always said that I was to be her godmother, but in fact she had so much on her mind that matters got a little confused. But I have always thought of myself as . . . Well, I have tried to be close. Such a talented girl. Perhaps we could come with you on one of your days in Geneva or Lausanne. She may find it dull here; I hadn't thought of that. I shall rely on you, Joseph. You always have such good ideas.'

His face brightened. It usually did, she reflected, plumping up cushions after he had gone. Mention a treat, an outing, a festivity, however modest, and he was a child again. But she wished he would not always talk of the past. The past to him was his golden treasure, all love, all happiness. Fortunate man to possess such capital! In comparison, her own past—she meant the past *before,* the pre-historic past—had been drab but dreamy, the sort of past that someone with no ascertainable history or parentage has, someone in whom the illusions of childhood outwit circumstance. With parents like children, frail, demanding, fearful, restless, as if some pleasure were being withheld from them. Only recently she had begun to think of them as adults, feeling pity for lives so haphazard, feeling gratitude that at last they were happy, that their old age was in some miraculous way their youth restored, that they no longer thought much of her, she who had interrupted their idyll so many years ago, and had more recently dealt them a terrible blow, just when they were beginning to think that life had been merciful with them, that at last—at last—they might make some concession to reality and admit that they were perhaps growing older, not old, not yet, but able in good conscience, and with due deference to their legendary youth, to relax, and with little more than a backward glance, to settle down.

3

UNLIKE Monsieur Papineau, her only friend in this curious aftermath to a life, she could not recall her childhood with anything like the quality of affection which he lavished on the past. And yet she had been quite happy, although always aware that her advent in the lives of her parents had not been entirely welcome. But parents like hers were not destined to become parents, had been too young, too feckless, too irresistible to each other to bestow themselves on a child, particularly the kind of child she had turned out to be, so, as they said when they contemplated her, unlike themselves.

What she knew of those parents she had had to reconstruct later, for they, understandably enough, only spoke of themselves in glowing cinematic terms. She could not, they thought, take in their wonderful romance; they had remained too close, two brave (they thought) people against the world. All their daughter knew was that they had always been good-looking. That was their birthright and their charm. As lovers they were picturesque, notable. She had been brought up on the legend of their beauty, although it was already diminished by the time she knew them. Her mother, Merle, had been a ravishingly pretty girl in the fashion of the time, petulant, provocative. As Merle Harrap she had been trained in pretty ways: singing and dancing lessons, deportment, nothing prac-

tical, for she was expected to marry young. She met Hughie
Blakemore in London, just before Hughie went to Oxford.
Both knew immediately that they were meant for each other,
that Oxford was an interval wished on them by outside forces,
that he would break free in order to spend his time with her.
In any event he was restless, weak-willed, evidently not a
scholar, though handsome, dashing, and conventional in
every other respect. He broke his widowed mother's heart in
leaving at the end of his fourth term in order to live with
Merle, who was then taking dancing and elocution lessons,
prior, as she thought, to a career on the stage. They lived like
birds, on Hughie's allowance, enjoying their youth. They
married, to everyone's relief, soon after, at a scandalously
young age (a fact they exaggerated in later life). Harriet was
born in 1939, by which time Hughie had joined the RAF.
They were so young, so dashing, that Harriet's birth passed
almost unnoticed. Except, 'Oh, Lord,' said Merle, when
shown the baby. 'It may fade as she gets older,' said the nurse,
pulling the shawl a little tighter round the baby's face, where
the red mark appeared so incongruous beneath the wide
innocent eyes. Merle felt for her, as well as love, a kind of
reluctant pity, almost a distaste. She was glad to leave the child
with her nurse and to put on the little black dress, the fur
cape, and the cocktail hat to go off to her young husband,
equally dashing in his air force uniform, with the officer's cap
pushed back from his forehead, and the white silk scarf draped
carelessly round his neck. How they drank! How they
danced! In smoky basements, in hotel ballrooms, very occasionally in the officers' mess when he wanted to show her off.
And she did him proud, with her neat figure and her high
heels, and her red, red lipstick which she renewed frequently,
lifting her eyes provocatively from her mirror to gaze into his.
He adored her, she him, although she was not having as good
a time as she suspected he was. He had the gift, had always had

it. But after she got a job as a mannequin at Marshall and Snelgrove things got a bit brighter. Then there was a bad period when she did not hear from him, and then came the news that his plane had been shot down over Osnabrück and he had been taken prisoner.

When she got him back he was different. The absence in his eyes frightened her; he seemed docile yet distracted. She resolved never to let him out of her sight again. With what she had saved, and his full disability pension and gratuity, she rented a little shop in William Street, filling it with the kind of smart black dresses that she herself liked to wear, and later with the dark greens and navies favoured by what she privately thought of as the old trouts in Pont Street. These splendid women were puzzled by the Labour government and the outbreak of an unspectacular peace. 'We held the fort,' they assured one another, disappointed when no one asked them how they had done it. Hughie sat in the room at the back of the shop, glad to be safe. As time went on he grew more confident, emerging for a chat with the old ladies—he was still very handsome—opening the door, carrying their parcels to the car, making coffee. The arrangement worked, well enough. The flat above the shop was small, which meant that the nurse had to go, and the landlord was somehow shady, lavish with extra clothes coupons, and perpetually mentioning that the rent would have to be reviewed. Merle grew very thin, smart, haggard, brilliant-eyed. Harriet went to school.

There were moments of peace, of unity, of something like sweetness. After school Harriet would sit with Hughie in the room behind the shop and do her homework. Hughie would place before her, with slightly shaking hands, a cup of weak tea, and later, even more tremulously, a doughnut on a cracked plate. He would subside into his chair with a sigh of contentment and address himself to his own tea, but sometimes his hand shook so violently that he could only raise his cup to his lips with a visible effort at control. After this he would wink at Harriet. 'Everything okay, sweetie?' he would ask. His slang dated from before the war. 'Everything tickety-boo?' Yes, she would nod, for she was a stoic in her way. 'Merle means blackbird,' she might say, looking up from her French homework. 'Blackbird, eh?' he would reply. 'To me she's Helen of Troy.' And he would get up and go into the shop, as if unable to be parted from her for another minute. And the old ladies from Pont Street would smile as he put his arm round her waist, although Merle herself was now too tired and too busy for this kind of thing. 'I can get it for you, Mrs Armstrong,' she would be saying. 'I saw the material the last time I went to Maddox Street.' In Maddox Street something mysterious went on once a month and resulted in the exchange of scarce cloth for illegal coupons. Merle gave the material to an outworker, and everyone was precariously satisfied.

It was demanding, it was even hazardous, but they managed. Regularly a car drew up and out stepped their landlord, Mr Latif, a sharp-eyed Lebanese businessman, come to pick up the post-war pieces in the form of derelict property. Those were the days when the Lebanese were rich, active, and influential, a merchant class of infinite resource. 'Hughie! Harriet!' Merle would call, agitation in her voice. They would present a smiling front, coffee and cakes would be brought out, and Mr Latif would lay aside his hat and his coat with the razored lapels and relax a little. Few people welcomed him these days, and he liked the girl, with her eyes flowering candidly above the birthmark. She did not wince when he patted her cheek, seeing no harm, as indeed there was none. He liked her for that perception. She was perhaps young for her age; he liked that too. *'Eh bien, ma petite, comment allez-vous ces jours-ci?'* he would say, in order to see

how she was doing in French. *'Très bien, merci, Monsieur Latif,'*
she would reply. It was all he could get out of her, but all the
same he was quite pleased. He was sorry for her, doing her
lessons at the back of the shop, with only the impotent father
for company, for so he thought of him. It was perhaps pity for
Harriet (or was it for Merle, who accepted his embraces?) that
kept him from raising the rent: the shop did not interest him,
although he had his eye on the flat, which he intended to
repossess. But he was in no hurry, and in his way he was glad
of the welcome they gave him. He thought them doomed,
but hoped that the girl would be all right. At Christmas he
brought her a large box of crystallized fruits. She thanked him
and put them on one side. Hughie's shaking fingers seized on
them with delight. He craved sweet things, as well as sweet
thoughts, sweet words, sweet music. There was not enough
sweetness in the world to satisfy Hughie, who aged only
physically, and that barely at all: his mind retained the ardour
and goodwill he had possessed as a boy. Merle, seeing him
smile with satisfaction as he performed some small task—a
cup to be washed, a parcel to be tied—asked herself whether
she had the strength to maintain this household all on her
own, and then told herself that she not only could but must.

Sometimes it was manageable. The little back room was
warm in winter, when the rain lashed the windows. Merle,
taking a break, would kick off her high-heeled shoes, and
Hughie would massage her feet. Harriet would close her
books and run next door for coconut macaroons. Tea would
be brewed and cigarettes smoked. When she saw her mother
relaxed Harriet would open her book again. They asked
nothing of her, seemed glad of her presence, did not enquire
into her thoughts. It was in many ways a sheltered upbring-
ing, so much so that Harriet had no longing for the outside
world. The shop and the back room, so warm, so peaceful,
and her simple father and her brave mother were company

enough for her. And then there was school, which she also
loved, and the public library. She was quite happy.

She had a friend, whom she worshipped, Tessa Dodd, a cut
above her, indeed a cut above the rest. The Dodds lived in
Cadogan Square. Colonel Dodd, a solid invincible-looking
man, went to Whitehall every day and did something patri-
otic. Mrs Dodd had her own dressmaker and did not patron-
ize 'Merle'. Tessa was tall and fair and commanding, a heroine
to her contemporaries. Harriet would be invited for tea, along
with Pamela Harkness and Mary Grant, whom she also
thought of as her friends, although there was an indefinable
difference. They were kind enough, though the three of them
were occasionally distracted by laughter which left Harriet
puzzled. Skirts would be tried on in Tessa's bedroom after tea,
blouses exchanged. The blouses were unbuttoned at the top,
to judge the effect. 'Tessa, you can't!' Mary would shriek, and
they would collapse. After that, exhausted, and perhaps a little
disgusted, they would kindly include Harriet in their conversation. 'What are you doing tonight, Hattie?' Mary or Pamela
would ask. 'Washing my hair' or 'Reading', she would say,
and be aware of a giggle suppressed. But they were kind, and
she was always asked again.

(Oh, my companions, thought Mrs Lytton, in her exile.
My lost companions.)

Yet of the four of them she was the one to marry first,
although there was little sign of this. She went to a secretarial
school in Oxford Street, where again she was perfectly happy,
happy above all after her day's typing, when she walked home
in the darkening evening, at one with the home-going
crowd. Even at the age of twenty she perceived the beauty of
this, the virtue of doing a day's work and receiving the reward, the legitimate reward, of the lighted streets and the
buses, and the girls—like herself—in their smart cheap
clothes. In the summer she walked through the park and

thought that this was all she needed, or indeed knew, of wider spaces and of fresher air. Tessa she still saw occasionally, but Tessa was busy most evenings, and in the daytime attended a cookery course with Mary and Pamela. But though distracted and high-spirited Tessa was still kind. The others she did not see, nor did she particularly want to, since Pamela had advised her to cover her birthmark—now largely faded, but still visible—with heavy make-up. Harriet overlooked this, but could not quite forget it. 'I must rise above it,' she said to herself in her bedroom that night, after shedding a few tears. 'I must simply live on a higher plane.'

She got a job typing invoices in a bookshop, which she also loved. Again, she was perfectly happy. From the back of one shop to the back of another seemed to her a logical progression, and a satisfactory one. She had no ambition. She still walked home, from Cork Street now, and still perceived the beauty of the procedure. One evening there was a visitor sitting with her father, a man who had been in his squadron and who had thought to look him up. He stood up when Harriet entered, and was introduced as Freddie Lytton. Both Merle and Hugh seemed excited and gratified by his presence, although Mr Lytton appeared taciturn in comparison. To judge from the fine sheen on his hair and his complexion he was wealthy. He seemed contained, thoughtful, a dry laugh merely escaping him from time to time. A man good at keeping his own counsel, making his way. He was with an oil company, he said: his large car stood at the door. Harriet, flushed from the evening air, was grateful to him for making her father laugh. There was a bottle of whisky on the little desk, and next to it the visitor's fine black gloves. He was perhaps forty-five or forty-six, elderly. 'Your father showed me how to make up my bed,' he told her. 'I hadn't a clue.' Merle and Hugh laughed. Harriet joined in politely.

'Can I take you all out to dinner?' he asked.

'No, my dear,' said Merle quickly. 'It's sweet of you, but after a day on my feet I'm whacked. But I'm sure Hattie would love to go.'

She went, again moved by a strange politeness, the quality that stood her in such good stead in the bookshop. He made her drink a glass of wine, and ordered for her. She found him agreeable, if a little uninteresting. But kind, very kind. Encouraged, she talked about her job, about the books she was reading. She was flattered by his attention, reminding herself to make this the main item of her weekly telephone call to Tessa. She was happy as she thought about this, her small contribution to the great game. After paying the bill he said to her, 'I have enjoyed myself. Would you like to do this again?'

'Oh, yes,' she said enthusiastically. 'I should love to.'

He walked her back through the beautiful evening, and rang the bell at the street door beside the shop. Merle appeared looking exhausted, but with a radiant smile, her feet encased in incongruous pink slippers.

'Here she is,' said Mr Lytton. 'Safe and sound.'

'Freddie, you are an angel. Did you thank Freddie, darling? Now we want to see you again. You've done Hughie so much good. And my poor Hattie doesn't get out as much as I'd like her to. Say you'll come again.'

'Oh, I'll come again, now that I've found you,' said Mr Lytton. He raised his hat and kissed Merle on the cheek, then held out his hand to Harriet.

'Goodnight, Harriet. Thank you for a very pleasant evening.' And he melted away into the night, forgetting that his car was still at the door. Five minutes later they heard him drive off.

In the dark hallway at the bottom of the stairs leading up to the flat Merle looked tensely at her daughter, then nodded.

'Go to bed now, darling,' she said. 'I've put one or two

things in your room. A couple of dresses I brought home from Maddox Street. I think it's time you took a bit more care of yourself.'

Harriet heard her parents talking on the other side of the thin bedroom wall for what seemed like a long time. The wine had made her sleepy, and she gave no further thought to her evening. If she thought about it at all on the following day it was in connection with Tessa, for whom she had at last an item of news.

And Tessa was intrigued, as were Mary and Pamela, all gathered together for once at Gunter's on a Saturday afternoon.

'Freddie Lytton?' asked Pamela sharply. 'My father knows him. He's been to our house. He's rich.'

'But if your father knows him he must be pretty old,' said Mary.

'He is. He's ancient. How on earth did you get hold of him, Hattie? He's been married. His wife left him, or something. He's *divorced*.'

'I always blame the man if the wife leaves,' said Tessa, with a worldly air.

'Oh, so do I,' they concurred, but Harriet, bewildered, said, 'I thought he was rather nice.'

All were alerted to the event while she was still in ignorance. New dresses awaited her in her bedroom when she returned from the bookshop, and sometimes Mr Lytton was there, sitting with her father. Harriet thought her mother might be attracted to Mr Lytton, so excited did she seem. In a dress which she privately disliked, Harriet prepared to go out with Mr Lytton, rather reluctantly, as she was tired and a little depressed. She was looking at her face in the mirror when Merle entered her room and stood with her back conspiratorially to the door, her hands spread out on either side of her. There was a smudge of cigarette ash on the bodice of her black dress.

'I hope you know what this is all leading up to, Hattie,' she said.

'Yes,' said Harriet, even more tired and depressed. 'I suppose I do.'

'Well, all I ask is that you do the right thing. Daddy and I aren't getting any younger, you know. We'd like to enjoy life while we still can. I'll soon be fifty, Harriet.'

'So will Freddie,' said Harriet, which was ignored, though registered.

'I can't work for ever,' Merle went on. 'And Latif definitely wants the flat. We can get a good price from him. We want out, darling, don't you see?' She began to cry. 'He's a good man. And he's besotted, although he doesn't show it. And not everyone . . . Although it's faded a lot . . .' She was crying in earnest now, ashamed of herself, bitter with impatience. 'Oh dear,' she sobbed. 'I can't go down like this. I'll have to stay up here. Don't keep him waiting, darling.' She took Harriet in her arms and kissed her, leaving a smear of damp on the girl's cheek. Then she sank down on to the bed, put her head in her hands, and wept.

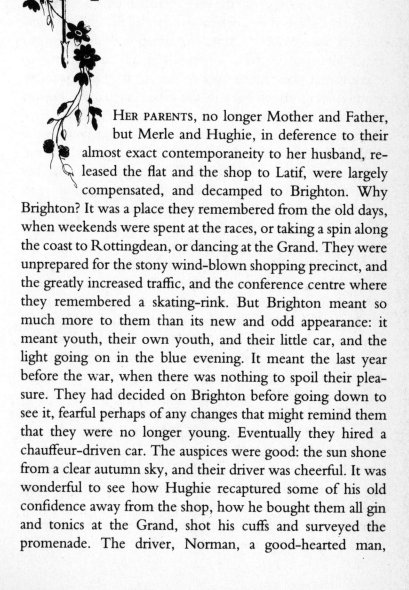

4

HER PARENTS, no longer Mother and Father, but Merle and Hughie, in deference to their almost exact contemporaneity to her husband, released the flat and the shop to Latif, were largely compensated, and decamped to Brighton. Why Brighton? It was a place they remembered from the old days, when weekends were spent at the races, or taking a spin along the coast to Rottingdean, or dancing at the Grand. They were unprepared for the stony wind-blown shopping precinct, and the greatly increased traffic, and the conference centre where they remembered a skating-rink. But Brighton meant so much more to them than its new and odd appearance: it meant youth, their own youth, and their little car, and the light going on in the blue evening. It meant the last year before the war, when there was nothing to spoil their pleasure. They had decided on Brighton before going down to see it, fearful perhaps of any changes that might remind them that they were no longer young. Eventually they hired a chauffeur-driven car. The auspices were good: the sun shone from a clear autumn sky, and their driver was cheerful. It was wonderful to see how Hughie recaptured some of his old confidence away from the shop, how he bought them all gin and tonics at the Grand, shot his cuffs and surveyed the promenade. The driver, Norman, a good-hearted man, guided them through the afternoon, waited for them outside shops, conveyed estate agents to and from properties which they rejected with a moue as old-fashioned.

Finally, just as the light was going, they found the flat, in a new block overlooking the promenade and the now mysterious sea, so placid, so uninteresting under the extinguishing darkness that covered it. Both exclaimed with delight at the dainty kitchen, the two, admittedly small, bathrooms, the balcony, the glass doors. 'We'll take it,' they said simultaneously, were driven back to the office, signed the cheque with the assurance of their new-found solvency, and insisted on vacant possession within the month. They wanted to be in by Christmas, which they dreaded. They dreaded change, and Harriet's leaving, for she was a dear good girl, and her marriage, which might well turn them into grandparents before they were ready, was, although an accomplishment of a sort, still something of a surprise. They knew so few people. But they would join a bridge club, even if it meant their having to play bridge, and they would find a few restaurants, and get themselves known somehow. They usually managed to be on friendly terms with barmen: that at least was what had happened in the old days. And they were both determined to make a go of things, for Harriet had been bound to leave sooner or later. Merle felt sorry for her, knowing that she was too young for her age, knowing that Freddie was probably too old. But what was she to do? It was not as if their way of life cast young men into their daughter's path. And this way she would never have the fear of bringing up a baby and supporting a husband who was an emotional invalid single-handed. This, to Merle, was the best dowry her daughter could possibly have. She was tired, as if the effort of willing it all to happen had been immense, disproportionate. Her heart broke when she thought of the girl on her honeymoon, and of her disappointment. But there was no help for it. Her own marriage, which had begun so rapturously, had ended in disappointment. Privately, she wondered if all women were disappointed, and concluded that this was probably the case but was never admitted. She felt better when she had managed to persuade herself of the truth of this. The prospect of spending money, after the years of careful parsimony, cheered her considerably, and in a while she forgot about Harriet, for the furnishing of the new flat made her feel as if she were the heroine of an adventure, a fresh start, while her daughter, who looked on solemnly and without comment, seemed oddly static, as though the roles were reversed and she were now the adult. Sometimes Merle hid the prices on the articles she now bought so feverishly, as if Harriet might disapprove and order her to return them to the shop.

The flat was to be pale green, Merle decided, *eau-de-Nil,* her favourite colour, and one that dated her, although she was never to know this. Harriet and Freddie were invited down to admire. Harriet knew that she had to reassure them, for the following week they would be gone, and she would be alone in the flat for the last few days before her wedding. Merle and Hughie had already booked themselves into the Ritz for that event, although the prospect did not excite them as much as their vast pale green velvet sofa, with matching armchairs, their ivory silk wall lights, their walnut cocktail cabinet, their glass-topped brass-legged coffee table, and their giant television set. A swirling green carpet led them to the bedroom, which was upholstered in ivory, this time, with a pink *en suite* bathroom. The triple mirror of Merle's dressing-table was already hung with necklaces; her kicked-off mules lay beside a button-backed pink nursing chair, with an ivory and pink cushion to match. Everything was shiny with newness. Merle's hand lovingly stroked her pink and ivory counterpane, a girlhood dream come true. 'And Hughie has a study and his own bathroom further along,' said Merle triumphantly. Harriet felt a twinge of pity when she saw her father's room, with the desk at which he was never to do any work but which she saw was fitted with a blotter and pen tray. 'I can settle down to some reading at last,' he said, incorrigibly cheerful. It was his greatest gift, she thought; his own youth had never decayed, gone sour, deserted him. He was still entire, frozen at the age of immaturity, and curiously unlined, filled with unlived life. 'You can send me some books from that shop of yours,' he said, momentarily forgetting that she was to be married. 'Keep me up to date. And don't worry about us, old girl. We'll have a whale of a time.'

And Harriet hoped that they would, although they had both seemed alarmed, even affronted, at the wedding, as if nothing had prepared them for this separation. Both had wept when she kissed them goodbye, when they realized that their factitious friendship with her husband was now at an end, and that their ways would now part and their meetings be rare. Merle's eyes brimmed and she bit her lip as she remembered moments of intimacy in the room at the back of the shop, the gas fire humming on winter afternoons, and the kettle on the boil for Harriet's tea when she came home from school. Hughie seemed about to beg his new son-in-law to take care of his daughter, but Merle put a stop to that and thrust another glass of champagne into her husband's hand. What was done was done, and, she thought tiredly, it was for the best. Harriet would now have to take her chance along with the rest of the human race, the female half of it, at least. She felt too old to sympathize. All she wanted now was the peace of her new bed, with the sea outside her window, and time to think of herself at last.

Harriet, in her new home in Cornwall Gardens, felt sorry for them, as she knew they felt sorry for her. This was both the depth and the limit of their love for each other. With her husband she was easier than she had ever been with her parents: the words 'Mother' and 'Father' now brought with them a kind of sadness that had to do with their frustrated lives and their pitiful domesticity and the reality behind their still handsome faces. But with Freddie Lytton all was solid, reassuring, prosperous. He was quiet, and pleasant, and she was fond of him in an uncomplicated way. Without the slightest feeling of strangeness she waited on him, served his breakfast in the morning, charmed by the novelty of seeing him respectable in his business suit after his behaviour of the previous night. When he returned in the evening she kissed him, took his briefcase from him, glanced at the *Standard,* then lit the two red candles on the dining-table and waited for him to pour the wine. Without warning, it seemed, she had become a married woman. She shopped and cooked and looked after the flat—his flat—and sometimes she walked through the fallen leaves in the fine afternoons, just sighing a little when the light began to fade and she remembered those homeward journeys of which she would now never be a part. The seasons changed, but nothing else changed. However, she liked her life. She liked Freddie, who was more of a father than her father had ever been. Her marriage seemed to her like a form of honourable retirement, with pleasant amenities to which she had previously had no access: the opera, the ballet. They talked objectively, on interesting topics. Feelings were rarely discussed. Nothing was expected of her except that she be reasonable and decorative. She had no trouble in being either. He, in his silent way, seemed devoted to her. He was an ideal husband.

But he was not an ideal lover. She knew this instinctively, although she was completely inexperienced. His taciturnity, so soothing and reliable in the daytime, vanished at night, when he was ardent, even violent, careless of her, briefly unknowable, occasionally foul-mouthed. Shock, and even a kind of excitement, gave way to distaste, to disappointment, to resignation, as her mild endearments failed to calm his fury. 'Quiet', she heard, and 'Keep still', and then, despite sensations of her own, which she was quite sure were in no way compatible with her husband's volcanic state, she would long for the return to calm and to some degree of respect for the night's integrity. He would subside and say nothing, for which she was grateful. She would not have known how to reply, whether to be gallant or to tell the truth. She lacked the mocking spirit, although some part of her was amused by her husband's doubleness. And in the morning she would bathe and dress and feel quite happy at the prospect of another day. Thus she reckoned that her marriage was a success.

They had friends to dinner, went to Glyndebourne, went abroad. Obediently she forgot her own life and adopted that of her husband. She had always hankered for stability and had always feared pity, the mournful pity she now felt for her parents, and thus found it easy to be her husband's creature, to dress as he liked her to dress, to entertain his business partners and their wives, finally to find herself on equal terms with her former friends, to cross the social gap of which she had scarcely been aware in the innocence of her youth but of which she now measured the significance. Looking back, she saw the pink woolly slippers her mother wore with her black dress at the end of the working day, saw the clutter of dirty cups and crumbed plates on the desk in the room at the back of the shop, heard Mr Latif ask, *'Et comment allez-vous ces jours-ci, ma petite Harriet?'* saw his hand on her mother's arm, saw her mother's eyes warning her to be pleasant. She had no difficulty in preferring to be Mrs Lytton. Freddie was courteous, stable, appreciative. On his fiftieth birthday they had lunch at the Connaught and then went on to an exhibition at the Royal Academy. Afterwards he bought her a silk scarf at Fortnum's, and when she protested, saying, 'But it's your birthday, not mine,' he replied, 'But when it's your birthday you will still be younger than I am. I feel I have to make it up to you.' She hugged his arm, and when they got home she took the champagne from the fridge, and they spent a pleasant evening.

Of his first wife there was no mention. Harriet did not ask about her, thinking the matter of no relevance, and indeed of little interest. He was simply not a man who could ever make her jealous. Despite his attentions to her she did not consider him a sexual being. Faithfulness was simply a natural condition, like breathing.

Of course she dreamed of a lover, but these were real dreams, in her sleep, and they troubled her only on waking, when she sometimes remembered them, and never in the daytime. This lover was faceless, but she knew that he was her own age, and that he both awoke and dispelled the loneliness that she felt in his arms. He made her aware of the strangeness of life, of its intrinsic strangeness, as they embarked together on that journey that only two can share. In her dream she wept and sighed, as if in acknowledgement of her real life and its unimportant compensations. The stranger in her arms knew her every mood, her every movement, felt as ardently and as sadly as she did herself, but took her away with him even as he vanished into the real light, so that on waking she was surprised and alarmed to find the body of her undisturbed husband in her bed. It will never be my bed, she thought, only his. He does not even know me, and he leaves me undiscovered. This is his loss as well as mine. But he knows so little, and is so well satisfied that this is not a regret that he will ever care to be acknowledged. Briefly she felt sorry for him, for his ignorance. She felt slightly superior, more his equal. With an unlived life of her own she felt reality breaking into the illusion with which her husband was content.

On such mornings, when she awoke, she felt a sudden ebbing of warmth and shivered slightly as she drew the curtains, although the spring morning was mild and damp, and the earth emerged from the night as if from a warm sleep of its own. Flat white light fell on buds and rustling birds, and although the cloud cover was low there was little doubt that the same unwavering light would persist until after seven in the evening, until nearly eight, in fact, and that she would no longer need to light the candles on the dining-table. Spending the evening in the flat with Freddie in this indeterminate season oppressed her a little: she felt a childish desire to be out in the streets, to stand by the railings in the park and watch the darkness come down, and see the trees lose their outlines to shadow. She did not quite know how to deal with these intimations of restlessness. Freddie, on his own admission, was too tired to take a walk, regarded walking as a pursuit for those who did not work, did not go into the city with a briefcase and return home smelling of cigars and exhaustion. Harriet deferred to this, but, remembering her own working days, felt wistful. Freddie, who sometimes dozed in the evenings when they were not going out, looked older when asleep; his hair was thinning and turning grey, and he had put on weight. Presumably he had seen his marriage as the one task heroically to be performed before the tiredness of middle age took over. Once married he could relax both his vigilance and his efforts. Harriet saw all this and felt sorry for him. She did not yet feel sorry for herself.

Freddie tolerated her friends, the girls, as he called them, and this toleration she took for encouragement to see them. These meetings all took place on neutral ground—in restaurants or hotel dining-rooms—as if the four of them, individually and collectively, wanted to be free of their new lives, their new homes, and to rediscover the solidarity of their youth, with which they had dealt so carelessly at the time. They were all older, and the threat of dispersal hung over them. Pamela, now a farmer's wife, and living in Northamptonshire, came

to London irregularly, which was always the signal for a
meeting. Harriet was surprised to find her looks so changed:
a reddened complexion, a chipped front tooth, and long
darker hair had replaced the bold blonde head of her earlier
days and also the commanding pronouncements on style
which they had accepted without question. With Pamela's
looks gone authority seemed lost. Mary was due to go to
Hong Kong with her husband who worked for Cable and
Wireless. Of the four of them she had perhaps changed the
least, was still confident, rushed, important. Tessa, after two
painful love affairs, was engaged to a television journalist
called Jack Peckham: no money, she assured them, but never
mind, he was a wonderful lover. Her wedding was to be
simple, at her own request, but her parents had bought them
a flat in Beaufort Street; after that they were on their own.
The marriage seemed ill-starred to Harriet, to whom marriage was a grave affair, but in this setting, among the four of
them, it was not what was new that was important but what
was already over, their common youth, their shared past.
Somehow what each of them had to tell about her new life
failed to arouse the same interest. What they appreciated was
the physical presence of the others, a sudden shared goodwill.
Together they monitored each other's progress towards maturity, towards middle age, or what they thought of as middle
age. When she was with them Harriet felt a girl again, and
when she thought of her present substantial position it was
with the onset of a certain bewilderment. They embraced
ardently on parting, saw Pamela, who was five months pregnant, into a taxi, made Mary promise to write regularly, kissed
and waved, turned and waved again, as if immense distances
were to separate them for ever, as if husbands would now
remove them from the pre-sexual conformity which they felt
to be their right, and as if this were suddenly a matter for
regret. Harriet stood on the pavement outside the Royal

Court Hotel and thought of a desolate telephone call of the evening before. 'He doesn't really want to marry me,' Tessa had said. 'But I'm pregnant and that's all there is to it. And I'm so tired, Hattie. I can't seem to get it right, somehow. Not like you.' Yet none of these reflections had come to light in the course of their lunch together, on the contrary; Tessa had been mordant, sprightly. It was another illustration, Harriet had thought, of the adulteration that had taken place in their original behaviour. None was what she had previously been.

Walking home, at the dead hour of three in the afternoon, she was anxious for the comfort and shelter of the flat, which she saw as both protection and dignity, in much the same terms as she viewed her husband. With him she need feel neither pain nor pity. Sorrow, the sorrow that she had occasionally glimpsed in earlier days, would never come to her from Freddie Lytton. The warmth that she had felt when she was with her friends—the girls, as she now thought of them, shading, perhaps unconsciously, into Freddie's way of thinking—was ebbing away from her, like those dreams whose disappearance left her so strangely chilled. But it was the warmth, she decided, that was illusory, unreliable, something of a snare. The real climate was moderate, even a little cool, and probably for that very reason less conducive to disorder, or distraction. Real life warned one to keep up one's guard, not to be seduced by attachments, certainly not those encountered in dreams. She wondered why she felt so sad. But they had all felt sad, she realized, sad for the very changes to which they were submitting, so difficult is it to leave childhood, and its innocence and courage.

Innocent: but this was an illusion too, she reasoned, as she walked the damp mild streets, with the haze of green in front of her that was the park. I was not so much innocent as undemanding, not knowing how to stake my claim, not even daring to think I had a claim to stake. She thought of the room behind the shop, and her childish father's smile, of her mother's harassment, of her own meekness. She saw this now quite coldly. She also saw the anomaly of her presence at the Dodds' house in Cadogan Square, always dressed in garments which had not sold in the shop and were therefore too old and too inappropriate. She remembered, with a rush of shame, a cherry red frock with a bow at the neck, designed for a matron, one of the Pont Street variety. At least that would never happen again, she thought, glancing down at her beautiful olive tweed suit. They must have been very kind to me, seeing at a glance that I did not fit in. Undoubtedly they were sorry for me, though I never knew it. Yet I became one of their set, even if I was the least important member of it. Pamela and Mary: I doubt if there was a great deal of affection for me there, although I failed to see it at the time. Tessa was always my ideal. And perhaps it suited her to have so disingenuous a friend. The friendship, she now saw, was based on habit, on her own assiduity, but also on something more, as if Harriet's very modesty, her lack of sexual awareness, had ensured that Tessa remained connected to a condition that was not shadowed by calculation. Had they ever discussed men? Or boys, as they were then called? Perhaps it was fortunate that they had lost sight of each other for a while, when she was at secretarial school and the others were doing their cookery course. Her own marriage had reunited them, and then Mary's later the same year. At Pamela's wedding they had made a joke of these reunions, yet each saw the others go with genuine emotion.

And now Tessa. And after that, no doubt, dispersal, for what could keep them all together when partners had to be considered? And they were no longer girls; at thirty Harriet looked back to an infinity of time past. Breaking in on her thought came a sudden feeling of muteness, as if there were no one in whom she could confide, even supposing that she might ever find the words to express what she wanted to say. She was aware of emotions that had never come to the surface. When she withdrew her hand from her glove to find her keys she was surprised to find it trembling. She told herself that these reunions were pointless if they derogated from her present contentment. She told herself that she had no need to keep a watch on Tessa's happiness, that in fact it no longer concerned her. That aching friendship that the four of them had briefly experienced, at the Royal Court Hotel, was to do with the past, with the sense of time slipping away, with the well-known effects of a spring day after a long winter, with different journeys to different homes, with a sense of no longer being fully known. Their bodies now held secrets, were no longer presented to each other for inspection. They had learnt to be silent on certain matters. Even Tessa, on the verge of an exciting marriage which was also perceived as a disaster, and already pregnant, could only joke and boast. After so long, after so many transparent years, they had grown opaque to each other. And this would—must—continue. The dignity of their husbands was at stake. Later, perhaps, when they were much older, they might confess mistakes, regrets. But Harriet saw them all bound in the meantime by certain rules. She herself had reason to be grateful for those rules.

To calm herself she went to the window, and saw directly opposite, across the oblong enclosure of trees and shrubs that was Cornwall Gardens, the mysterious window that was always closed yet always lit up. She had seen the light blazing there at five in the morning and at midnight. Sometimes a figure could be seen moving rapidly across it, as if in agitation. Was it a sickroom, a nursery? Somehow that agitated figure seemed to Harriet like a prisoner, for whom she felt a terrified sympathy. Soon the branches of the trees would thicken with foliage, and she would no longer be able to see clearly. On this particular afternoon, still light, still bright, but very quiet, she could discern no silhouette. Yet the light was already on. Suddenly the figure appeared, as if from nowhere, and took up a position at the window. With a qualm of fear she turned away, for even worse than seeing the stranger was the thought of the stranger seeing her, lonely, at the window, and gazing with longing at a world which was beginning to disclose concealment, estrangement, silence.

5

WHEN Harriet first saw Jack Peckham she put up her hand, instinctively, to shield her face. With no one else had she ever done this. The gesture was symbolic, as if she were hiding more than her face, as if she were hiding herself, for she recognized in him the stranger of her dreams, and in the light of day did not wish to be found. The four of them were in a restaurant, a week before Tessa's wedding. Freddie had grumbled at the idea of this dinner, which, he thought, had nothing to do with him, but Harriet had insisted on this being their treat, and the most graceful way to show the recalcitrant Peckham that there were witnesses to his dubious entrance into Tessa's life, and as if to warn him against a too precipitate departure from it. Theirs was apparently already a tired arrangement: he would stay with Tessa until the baby was born, and then they would separate. He had it in mind to be a free man within a couple of years.

'I'll never divorce him, never,' Tessa had said to Harriet in the Ladies' Room. 'Anyway, he might as well be married to me as to anyone else. You'll see what he's like. He'll never settle down until somebody makes him. And when he sees the baby . . .'

Harriet, apart from noticing the antagonism in Tessa's voice, and understanding it, knew that she was wrong, that

Jack Peckham was unlikely to be seduced by a baby, or by
a simulacrum of marriage, or even by a woman's longing for
him, because he was a prodigious man who was made for
adventure in the wider world, and whom the same four walls,
however welcoming, would irritate beyond endurance. He
was already irritated by having to dine with this friend of
Tessa's and her pompous husband, a man of the kind who
normally made him utter a short bark of laughter. He seemed
to create annoyance wherever he went and to be indifferent
to it. He had arrived late, wearing jeans and a leather jacket:
light caught the very fine reddish stubble on his jaw, and his
longish hair was untidy. Harriet became aware simultaneously
of her husband's disapproval and of that same husband's cos-
tive navy blue suit and striped tie, his sparse hair, and the
cologne which he used and which she now realized she had
never liked. She switched her attention as best she could to
Tessa, who had coloured hectically at Jack Peckham's arrival
and had caught at his hand, which was unresponsive.

'Too bad of you to be so late, darling,' she had said, in a
tone which attempted to convey that they had been happily
married for years.

'I'm afraid I shall have to leave rather early,' was his reply.
'I have to go back to the office.'

'Then we had better order now,' said Freddie, who seemed
to find Peckham's presence displeasing. 'Will you leave the
wine to me?'

'Delighted,' said Jack Peckham, sitting sideways to the
table. 'Tessa mentioned that you were in the oil business. Can
you fill me in on Riyadh? I have to go there in a few weeks.'

It was then that Harriet made a sign to Tessa to join her in
the Ladies'; it seemed to her urgent to find out more about
this strange alliance which had previously seemed to require
from her nothing but sympathy.

'He is very handsome,' she said moderately, while combing

her hair. In the mirror she noticed, with a feeling of instant rejection, the white crêpe de Chine shirt, the black skirt, and the pearl stud earrings which she usually wore on such occasions. She felt she never wanted to see them again.

'I hope I'm going to be able to manage this,' said Tessa. 'I usually feel sick in the evenings.'

'I'm afraid Freddie is already a little put out,' Harriet observed. 'This is not going to be easy. Yes,' she added, after a moment in which both scrupulously washed their hands, 'he is marvellous to look at. He will break your heart, you know.'

'He already has. He was bound to. I adore him. I hate him too.'

Both silently acknowledged the rightness of this last remark. Yes, thought Harriet, as they turned to go, you hate him because you will never master him. He will leave you and you will wait for him, and maybe he will come back but too late, and you will not look as he remembered you in the brief moments when he ever thought about you. I should be the same. No, I should be even more abject; I should be contemptible. I should wait for ever, so that my life would resemble a long widowhood, and I should still be proud to have captured—for however fleeting a moment, a second, even—such a man's attention.

They went back to the crowded restaurant to find Freddie discoursing quite amiably to Jack Peckham, who was taking notes. So his time was not entirely wasted, thought Harriet meekly. Throughout the meal he continued to sit sideways to the table, as if he had no intention of staying. He ate decisively, economically, staring at his plate for a few seconds before making a strategic incision, then laying aside his knife as if of no further use to him. She studied him covertly, under her eyelashes. Although large he was very graceful. He was, she decided, the villainous hero of romantic fiction, the cruel lover who breaks hearts and thrills women, so that they look with disdain on the humbler, more available variety of men

for ever after. Thus did the virtuous Jane Eyre spurn St John
Rivers, who would have made her a much better husband
than Mr Rochester. Mr Rochester, she thought, has a lot to
answer for, both in the book and in real life, where his legend
lingers on. Only when he was blind and impotent did Charlotte Brontë let Jane have her way with him, and what kind
of a victory was that? To master such a man demands extraordinary resources, of which undoubtedly the most effective is
indifference. Jack Peckham had the unforgivably memorable
looks which provoke a certain respect, from men as well as
from women. Tall, big-boned, and of a reddish fairness, he
lowered his head as if bored with admiring glances, and was
taciturn, even rude, for the same reason. His extraordinary
looks and his abrupt manners gave no clue to his character,
but then his character would always be of less interest than his
appearance, she thought, and so thinking, had no feeling of
strangeness but rather one of familiarity.

Of course, he was not made for a conventional marriage,
particularly of the kind which Tessa envisaged: her jokey
coyness must make him grit his teeth with fury. He would
have to be greatly diminished, like Mr Rochester, to allow a
woman like Tessa any access, and then no doubt a woman
like Tessa would ignore him, for conventional women like
Tessa also had their cruelties. As it was, his very refusal, his
obvious reluctance, had conferred on Tessa a certain depth,
even a foreshadowing of tragedy, which did not become her.
The very incongruity of Tessa's passion and her well-
brought-up obstinacy made Harriet uncomfortable. She was
aware of tension, a tension which was in some perverse fashion attractive. Pity would come later, for pity was what she
was supposed to feel, the solidarity of women in such a
predicament. But the time at her disposal was too precious.
For this hour it was almost permitted—and at the same time
it was even a necessity—to contemplate Jack.

Feeling a pulse beginning to beat in her throat she laid

down her fork, and took a sip of wine. She found herself looking at his hands. Instinctively he raised his head; his gaze was quite dispassionate. It was then that she put up her hand to her face.

He is only the same as other men, she admonished herself, remembering her husband in the dark and his clumsy hands. Why should it be different? Yet she noted that her thoughts had immediately turned to the act itself, as if any other context were irrelevant—she, who out of fastidiousness, out of shame, even, would never allow herself to speculate on anyone else's sexual activities, and who could hardly bear to think about her own. But this was a man with whom she would never want to walk or talk, or pass agreeable but unconsidered time: she would want to lead him straight away to a bed, to a secret room, and the odd thing was that in her imagining it was she who led the way, while he, prodigious though he might be, merely followed her. It took no further imagination to see them naked, as if all this were pre-ordained, as if her present life were a superimposition of no importance, which an expert hand had cleanly removed.

While thinking these thoughts she felt taller, stronger, more armoured against the world than she had ever felt before. She looked at her husband perplexedly, as if he were someone she barely remembered, saw his speckled hand pour the last of the wine into Jack's glass. He was captivated too, she saw: his initial defensiveness had already dissolved into a kind of admiration, as if the stranger's grace and force, his careless presence, his indifference, even, exacted their own tribute. So must Freddie have been at school, thought Harriet, clumsy even then, and flattered by the mere existence of beauty. He is such a decent man, she told herself, and he must never know what I feel at this moment, what I felt when Jack Peckham looked up and caught my eye, what I have been feeling ever since he came into the room. She saw Tessa trying to suppress an ominous hiccough, laid her hand on Freddie's arm, and said, 'Dear, it's getting late. Shall we make a move?' and, turning to the others, said, 'We are so looking forward to the wedding.' (Indeed, she was anxious to see what Jack Peckham would look like in a formal suit. She was excited by the idea of his being momentarily subdued.) 'Tessa, shall I come over to the flat tomorrow and give you a hand?' She did not much care that her wishes and her remarks were dominating the proceedings. She did not at that moment feel guilty that she had eclipsed her friend, who admittedly was not looking her best, nor was she much impressed that their roles seemed to be reversed. Childhood now seemed far off, irrelevant, discarded. Now, for the first time, she had passed into a different phase of being.

Later that night cold realization came to her and she felt terrible. Better that she should remain in lifelong ignorance than yield to insights so destructive of her real life, her real husband, who now seemed to her to be definitely altered by her recent perceptions. He was not young for his age: he would get older, and his hands would get clumsier. And she would never know anything other than this. For her imaginings were not to be borne, not to be tolerated, as if they were dangerous. And they were, exceedingly dangerous; they were a danger to order. She saw that the power of Jack Peckham was to spread this grand disorder into other lives, not seeing, or not caring, that although disorder was his natural climate it might not be so for those with whom he came into contact. Already Tessa was damaged by it, had, like any girl victim in a melodrama, succumbed, and was diminished, never again to enjoy freedom. She had looked frail, mournful, behind that façade of defiant high spirits which so annoyed Freddie. Part of Harriet's anguish originated in the knowledge that she must henceforth support Tessa, and Tessa's interests, and that Tessa's interests were not those of Jack Peckham, were in fact diametrically opposed to them. Here was her chance to be the friend she had always longed to be, loyal and good and faithful unto death, like those valiant friendships she had read about in her fairy books. An immense sense of the fragility of human destiny enveloped her. It occurred to her briefly that she might choose another path. In her mind she chose it, then, blushing, put it away from her for ever.

The following day she telephoned Tessa at Cadogan Square, where she seemed to spend most of her time. 'Will you be at the flat at about four? Could I come for a cup of tea? I'll bring a cake. Line up something useful for me to do.' A pause. 'Longing to see you.' And by then it was true.

'Freddie tells me that Jack is going to Riyadh,' she said, on that afternoon, picking her way through a jumble of boxes in the hallway of the flat in Beaufort Street. She noticed uncurtained dusty windows in a room at the far end of a cluttered corridor. The flat, what she could see of it, was large but empty of all the necessities of life. The arrangements had aborted, or had always been makeshift. She put her box of cakes down on a packing case, and followed Tessa into what she supposed would be the drawing-room. Abundant light appeared balked by the coating of grime which seemed to press in from outside; dust swirled in sharply defined cones of sunlight which spread briefly along the floor and died.

'Yes, well, he's a journalist, he's got to go where the news is. I don't mind. I knew all this when I met him. To tell the truth, I'm quite glad he's not here while I'm being sick all the time. I'm not at my best.'

'Where is he?' asked Harriet.

'He's got a flat in Judd Street. He's usually there.'

'He'll make you unhappy,' Harriet said abruptly. 'He may not be good for you. You may be going into something that is not necessarily in your best interest. Will you ever feel comfortable with him? Relaxed, like couples are supposed to feel?' None of this is what I meant to say, she thought. I meant to say, he will destroy you. Or rather that you will destroy yourself for him. Already you are less than you once were, when you were my friend, and I looked up to you. I hate this.

Tessa stared at her. 'What's come over you? Whatever made you say all that?'

'I'm sorry. I don't know why I said those things. I just had a sort of feeling that you were doing the wrong thing.'

They were both silent. Tessa, sitting on one of the two dining-room chairs, which were all that the room contained, attempted unsuccessfully, haplessly, to screw together the two halves of an electric plug.

'Why did you say all that?' she asked eventually. 'It's not like you. You were always so, well, pleasant. My mother always said you had nice manners. Nicer than mine, was what she meant. I got a bit sick of it, I can tell you.'

'I just don't think he'll make you happy,' repeated Harriet, flushing with embarrassment and shame.

'Do you know what it sounded like? It sounded as if you were jealous.'

'Jealous?' said Harriet, horrified.

'Well, envious, then. Because he's young, good-looking. Because he's the kind of man women dream of, the kind of man women like you dream of, Harriet. I can see it in your face. Because you ended up with Freddie. Perhaps even because you can't have children, at least you don't seem able to. Sorry to say all this, but you did rather ask for it. Is it because Freddie's too old? Well, you knew that when you married him.' She relented when she saw Harriet's bent head. 'I don't blame you for being envious,' she said. 'I'd be the same in your place.'

'I do envy you a little,' said Harriet, clenching her shaking hands and praying for the moment to pass. 'It's the baby, you

see. I do love babies, always have done. But it would disturb
Freddie to have one in the flat. Otherwise I'm perfectly
happy.' After that she did not dare to mention Jack Peckham's
name again.

Tessa pushed back untidy fair hair, got up with an effort.
'Well, I'll expect you to be godmother; you can see the
baby as often as you like.'

This, Harriet reflected, had been exactly the tenor of her
friendship in the old days, gracious, graceful, with an aftertaste
of protection. Or was it patronage? Yet she was lovable, and
Harriet felt love for her even now, in this chastening moment. But she also felt acute sadness, as if the innocent part of
their friendship had been supplanted by something more
watchful. I must be circumspect, she thought; even more
important, I must grow up. She saw in Tessa's tired face a
vulnerability that had not been there before. She felt no
resentment, felt indeed a weary tenderness. Out loud, she
said, with a certain dignity, 'You must let me help in any way
I can.'

The moment passed; faces had been saved; the truth, on
both sides, contained, if not entirely suppressed. Harriet,
walking home, knew that an alteration, however slight, had
taken place, felt a coldness. Freddie is my only friend, she
thought. He is my husband. I should talk to him more. I
should ring my parents. But they seemed to have no need of
her any more, and she had little of interest to tell them. They
found her dull. They had made a life for themselves that
excluded her, had handed her on gratefully to her husband,
with whom they were on friendly but increasingly absent-
minded terms, as if he were someone they had once known,
as perhaps he was. They seemed to be out a lot, particularly
in the evenings. They were on good terms with a couple of
neighbours, whom they met for drinks on a more or less daily,
or rather, nightly, basis. It was natural to them to frequent the

bars of the bigger hotels: spruced and polished, they could put
the day behind them, able at last to sparkle and laugh, and
conscious, as before, that they were appreciated for their
looks and their easy-going ways. When Harriet had last telephoned they had referred to a host of people whom she could
not place, had spoken of restaurants, had indeed expressed
concern that they might be late for some function or other,
a dinner dance, she thought they had said. She imagined the
flat as full of smoke and scent, ashtrays repeatedly emptied,
damp rings on the glass of the coffee table. No plans were
made for a visit to Cornwall Gardens, no invitations to Brighton forthcoming. In the background she could hear music,
pop music. They affected a jokiness which in them was more
than affectation. It was as if they were on leave from the war,
and their spirits were artificially high, with the added bonus
that this time there was no danger to contend with. They
seemed perfectly happy. When she had last seen them they
had impressed her as being younger, younger than she felt
herself to be.

Freddie, on the other hand, seemed old. He had taken to
addressing her as 'old girl', as if to minimize the difference in
their ages. On the evening of her conversation with Tessa he
had come home tired and exasperated.

'That dinner last night was the last straw,' he said. 'I'm not
too keen on that friend of yours, if you really want to know.
And the duck was tough. I had indigestion all night.'

'Well, it's only a light meal this evening,' she replied.
'Roast chicken.'

'Very little for me, then.' He loosened his tie. 'I think I'll
have my bath now. And then an early night. There's nothing
on television; I've looked. You seem a bit tired yourself. Pale.
All right, are you?'

'And what did you think of Jack?' she asked, after a largely
silent dinner, as they were peeling their pears.

He smiled, reluctantly. 'Amusing fellow; I rather took to him. He'll ditch her, of course. She's forcing his hand.'

'But what could she do? With the baby coming, I mean.'

'She should have thought of that earlier. That's what got on my nerves, the pretence. Her pretence. Anyone could see he was fed up to the back teeth.'

'You're very hard on her. Women want to get married, you know.' And they get restless, too, she thought, sometimes even when they are married.

'Well, don't get too involved. There'll be trouble there, and I don't want you running round every five minutes.'

She had no desire to displease him. He was her protection, her support, her very respectability. If she was beginning to see him more objectively it was because the day had brought disaffection. She knew that she did not want to be the sort of dignified but essentially downtrodden woman who dotes on other women's children and secretly yearns for their husbands, never letting a complaint pass her lips. Pitiable! Yet to be the wife of a man who saw her merely as a restful presence and a compliant body was equally pitiable. It was pitiable to be discontented when one was in good health and had so little to sadden one. And yet she had never felt so bereft, as if her presence in other lives were entirely illusory, as if she herself were a kind of facsimile, pleasant but inauthentic. Before she got too old she must wrest some part of her life for herself, or she would fade, vanish, before anyone had noticed her disappearance.

When she emerged from the bathroom Freddie was already in bed and dozing, his reading glasses still on, his book face-downward on the sheet. She looked at him steadily, and then went to the dressing-table to brush her hair. As she brushed she felt the onset of a certain useless energy, so that she brushed on, past her usual hundred strokes. She had fine thick hair, almost black; it curled and rustled around her head with electricity. Finally she turned from the dressing-table, went across to the bed, removed Freddie's book and glasses, careless of whether she woke him or not. Later, she thought that must have been the night her daughter was conceived, for after that her husband seemed to her less familiar, less impressive, less important, as if he had come to the end of any useful function he might have had, and might now be perceived as an old acquaintance, sometimes a stranger, sometimes still a friend.

6

THERE FOLLOWED weeks, months even, of a
discreet excitement. Life, formerly an affair of
settled and sedate order, became delightful. Activity, once decreed for her by others, was for a time
her own prerogative, and feelings, no longer the
residue of others' anxieties and expectations, flowered into an
energizing accompaniment to her days. She felt strong and
calm, calm enough to deal with Freddie's appalled realization
that he was to become a father, wily enough to praise him for
something which she regarded entirely as her own affair. She
invited his friends to dinner, watched him grow flustered and
finally proud under their ironic congratulations. 'But have
you room here?' one of them thought to ask. 'No,' she said,
across the table and in front of witnesses. 'We shall have to
look for a house.' In fact she had found one, or rather had seen
a For Sale board outside a house in Wellington Square when
out on one of her afternoon walks. As soon as she saw it she
knew that she must have it, that she would not bother looking
for anything else. It was too big, but she thought that the
basement could be made into a flat for a nanny or housekeeper, while the top floor could be turned over to the child,
when it grew up and craved independence. That way there
would be no separation. The house was in good order, had
only just been vacated. She would even keep the long flow-

ered damask curtains: the walls could be plain white, the
carpets pale blue, with Freddie's precious rugs relegated to a
room which she designated vaguely as his.

He raised a few objections, but she made light of them. 'I
am not made of money, you know,' he protested. 'We spend
nothing,' she countered. 'And I have never liked this flat.'
Indeed she was only just beginning to realize how much she
disliked it. It seemed to her elderly, the home of an elderly
person, and she had no wish to be that person. She was
thirty-two and had never felt so young in her life. And she
discovered that she had found an appropriate attitude towards
her husband: a tender but detached amusement. A dissocia-
tion had taken place which had essentially freed her from the
past.

It no longer bothered her that Freddie looked unsightly in
his sleep, or that his step was heavier than her own. She felt
physically in a world apart, not only from Freddie but from
everybody else, unnaturally well, flushed with healthy blood,
and despite her barely perceptible new weight, light, impalpable. She was tireless as she walked all afternoon, round the
silent squares and terraces, no longer gazing wistfully at the
park but on smiling terms with all inhabited spaces. In her
inner contentment she became almost wordless, greeting
Freddie in the evenings with smiles and murmured phrases,
sometimes laying a hand gratefully on his own. She saw that
he was disarmed, finally, not by the prospect of the child but
by her own happiness. He took to settling her in her chair, as
if she were very tired, very frail, whereas in truth she could
have got up, gone out into the moonlight and walked, she
felt, until the small hours. 'Don't overdo it,' he would say, as
she got up to put on a kettle for tea, and 'All right, old thing?'
searchingly, as he departed for the day. She saw him go with
relief, although she, in her turn, became anxious for him in
the evening. For this reason alone—the sudden pang of sepa-

ration after hours of quietude, the sense of having moved away too far from what was familiar to her—she was at the window to look for him, at the door to greet him. He was bemused, attracted again, indulgent. They got on very well.

But she knew that she was in some way divorced from him, and dated this from the moment her hand had flown up to shield her face from Jack Peckham. There was no disloyalty in her thoughts, simply an acknowledgement that something long dormant had come to life in that instant. She saw this as secret knowledge, devoid of intention: she was not a woman who knew how to pursue her own satisfaction, particularly at the expense of someone else. She was unaware of any skills she might possess, but knew that should they ever be wanted they would be adequate to the task. She looked in the glass and saw a pleasant face, saw the red stain on the jawbone: she accepted herself, mark and all. Never again would she attempt to hide herself. All this was of very great interest to her, as if she were coming to life after a long sleep, or being allowed her freedom after long claustration. No friendship suffered, rather the contrary. Goodwill suffused her. She thought of it as the elixir of life, which she had found at last, not knowing that it had been lacking.

In this manner she was able to call on Tessa most afternoons, in the course of her long walk, or on her way to see the house. She had never been so fond of Tessa as she was at this time: it was delightful to have steered this long course from girlhood to pregnancy, to share symptoms, remedies, advice. The sheer sexlessness of these afternoons, passed in the dusty sunlight of Tessa's still half-furnished flat, enchanted her, for it seemed as if they were very young again, in the schoolroom, before growing up had taken place. Tessa was not enjoying her pregnancy, complained of permanent nausea, of fatigue, of lack of energy. She was grateful for Harriet's visits, grateful for her new and apparently immovable confidence, would allow her to make the tea and unwrap and slice a cake, while she sat brooding. They both ate voluptuously, proud of their appetites. In this too they regressed slightly.

They discussed the move to Wellington Square, which would lessen the physical distance between them, making Harriet's afternoon walk shorter, for she did not see herself ever breaking this agreeable habit.

'Simplicity itself,' she replied to Tessa's questions. 'I'd have done it before if I'd known how easy it would be. Luckily the place has just been decorated; I shan't change anything at first. It's only a question of packing up and unpacking. I've told Freddie to go off to work and forget all about it, just to come home to a different address. We can eat out until I'm straight. Have you written down that new telephone number?'

'You seem happy,' said Tessa curiously. 'Are you happy?'

'I am now,' she replied, with evident truth. 'I may not have been before, but I am now.'

There was silence while they drank their tea.

'You're lucky,' said Tessa, in her new fretful voice. 'I wish I could say the same. I don't want this baby, poor little wretch. Look at this place! It'll never be finished. I don't even like it. I'd far rather be sharing with those girls again in Redcliffe Square. For two pins I'd put it on the market and go back to my parents. I never realized how lonely I'd be. I've never been lonely before.'

'Where is Jack?' asked Harriet finally.

'In the Middle East somewhere. I occasionally see him on the television news—I don't know where he is at this precise moment.' She laughed mournfully, got up and moved to the window, her hands easing her back, as if she were a middle-aged woman. Her body took the full force of the blazing sun and darkened the room.

'But he'll be back before the baby . . . ?'

'Oh, I dare say. But he won't stay long. He hates this flat, goes on at me for not getting it together. But I don't like it either; I just put up with it. Not he. Very fussy is Jack, very keen on his comforts. He'd rather go back to his place and ring up some old girl friends to come and feel sorry for him. It's not going to work out, Hattie, I can't kid myself. Not that I'd ever admit it to him. He's my husband, whether he likes it or not. Though it's probably not, I have to admit.'

'You were always brave,' Harriet surprised herself by saying. She had a sudden impression of dereliction, as if Tessa, despite her essentially immature protestations, had become older, more experienced than herself, as if she had met a fate that was noxious to her, although there was no mistaking the longing in her face.

'I always admired you,' she went on. 'You had no anxieties, about school, or about boys, men, I should say. I can see you now, in those kilts you wore, that your mother had made for you in Scotland. You were so fair—that lovely skin. You never had a spot! I took that as a sign of your superiority. I thought you were invincible.'

'I was,' said Tessa. 'Until I met Jack. I knew straight away that he'd always been unfaithful, but I had to have him. I was used to having things, you see, and when I saw what I wanted I simply persisted. I ignored all the warning signs, like his going back to Judd Street instead of staying with me. Oh, yes, he did that a lot. Still does. He'll sleep with me, and then take off. And I put up with it. I sit here all day instead of getting a move on, and I think, what can I do to make him stay? How can I make it come out right? Because that's what I want.'

She moved back to her chair and sat down heavily, her face drawn. Her hair, Harriet could see, was not clean. How often she had envied that fair hair, when it was held back by a velvet band, when it bounced with cleanliness on Tessa's shoulders . . . How commanding she had been, how one vied for her favour, her commendation! And yet gracious, intimate when it suited her. A glamorous friend. And she had had her pick of young men, was irresistible to the easily impressed. If she had married a weak man she would always have retained the upper hand. Not perhaps have known true happiness, but on the other hand never have known doubt. She would have stayed in character, stayed safe. Instead she had lighted on a strong man, and had instantly gone under. The doom, the terrible doom of a woman like that in thrall to the wrong man! Unused to circumspection, she had been revealed as simple, obstinate, and finally without resource, disarmed. This discovery had left her with a kind of hatred, which, as surely as anything else, would militate against any kind of happiness, which concessions might just bring about. But with a man like Jack, she thought, one could not count on happiness anyway. Women would find him attractive, and he would find them convenient. He was not made for conventional alliances.

'You'll be all right once the baby is born,' said Harriet, with a conviction she did not feel. 'Once you've got a bit more energy, when you want to go out again. If you got a nanny you could go back to your old job. Are you all right for money?' It was not a question she had ever thought to ask.

'Oh, money's no problem. The parents are very good. And Jack, to give him credit, puts quite a bit in the bank from time to time.'

'Well, then. I'm sure Angie would have you back.' For Tessa had worked for a friend who was an interior decorator, which made the dilapidation of her own flat even more worrying.

'I could, I suppose. Yes, I might do that, if things work out. I need to see more people. I just don't have the energy somehow.'

'We shouldn't eat all this cake,' Harriet said abruptly. 'We should eat fruit. I'll bring some tomorrow: apricots, or something.'

'I couldn't face them. I only want stodge.'

'But you're putting on too much weight! What does the doctor say?'

'He says what you're saying. Oh, don't worry, I'll be all right. I'm as strong as a horse. Let's change the subject. Tell me about the house.'

But she had felt ashamed, ashamed to talk about carpets and curtains in this dusty place. And later, standing in the clean empty rooms, she found her pleasure in the house slightly dimmed. It seemed wrong to have so much when her friend had so little. Little of what I have, perhaps, she thought: she has Jack. The thought came unbidden. Nevertheless she felt an anxiety, even a disappointment that their roles had been reversed. The point is, she thought, that she was brave and confident, and I never was, and now, I suppose, I must be brave and confident for both of us. The idea was strangely disturbing. She went home and read *Little Dorrit,* which intensified her feelings of anxiety. And of sadness. For a moment, in spite of everything, she felt quite sad.

'And how's my girl this evening?' asked Freddie, giving her a kiss. As her pregnancy advanced she was his girl again, allowed to be young once more. 'Nice day? What did you do?'

'Nothing much,' she said, for she knew that he disliked her visits to Beaufort Street. 'I got two beautiful soles for our dinner. We should eat more fish; all the doctors say so.'

'Fine by me,' he said, although he was of a meat-eating generation; a meal was not a meal without steaks or chops.

'And I thought I might go down to Brighton tomorrow,' she said. 'I haven't seen them for quite a while.'

'As long as you don't stay out too late,' he said.

'Don't worry,' she smiled. 'I'll be back in time for dinner.'

But next day, in the train, she rather regretted her decision, regretted those afternoons in the sunny dusty flat, pouring tea out of a brown pot surrounded by cake crumbs. She felt

homesick for the kind of pleasure she took in Tessa's presence, which restored to her some semblance of the authority she was now about to forgo, had always forgone, in the company of her unrealistic parents, like no other parents she knew, with their flimsy frivolous tastes. In contrast to the weather of the past few days the morning was overcast, moist and heavy. As the train left Victoria she felt a qualm of nausea, her first, and wished that she had stayed at home. She had come to cherish her quiet days, now that their end was in sight. She felt a little wistful as she thought of the trials ahead of her, as if she had not yet fulfilled her quota of independent activity. About her baby she had no qualms; her baby would be perfect, and unmarked. But walking from the station she longed for a moment to have no one to go home to, to have no parents, no husband, no baby, just a day to herself, as if she were a girl again.

They saw her before she saw them. They were on the little concrete balcony of their flat, tremendously dressed up, as if she were a real visitor. Merle wore a smart cream coat and skirt, Hughie a houndstooth jacket that was obviously new, perhaps donned for the occasion, to mark a day on which something happened. They had always thought that smart clothes formed part of their effectiveness, assumed in the teeth of occasional misgivings. Both were smoking. When she looked up, it was to see them both waving. She waved back, feeling love and something like relief. They had abandoned her lightheartedly to her fate, and she, perhaps unconsciously, had done the same, yet all had survived. And in the mere recognition of each other's outlines—a gesture, an attitude— they knew that they were from the same mould. They loved her, it was now quite evident; they loved her now that she was gone. They loved her awkwardly, inexpertly, and with a certain regret. They were still lightweights, but now they were growing older. They seemed touched by a new serious-

ness; bored, and without resource in their limitless freedom, they had only their legend to fall back on and their evenings to look forward to. The days were uneventful; time sometimes dragged, was becoming a problem. All this she saw at a glance, in the smoker's languid and somehow disillusioned motions, in the stiffness, unremarked before, of her father's shoulders, as he shot the cuffs of his heartbreakingly new jacket. She remembered a line from *Little Dorrit,* which she had left at home, beside her bed, 'Her father! Her father!' as the pious heroine repeatedly refused to attend to her own interests, and Dickens himself threw up his hands in impotence. Though she felt none of this she knew that for her own father she would always retain an awful pity. Perhaps no sacrifices would be necessary—for that she had Freddie to thank—yet she knew him better than she had ever known her mother, knew him instinctively, because she had some of his own longing for childish homely ways, for soft answers, and for protection. She realized how dependent they were, and always had been, on her mother's competence, a competence they had always taken for granted, had sometimes found too harsh. She feared for them both; saw the brittleness of the arrangement, although they did not see it themselves. She supposed that they still loved one another, although the idea seemed strange to her. The loves that lingered, that entered memory, were not the ones she would have expected. Such loves were sometimes painful, which was why, she supposed, one moved on, moved outward. Old longings were only safe when they were submerged, allowed to escape much later in the form of memory. The figures of her parents, so smartly dressed, on their minuscule balcony, stirred depths in her, as their mere presence never did.

They were the same age as her husband, yet Freddie still lived in the real world, was busy, prosperous, well thought of, and from time to time, when the occasion demanded it,

convivial. He had, with relief, begun to assume public attitudes, in which no intimacy was demanded of him, was, in
fact, at his best, in company which was largely indifferent to
him. By contrast, these two struck her as unprotected, inexperienced, fatally let down by the lack of any kind of social
structure. Once they could act in unison, turning smiling
faces to her and holding out welcoming hands, she could see
their genuine attraction. But they needed some stimulus,
some little excitement to animate them. Without that, she
could see, they might easily fall into disappointment. She
wondered how they filled their time.

Thus softened—by the turn of her mother's head, her
birdlike, still bright eyes, by the jauntiness of her father's new
jacket—she was further moved to see that they had gone to
some lengths over the preparation of the tea. An array of
cakes, none of them home-made, reminded her of days in the
room at the back of the shop, and, 'I thought a little buttered
toast . . .', said Hughie, getting up with alacrity as she nodded
anticipation. Nobody knew quite what to say. It was clearly
out of order to ask, 'Are you happy?' They saw her as someone more dignified than themselves, a little more staid than
they would wish, or could understand, while she, quite simply, saw that they were lonely. For this reason alone she was
glad that she could make them the present of her child: a new
preoccupation, a new cause for the congratulation they could
never quite forgo. She could see that a grandchild, however
unexpected an occurrence, would absorb any tenderness, any
ruefulness that might be making inroads into their lives: a
grandchild might thus be an improvement, from their point
of view, on a daughter. And certainly more timely.

'Are you really all right?' she asked, as her father cut her
toast into strips for her.

'We're pretty good,' said her mother, taking a fresh cigarette. 'What about you, dear? No sickness? No, of course not.

I was as fit as a fiddle with you.' She was mildly embarrassed by this conversation, Harriet could see. 'But you must exercise, Hattie, or you'll never get your figure back. Your figure was always good. Sit down, darling,' she said to her husband. 'Don't make her eat so much—she'll put on too much weight.'

'And yet look at all this food,' Harriet smiled.

'That's Daddy's doing. Normally we just have a cup of tea. But he had to go out shopping for all this—nothing less would have done. Some more hot water, darling,' she said to him.

'Some days,' she said in a lowered tone, when he was out of the room, 'he doesn't feel too bright. That's why we're so pleased about the baby. It'll be a new lease of life for him.'

'Is he ill?' asked Harriet, alarmed.

'No, dear, not ill. Old. Or rather, older. You think back more than you should. And he's got some unpleasant memories, don't forget, although he's never spoken about them. Maybe he can't. The doctors don't seem to have done him any good. I've always had a job to keep him from feeling depressed, though now he's got the pills he's more stable. But we're lucky, really; we've got our own home, and we've got each other. And you, of course. Only I can't bear to think what would happen to him if anything happened to me.' Her face fell into a grimace of pain which straightened out into a vivid smile as Hughie came back with the teapot.

They walked with her to the station, anxious now in her presence. As Merle fell behind to greet a neighbour on a balcony adjoining their own ('Our daughter', they heard her say), Hughie pressed Harriet's arm and said, 'Keep in touch with us, dear. It's a little dull for her sometimes. I'm not always good company, you know. I know that. I think it's wonderful of her to put up with me. But then she was always wonderful.'

Don't change, don't change, she silently begged them. Don't grow up, grow old. Be frivolous, as you always were meant to be; be flippant, pleasure-loving, insubstantial. Preserve yourselves until I see what is going to happen to me, if anything still can. The thought that they might ever die released panic; she surprised herself by finding tears in her eyes when she said goodbye to them.

'Ring us when you get home,' said Hughie. Cross, now, at the fuss being made, her mother told him to calm down. Harriet watched them as the train receded from the platform, knew that for all their stylishness they had taken a step along the path that led to the final decrepitude. She put her hand to her heart, surprised to find it beating so strongly, then, simultaneously, all three of them waved, until she, and they, were out of sight.

7

WHEN did the feeling of dread begin? She could neither quite date it nor place it. She thought it might have been the consequence of the visit to her parents, and of the memories it aroused. Or possibly of the move to the big house, which did not seem entirely favourable. 'I hope you know what you're doing,' Freddie had said on their last evening in Cornwall Gardens. 'What *we're* doing,' she corrected him. He did not answer. This, he implied, was not why he had married her; he had not bargained for upheaval, expense. Momentarily she wondered what on earth she was doing, sitting in this denuded room with a man who seemed to her a complete stranger, like someone with whom she was forced to spend time while waiting for a train. Their first evening in Wellington Square left them similarly estranged. The room was glassily bright; not all the lampshades were yet in place. They were too tired to talk, nor could either think of anything encouraging to say. After a while she roused herself, went into the kitchen and scrambled some eggs, which they ate from unmatched plates. Then, since there was nothing more to be done, they went to bed. At least the bed was familiar. But the window was in the wrong place, and when Freddie got up in the night he walked into a wall where the door should have been.

Her tiredness of the following days she put down to natural

causes. There was so much to do, too much; she would not be able to resume her dreamy existence for some time. The activity, although unwelcome, concentrated her mind; she feared an encroaching dullness, which her ordinary life did nothing to discourage. But in her fatigue she found the house exorbitant, overwhelming. She longed for a small remote sunny room to which she alone might have access. The picture of this room was quite clear in her mind; it was the private place which she had never quite been permitted. The new house, when measured against this fantasy, alarmed her. I am not quite up to this, she thought.

Because he had been led unwillingly to the house Freddie failed to sympathize with her fatigue, but merely carried out the obvious tasks assigned to him. He was discomposed; he did not see why they should not have stayed in Cornwall Gardens. 'But babies need a nursery,' Harriet had protested. 'They have a lot of equipment. You wouldn't have wanted it all in your bathroom, would you?' He had not replied. He thought at this time that there was a certain dignity in silence, his usual resource when outfaced by events. His earlier pleasure in Harriet's pregnancy (or rather the announcement to his friends of her pregnancy) had evaporated silently, leaving a certain bewilderment behind. He had bargained for none of this. His first wife had been a woman of uncertain temper, well-bred enough to be fearless; he had been criticized at every turn, frequently humiliated. Marrying a much younger woman had been the first and last romantic action in a dull but reasonable life; he did not see why he should not be allowed to relax completely once the deed was done. Harriet's simplicity had appealed to him. With a shrewd and self-preserving instinct he knew that she would never do battle with him, betray him, make fun of him. He had appreciated all this and had come to cherish her. He would not now willingly live without her.

But he wanted her to remain cherished, and as simple as she

had been when he had first found her. Independent action on
her part, as he saw this pregnancy, and this removal, disturbed
him profoundly. He also suspected that she herself was disturbed by it. She was not bred to this, he told himself silently;
he was too honourable to tell her the same thing. From time
to time he had seen young men in his group of companies,
men with excellent qualifications, simply overreach themselves, make some error through sheer enthusiasm, mistaking
enthusiasm for judgement, without the proper controls to
slow them down. He usually saw to it that they were rede-
ployed, not wanting to risk them in situations which might
reveal their lack of background. He could not do this with his
wife, since there was a certain logic in her behaviour. He was,
in addition, ready to concede that the new house was in every
way desirable. Simply, he had preferred his life as it was, with
just the two of them. Harriet had allowed him to retain all or
most of his bachelor habits; his house was well run, his wife
was agreeable in the ways in which he thought a wife should
be agreeable. In return for her docility he wanted to protect
her from those who might wear away her confidence. He saw
the frowns of anxiety on her face as she surveyed her domain,
saw her fatigue, her thickened figure. All of which, he
thought, could have been avoided. He was too kind to tell her
so, except in moments of unusual exasperation. He knew, and
was disarmed by the knowledge, that she wanted what all her
friends had long possessed: a proper house, a proper family.
He saw that she would lose some of the simplicity which had
first attracted him to her in her efforts to be like everyone else.
He saw that in some ways she was not qualified. He was
familiar with the phenomenon, which he could never explain
to her.

　She saw none of this, although she was aware of a certain
disharmony. This she attributed to her condition, to which
she was now obliged to make certain concessions. In the

afternoons she rested, tensely, in her spacious new bedroom. In the evenings, bathed and changed, she awaited Freddie in her new and rather too grand drawing-room. Furniture looked stranded on expanses of pale blue carpet, which she now saw should have been pale green: Freddie's Persian rugs, over which she had tripped continually during the first year of her marriage, must now be laid end to end until she plucked up the courage to change the whole room. Fortunately the white curtains, with their pattern of flowers, looked well, and the windows were wide and high. Her commitment to this house was not total; part of her retreated in her imagination to that small empty room of her own devising, in which she might read unpretentious books, think unpretentious thoughts, even eat unpretentious meals quite unlike the ones she conscientiously prepared for Freddie, although her own appetite suffered. Like her father, she craved sweetness, and was forced to make do with a healthy diet. Their evenings were a little forlorn, neither wishing the other to see disappointment. Sometimes they took a walk round the square. Leaning on his arm she felt secure, as she no longer felt secure when she was alone.

In the morning she was out a great deal, mostly in department stores, buying towels, pillowslips, kettles, soap dishes for the basement flat, which she now saw would have to house someone quite specific, someone strong and cheerful and experienced to look after the baby; she felt suddenly unequal to looking after anybody other than herself. Freddie, anxious to restore some semblance of home comforts, the onus of providing which he would willingly have discharged on any half-way competent stranger, drafted an advertisement, and within a week they had interviewed and acquired Dawn Molyneux, a South African girl with dazzling teeth, who was working her way round the world. Just to know that Dawn was in the house made Harriet feel better. The girl had

completed two years of medical studies before deciding that
she would rather see the world outside Durban, where her
father was a fashionable dentist. She had promised him that
she would be back within a year, eighteen months at the
outside. 'Eighteen months!' Harriet had exclaimed. 'But we
hoped you might stay longer.' 'Not me,' said Dawn. 'I've got
something lined up in Italy for next year. Of course, if it falls
through I'll let you know. Now, what about a cup of tea?' It
was ten o'clock in the morning, but the nice thing about
Dawn was her homeliness. Cups of tea were drunk all day,
biscuits were proffered. Harriet soon found her way down to
the basement on most mornings, and sometimes in the afternoons, when she had rested and changed. She loved to see
Dawn making herself up for her nightly forays into town,
where she met up with other girls like herself, or with her
boyfriend, Ronnie. On boyfriend evenings circles of colour
were applied to eyelids and cheekbones; lipsticks nestled next
to the teacups. 'You've got your key?' Harriet would ask.
'And enough money? Always keep enough money for a cab.'
She liked to think of the girl having a high-spirited time,
knowing that she would hear all about it the following morning. 'And what about yourself?' Dawn would ask kindly.
'You out tonight?' 'No, I expect we shall stay in,' was the
usual reply, for now she craved her bed, and silence. She tired
swiftly these days, and her sleep was dreamless. Only her
waking hours contained dreams.

   She could not remember such a splendid autumn. While
the leaves fell in the windless air the sun still shone out of a
blue sky. Gradually she regained a little energy, and thought,
belatedly, of Tessa, from whom she had not heard. This was
not unusual; it was usually she who did the telephoning. She
rang the Beaufort Street number and got no reply, walked
round there once, only to hear no movement from inside the
flat. She was a little surprised not to have been informed of

any absence; she was sure that she had sent out change of
address cards. When Dawn came up with tea and said, 'There
was a telephone call for you,' she automatically replied, 'From
Mrs Peckham? What did she say?' 'Mrs Collins,' said Dawn,
adding sugar to her own tea and energetically stirring. It took
Harriet a minute or two to remember that Mrs Collins was
the former Pamela Harkness, whom she had not seen for a
couple of years. She tried the number twice before Pamela's
discouragingly brisk voice answered. Make it snappy, it
seemed to say. What you are interrupting is far more important than anything you have to impart. One did not telephone
Pamela; one was telephoned by her. In the old days Harriet
had preferred to find out what Pamela was thinking or doing
indirectly; mediated, the news seemed less peremptory, more
normal.

'Harriet? Message from Tessa. She's gone away for a few
days. Jack turned up, apparently. I think she said Paris.'

'Oh,' said Harriet, bewildered. 'Did she not have my number?'

'No idea. That was what she said to tell you. Of course she
dropped everything when he materialized. She rang from the
airport, actually.'

'I see. I expect she'll get in touch when she gets back. How
are you?'

'Surviving. I'll be in London next month, probably see you
then. Are you still presentable?'

'Getting rather large. But it will be lovely to see you. Ring
me when you get here. Or I expect Tessa will.'

'Okay. Keep well. Bye.'

So I did send the change of address cards, she thought, as
she replaced the receiver. I thought I did. I must have been
out when Tessa called. Oh well, never mind. I'll stay at home
for a bit. It will do me no harm.

'Dawn,' she said. 'I think we might go out this evening. I don't feel like cooking.'

'Good idea,' said Dawn cheerfully. 'I'll do the ironing, shall I?'

Such a pleasant girl, thought Harriet. More my own type, was what she really thought. Pamela always had that effect on her.

'You're looking pretty,' said Freddie, breaking a roll. In fact she was not; her face was too thin, her eyes too big. He loved her diffidently, although he could never quite say so. Her unhappiness, he thought, was due more to moral than to physical upheaval. All he could do was ease her through it. No doubt she would want to give parties for her friends as soon as she was back to normal. But whereas his own friends always found her delightful, he saw that she would be in some ways inadequate when faced with another kind of hierarchy. Contact with her own friends brought on, or left behind, a complex of feelings which made her look older than her years. He resented anyone or anything that took away her youthfulness, which was to him unique, not to be compared with that of her contemporaries, whom, he thought, she did not resemble. He wished to bestow on her calmness and good order, and sighed inwardly at the thought of all the changes she must undergo, and he with her. At this rate I shan't be able to retire, he thought, although the idea attracted him. All his travelling had been done when he was in the forces, or away on business. He would have liked to explore different worlds, at his leisure. India appealed to him, Malaysia. Without the child he could have afforded to take things a little more easily. They could have followed the sun: the West Indies in winter, Greece in the spring, and summers in a house they might even have bought in the country, or near the coast. He was a discreetly wealthy man, and none of Harriet's current expenditure seriously inconvenienced him, but he could see that it was not making her happy. And he had always had a desire to see the autumn leaves in Vermont, or Canada. He sighed again at the prospect before him: unremitting work, and short trips on Concorde.

'Very pretty,' he said.

'You never speak of Helen,' said Harriet. She felt on edge, ready to provoke, and at the same time ashamed of herself.

'I never think of her,' he replied, although he did, remembering her harsh hilarity, her frequent jibes at his cautious manners. The differences between his first wife and his second were so profound, and at the same time so obvious, that he did not see how he could ever explain them to her. Hearing in his mind's ear Helen's laughter in the bedroom—and it was always that laughter, or more properly speaking the cruelty of that laughter—he wished to spare them both what to him had been almost constant humiliation. A marvellous hostess, of course; her household was impeccable, her dinner parties brilliant. 'Without me you'd be nowhere,' she had flung at him. 'You'd have no friends at all if I didn't attract them.' He thought she was probably right. But he had found the task of living up to her onerous and increasingly uncomfortable. After Helen, Harriet had had the appeal of disembodied kindness, of timidity allied to the desire to please. He had felt himself gently released from the restrictions and the disruptions of his earlier marriage. He knew that he did not make Harriet happy, but tended to disregard this. Happiness was what young people wanted; at his age he knew that comfort was more important. He had made her comfortable, and in that he was prepared to take a grim pride. After all, nobody else had done as much. He had no regrets, no misgivings: at least, he would have said as much a few months ago. Now, of course, it was all in the balance, as it had never been before.

'I believe that Helen is extremely well; at least, I have no reason to suspect otherwise. When last heard of she was living with a woman friend near Newbury. Why do you ask? She can be of no interest to you, particularly now.'

'I sometimes think I don't make you happy enough,' confessed Harriet.

But he knew she was thinking of her own condition, and said gently, 'I am perfectly happy, you know. We're both a little overwrought at the moment—you must allow for that. Now, what about some raspberries?' He put a hand on hers. 'It will be all right, you know. You're not frightened, are you?'

She smiled at him, grateful as always for his kindness. 'No,' she said. 'I'm not frightened.'

They walked back, on a mellow evening not appreciably cooler than the preceding afternoon. The radiant autumn had lasted well into October; the sun at midday was nearly as warm as August. The baby will be born in the winter, she thought, and felt a little cold herself. 'You should have worn a coat,' said Freddie. 'That jacket is too light.'

'But it was so warm this afternoon . . .'

'And now it is unsettled. The fine spell may be over.'

How shall I stand the winter, she thought, and at that moment her baby moved imperiously inside her.

'Freddie,' she said. 'I'm really very well. Take no notice of my moods. I'm fine, not even tired any more. Would you like to ask anyone to dinner? It'd be no trouble; I'm more or less straight. I haven't paid you nearly enough attention recently. You've been wonderful,' she said, in all sincerity. It did not occur to her at that moment that any other kind of happiness existed.

Freddie's predictions were correct. The following day dawned dull and grey; cobwebs on the rose-bushes in their garden were spangled with opaque misty drops.

'Not much point in going out today,' said Freddie, departing for the office. 'What will you do?'

'Nothing much. Finish my book, I think.' But *Little Dorrit* was beginning to horrify her, as well as move her to frequent tears. The tenderness, the pity of the girl! And to end up with that wreck of a husband! An impossible woman, she thought, with a slight but definite sorrow. But good, as I always wanted to be good, believing that if one wished it so one could become perfect. Dickens himself wanted it to be true. Maybe it is merely a matter of doing one's best, all the time. The thought cheered her. I shall behave as if I were a better person, she decided, and that way I might turn out a credit to Freddie. But I must be cheerful! Cheerfulness is what is needed now, and humility. Let nothing you dismay, she thought, walking round the garden, and feeling drops of water on her skirt. In the distance she heard the telephone.

'Mrs Dodd,' said Dawn, as she came into the house. 'Left a number for you to ring her back.'

The number was Tessa's old number in Cadogan Square. But the caller had been her mother. Had something terrible happened? Why had Tessa not telephoned herself? Are we, awful thought, estranged? Or, worse than all other thoughts, has she seen through my indifference when Jack's name is mentioned? There was a dangerous conversation once . . . But there was never any intention on my part . . . She could not have thought . . . She blushed, took a deep breath, and picked up the telephone. 'Mrs Dodd?' she said. 'This is Harriet Lytton.'

'Harriet! So good of you to ring back so promptly! Such exciting news! Tessa's had a little girl, prematurely, but quite all right. They just got back from Paris in time. *Wasn't* it lucky?'

Harriet had forgotten the amount of emphasis and punctuation in Tessa's mother's conversational style. A noble and commanding woman, she had always thought her; her voice matched her unusual height and distant kindness. All kinds of public duties could be assumed from the very fashion in which she entered a room.

'A girl!' she said, sitting down. 'How wonderful. Was Jack with her?'

'Of course,' said Mrs Dodd, with immense enthusiasm. She did not like Jack, but would have considered it disloyal to admit it. 'Well, I must get on and let everybody else know. Nice to have made contact again, Harriet. You're keeping well, I hope?'

'Thank you, yes. I'll go and see Tessa this afternoon, shall I?'

'Oh . . . how kind. But you won't stay long, will you? She's very tired still. And Jack's there, anyway. Now, you take care of *yourself*. Goodbye, my dear.'

Excitement, long dormant, brought her to life. 'Dawn,' she called. 'I'm going out. Could you leave me a sandwich for later? I don't know what time I'll be back.'

She half ran down the King's Road in her eagerness, then pulled herself together, reflected that she should have brought an umbrella, smoothed her hair, buttoned her white coat, and walked on sedately. Both she and Tessa were booked into the same private hospital, under the same consultant. She floated up the stairs, disdaining the lift: she knew the rooms, the efficient corridors. Knocking on Tessa's door, she tried to compose her radiant face, which was what Jack Peckham saw, before once again her hand flew up to her jaw.

'Mrs Lytton,' he said gravely. 'Have some champagne.'

'Hattie! How did you get here?' Tessa was sitting up in bed, her hair washed, a white cotton nightgown slipping from her shoulders. She looked, Harriet thought, almost dishevelled, alert, quizzical, as if she had not bargained on the interruption.

'Your mother telephoned. I'm so happy for you, darling. Where's the baby?'

'Downstairs, in an incubator. Oh, she's fine, quite small,

but that's to be expected. Elizabeth, we're calling her. Elizabeth Charlotte.'

'Elizabeth after my mother,' said Jack, handing her a glass of champagne.

Harriet sat down, feeling suddenly tired. Jack's presence inhibited her from asking the questions she longed to have answered. She drank her champagne, told Tessa how well she looked, and, aware of Jack standing with his back to the door, his arms folded, said, 'I'll come back tomorrow, shall I? Oh, I didn't even bring flowers! I think I must be more excited than you are.' When is Jack going back? She wanted to ask. When can we have a proper talk?

'Well, actually . . . I don't want too many visitors while Jack's still in London. Of course, it's always good to see you. Dear Hattie. Have some more champagne.'

'No, I must be going,' said Harriet, smoothing her fine dark hair back again; her hand, she noticed, was very slightly trembling. 'Well . . . let me know when you'll be coming home. Is there anything you want? Anything I can do?'

'Nothing. Now I *am* a bit tired. Good to see you, Hattie. Thank you for coming.' She sank down in the bed, apparently torpid, her eye watchful. Jack opened the door with exaggerated courtesy. 'Good of you to come,' he said. She detected a faint irony in his elaborately good manners. As the door wheezed slowly behind her, she could just make out, 'She can be a bit dense, sometimes.'

She walked slowly home, through what was now a steady drizzle. Dawn had left her watercress sandwiches. Ignoring these, she made some coffee, then sat by the window, looking out on to the silent square. It's just that one feels a little lonely from time to time, she thought. So stupid. And it will be hours before Freddie gets home. Always I turn back to him, she thought, and almost managed not to think, and usually after disappointments.

8

On Freddie's face, unseasonal merriment. 'A girl!' she heard him say before she drifted off. When she woke again, the sight of her furiously sleeping baby led to instant possession of herself. There was a certain hilarity in the room; she was thought to have done well. 'A very easy delivery,' said Mr Cambridge, looking in. Her father and mother were joking with Freddie; Freddie was joking with the nurse. What larks, thought Harriet, amused. Now they will all take the credit. Nothing could upset her now; she had belatedly come of age. 'Imogen', she announced to the room. 'She is going to be called Imogen.' Surprised, they acquiesced; what a pretty name, they said. 'Imogen Claire,' she added later, after drinking a cup of tea. But when they had all gone away, at last, she bent over the little crib and whispered, 'Immy. My Immy.'

There never was such a child, she thought, both then and later. Her beauty was astonishing, even more astonishing in that it proceeded from two such ordinary people: such perfection of feature, such silkiness of hair seemed to them miraculous. In comparison poor little Elizabeth Peckham looked like a waif, spindly, blotchy, her pale blue eyes faintly crossed. 'Oh, that's nothing,' said Harriet generously. 'She'll grow out of that.' Her own child gave no trouble, so little that they marvelled at her. There was no thought of disciplining her:

she was too unexpected, too undeserved. Although the child slept through the nights her parents did not, alert for possible calls, for possible dangers. Dawn thought them crazy. Freddie, permanently tired, found himself smiling throughout the day.

Harriet, with magnificent impartiality, allowed others to admire the child. Her own father was restored to euphoria; her mother was pleased but impatient, anxious to dissociate herself from so ageing an event. Nevertheless, exquisite clothes continued to arrive by post. The baby was immaculate, changed several times a day. It seemed a pity not to spoil her, to gratify her. There was never any thought that she might be denied whatever it was she wanted. And they were rewarded, they were quite sure of that. Imogen never cried. On the contrary, she laughed. When Harriet wheeled her out in her pram she laughed at the women who were drawn to her. Sitting up, and able to use her hands more purposefully, she grabbed what was available to her on supermarket shelves. 'Imogen! Put that back!' Harriet would say. Imogen laughed. Others might see defiance in that small face. Harriet saw the life force.

There was no more boredom, no more loneliness. Unsuspected energies constantly renewed themselves; self-pity was a thing of the past. And sometimes there were two children to look after, for Tessa took advantage of the garden in Wellington Square to leave poor Lizzie Peckham for the afternoon, or for the day, or occasionally for the night. 'You don't mind, do you?' she would say. 'Only it's Dad's retirement party.' Wish it were mine, thought Freddie, who was now rather more tired than he had bargained for. Dawn was not best pleased, although it was really no trouble to cook two fillets of plaice instead of one, to put two sets of clothes into the washing machine. 'That kid's not properly fed,' she might remark to Harriet. 'She doesn't know how to eat.' 'I think her mother still gives her baby food,' Harriet would say. 'That's why she has no appetite. The food is unfamiliar to her. Come on, Lizzie, another little mouthful.' Imogen would look on amazed, then would start to eat the strawberries put on a plate for Lizzie. 'Immy!' she would protest. 'Those are *Lizzie's* strawberries. You've had yours.' Imogen laughed.

Curiously, the two children did not get on. Lizzie was a nervous child, pale, and sometimes, when she could raise the energy, fierce. She would sit in a corner of the room, nursing the toy she had brought with her, visibly anxious that it might be taken away from her, longing for her mother to come and end her ordeal. For that mother she had a love and a hunger that were not entirely reciprocated. Tessa viewed her daughter with a certain perceptible disappointment. Where was Jack's beauty, where were her own high colour, her sense of what was due to her? She grew bored with the tasks required of her, decided that she must go back to work, left Lizzie at Wellington Square for a whole day while she had her hair done, and, while she was about it, treated herself to a manicure and a pedicure, and—why not?—something new to wear. For Jack might come home, unannounced, at any moment, though he showed no signs of doing so. 'Somewhere in Israel,' she replied to Harriet's question, sitting in Harriet's drawing-room, accepting a glass of sherry from Freddie, while Lizzie plucked fretfully at her short and unmaternal skirt. 'But he'll be back as soon as he can manage it.' 'He won't, you know,' Freddie remarked to Harriet, when they were preparing for bed that evening. 'She really is a tiresome woman. And why can't that child go to its grandparents?' 'You weren't listening,' said Harriet. 'They've sold Cadogan Square and moved to the mews. Now that he's retired they plan to spend most of the year at their place in France. Tessa will be entirely alone.' 'Why don't you think Jack will come back?' she asked, a little later. 'Why should he?' Freddie

retorted. 'He's not my idea of a married man.' He resented
Jack's freedom on behalf of married men like himself. 'He's
never spent any time at home, if you can call it home. And
neither of them seems particularly interested in the girl.' For
Lizzie was 'the girl' to him. He could not, perhaps would not,
take to her. She was inferior in every respect to his own child,
who was quite enough, sometimes too much for him. Lizzie
Peckham was an annoyance, a distraction, with her woeful
face and her grubby track suit. She did not seem to care for
him, or indeed for anyone except her mother. She sat out her
periods in Wellington Square as if they were a long exile.
Harriet was sorry for her, but Immy came first.

Imposing Lizzie on Freddie meant imposing Tessa as well,
for Lizzie had to be collected at the end of a long and tiring
day, when the child's face was already wan with fatigue. And
Tessa was not easily dispatched; Freddie fumed. It seemed to
Harriet that her friend was endangered by various antago-
nisms; Dawn too rather disliked her, thought her a bad
mother, and to Harriet's amazement remarked that she
thought Tessa frivolous. 'Frivolous?' echoed Harriet. 'But in
fact her life is rather hard. She never knows when her husband
is coming home.' (Or indeed whether he is coming home at
all, she said to herself.) 'And her parents are leaving London,
going to live abroad—she will hardly ever see them. And
Lizzie does rather cling to her. I think perhaps she's a little
unsettled,' she said moderately. 'She was talking about going
back to work.' 'Lizzie might as well be a weekly boarder
here,' said Dawn, who liked the child. 'And she's not happy.
Anyone can see she's unhappy here. Women like that
shouldn't have children,' she added virtuously, as the young
sometimes will.

Women like that? But Tessa was not like anything, thought
Harriet, for whom Tessa had lost none of her prestige, indeed
had rather gained a little more by virtue of having married

Jack, and married him against his will. Tessa spoke of him only in the airiest terms, which particularly angered Freddie, although Harriet knew that it was all an act. But it was the kind of act which confers a certain glamour on a woman, a recklessness, a restlessness, even a depth denied to staid wives like herself. And Tessa responded to her strange condition of abandonment—if that was what it was—of ambiguity, certainly; she even played up to it, saw herself as an object of interest, of speculation. In her heart of hearts she knew that her marriage was threadbare, was inferior in quality even to Harriet's own, knew that it was over, knew that the child was irrelevant, since it had not served its purpose of winning back the errant father. In the light of such terrible knowledge, Harriet saw, Tessa had decided to be airy, inconsequential, self-indulgent. She had the strange satisfaction of being publicly acknowledged as her husband's wife, and with the solid conviction of her class was beginning to consider herself something of an asset, as if she and Jack had married on an equal footing, as if she had never confessed her unhappiness. She avoided the truth of her imperfect condition these days, berated herself smilingly for being depressed, or, more usually, 'quite angry'. This anger of hers, always referred to with an air of complaisance, she thought an advantageous quality, heroic almost, something that did her credit. 'I'm beginning to feel my anger,' she might say to Harriet, who, in passing, was quite glad that Freddie was not at home to hear this. The anger was always referred to with the sort of smile a therapist might have worn, a steady, patient, professional smile. And there was pleasure in it, as well. The anger would rebuild Tessa's self-esteem. And while it went about its essential work—a long task, for that self-esteem had never previously faltered—it received a certain amount of help in the form of new clothes, beauty treatments, and, tentatively at first, the attentions of other men.

These days, after leaving Lizzie at Wellington Square, Tessa would take herself off to renew 'contacts', high-spirited women like herself, for whom she had worked energetically but for brief periods before she was married. Thus, for three months she had been an expensive florist; for six months had helped Pamela cook directors' lunches; for a year had worked for Angie, the interior decorator. Angie was her most substantial contact, although nothing seemed to come of these meetings. Perhaps Tessa simply liked going into Angie's overstuffed little shop ('blowing in', was how they both put it) and pretending to be working there without actually having to do any work. Perhaps she found it an ideal way to fill in the morning and see a few people, before embarking on the most important matter of the day, which was lunch, in a good restaurant, or a hotel dining-room, the sort of place where businessmen forgathered and where she might find just such a man on his own. Hotels were better for this, although she preferred the more fashionable kind of restaurant.

She attracted attention because she looked purposeful, and also unafraid. She had regained her major asset, her lean long-legged figure, and was now well dressed, her hair groomed. Occasionally there was what she considered to be a permitted distraction in the afternoon. She was discreet, although it did not matter much to her whether she was discreet or not, but her partners preferred it. For herself, she rather hoped that Jack might get to hear of her conduct and become furiously possessive. This was the whole point of her manœuvres. It was difficult to tell whether she enjoyed them or not. Certainly the attention (and the champagne, which was obligatory on these occasions) keyed her up, brought colour to her cheeks, made her a little self-conscious, so that when she arrived at Wellington Square to pick up Lizzie (whom she had entirely forgotten: thank God for Harriet) she would sometimes be quite self-absorbed, mock-ashamed, inclined to take long exaggerated breaths, raise her eyebrows, roll her eyes, as if to say, yes, I dare say this is scandalous behaviour, but you see I am acting out my anger. I am making my anger *work* for me. And anyway, Jack can hardly expect me to sit here like patience on a monument, can he? I have a pretty good idea what *he's* up to. Israeli women can be quite attractive, I hear. Anyway, *he's* not particular. In this way she set Jack up as an enemy, to suit her own purposes. As if in recognition of the hopelessness of the task (to make Jack come back and be a good husband and father and settle down and let the parents find him something suitable to do) she lavished more attention (and less thought) on her own concerns and turned up at Wellington Square looking merry, secretive, rakish, and longing for someone to ask her what on earth she had been up to.

To Harriet this was all derisory, pitiful. More alive to symbols than Tessa ever could be, she saw symptoms of decadence in tiny incidents: the combing of the hair in the mirror in the hall, the removal of a long alien hair from the exaggerated shoulders of the new suit, the hasty brushing down of the skirt, as if she had just emerged from a *maison de passe,* thought Harriet, yet it cannot have been as sordid as that. It was difficult for her to conceal dismay, and also shame, shame not only on Tessa's behalf but on her own, for in comparison she thought she must appear hopelessly suburban, retarded, almost. She knew that the reunions to which she had formerly so looked forward—Tessa, Pamela, Mary, and herself—were now compromised, for she would never be sought after as a co-conspirator in adventures of this sort, although the former Pamela Harkness might, while the former Mary Grant would have joined in enthusiastically. And of course Harriet saw dereliction where there was simply a certain verve, reasserting itself after a long period of aberration. Harriet suspected that at some point a letter had been

received, giving grounds for divorce, and that Tessa had smilingly chosen to ignore it. Always that smile! Always that
fiction that the marriage, although awkward, was particularly
intriguing and fascinating. Always that slight air of pity for a
friend who, while absolutely marvellous, simply didn't know
enough to come in out of the rain. But then look who she had
married! A man old enough to be her father, and nothing in
the way of charm to carry it off. Moneyed, but if that was all
she had wanted . . . Yes, Dawn's use of the word frivolous was
probably justified, decided Harriet, to whom Tessa's thoughts
were perfectly visible.

Dawn was of great value to Harriet, since she incarnated
those bourgeois values which Tessa was currently putting to
flight. Apparently the circles in which Dawn's parents moved
in Durban were particularly down on that sort of thing. And
Dawn felt sorry for Harriet, whom she saw saddened by the
knowledge of such behaviour. In any case Dawn was fed up
with washing whichever of Lizzie's two track suits she happened to have dirtied the previous day; it seemed simpler to
keep the clean one in Immy's cupboard, where it scarcely
found room among the latter's many toilettes. 'At least she
can go home looking clean,' Dawn said to Harriet, who sadly
acquiesced. Dawn was seriously thinking of moving on.
'Don't go,' begged Harriet. 'You know we love having you.
And Immy is devoted to you.' 'I can't stay here for ever,' said
Dawn crossly, but she put the kettle on, and added, 'You
ready for a cup, then?'

In the meantime Immy grew, in beauty, in boldness, a
boldness which her mother delighted to see, having none of
her own. It did not occur to her that this quality should be
checked, since its very existence seemed a certificate of viability, a passport to a successful future. It was Immy who
brought a smile to Freddie's harassed face; to be the father of
a turbulent two-year-old at fifty-nine was otherwise no

laughing matter. Immaculately presented in the clothes her grandmother sent her, the child apparently had a foreknowledge of all the social graces: how to receive, how to entertain. There was an interval in the evenings when, freshly bathed and dressed, she would greet her father with cries of 'Daddy!', and laugh. This laugh indicated pleasure, excitement, though her attention was quickly withdrawn if Freddie turned his face to Harriet. Lizzie, having made one attempt to join the celebrations and been repulsed—'*My* Daddy!'—would look on, until Harriet, reminded of certain solitary days of her own, bought her a couple of picture books. These concerned the behaviour of an infant of indeterminate sex who put saucepans on its head and climbed into its parents' bed. 'What's that naughty baby doing, Lizzie?' Harriet would call, when she saw the child lapse into disappointment. The book would be opened; Lizzie would smile. Sometimes Imogen would snatch it away, and then Lizzie's face would crumple. 'She's tired,' Harriet would explain, taking Immy by the hand. 'Dawn, perhaps Lizzie would like some milk,' she would call over her shoulder as she mounted the stairs. 'Daddy will come and see you when you are in bed,' she would console. For this too was a moment savoured by all three of them. The child had certain innocently lewd gestures; she would pull up her nightgown, and watch her father's face. Freddie, Harriet was amused to see, was even a little embarrassed. Lizzie, in all this, waited out her exile downstairs.

'Have some compassion,' she said to Freddie later, pushing back her hair, which had grown long. 'She has no father to speak of.' 'And I suppose it'll be you who takes her to school and collects her afterwards?' He dropped the shoe he was taking off. 'It's no trouble, now that I've got the car.' 'Something ought to be done about that girl's eyes,' he also said. 'I believe they give them exercises,' she replied. 'But she's too young to understand them. It'll all straighten out when she's older.' She placed great faith in Lizzie's growing older, as if childhood were wasted on her, as indeed it seemed to be. Only the books, reverently placed on a shelf in Immy's room, engaged her attention, the books and her mother. Immy tried to throw the books away, but Dawn found them and put them back again. Harriet hoped that school would make them better friends and teach them both the virtues of citizenship (or interaction, as the head teacher had informed her such a condition was now called). Occasionally she perceived both children as entirely unmanageable, as if their characters were formed, their destinies plain, their successes or their failures adumbrated, waiting to be developed. She was aware of Immy's hilarity, of Lizzie's bleakness, felt time rushing away from her as they seemed to grow up, grow older, as if there were nothing more to discover, as if all she could do would be to follow humbly in their wake. She even thought she might be too tired to contain, eventually, Immy's energy, for the child was merciless, issuing commands and demands like the courtesan she seemed destined to become. And Lizzie, always lagging behind, disadvantaged.

What cruelty had placed two such disparate children in such close proximity? At last Harriet began to think like Freddie: that Tessa should occupy herself with her own daughter more than she evidently desired to do. But this, she could also see, was a hopeless idea, for Tessa consistently failed to interest herself in Lizzie, having written her off as a mistake, someone who would fail to win Jack's affection or approval, someone so lacking in prestige, in natural charm, that Jack, if he ever reviewed the situation, would decide that it was Tessa who was defective in presenting him with such a daughter. Therefore Lizzie was perceived as disgraced, although this perception was never overt. Tessa herself, if she allowed herself to feel anything but tolerance, would have felt pity, but pity was something she strove to ignore. In any event, nothing in her make-up provided the right conditions for pity to be registered. If she ever felt the onset of a certain impatient ache—for the child's poor appearance, her limp hair, her clumsy movements, her wandering right eye—she knew that it was time to take herself out again. 'I mustn't let myself get depressed,' she thought. 'I need distraction,' she told Harriet. 'I don't see enough people. It's all right for you—you've got Dawn. And Freddie, of course.' Freddie she despised. Harriet, noting the sheerness of the dark stockings on the long legs, and the slight exaggeration of the arched brows, replied, 'Oh, that's all right. You go. I've got to be here with Immy, anyway. Only do try to get back earlier. Lizzie gets so tired, and it's bad for her seeing Immy being put to bed. The sooner she learns to read the better. She loves her little books.' 'Yes, it was good of you to buy them. Well, I'm on my way. Goodbye, poppet.' Harriet, as always, turned aside, so that she could not see Lizzie's blank expression.

On their first day at school Immy wore a pink dress, with a pink sweater knotted loosely around her neck, and Lizzie one of her track suits. Immy at once acquired a boyfriend, a surly child called Vincent. Lizzie, who was bewildered, was allowed to hold the teacher's hand. At the end of the first day both decided that they might give it another try. Harriet, waiting tensely for their reappearance, was relieved to see them emerge unscathed. In the car they were vociferous, vainglorious; even Lizzie had something to tell her. She realized that it was going to be all right, and then understood how very tired she was.

'Angie's thinking of taking me on again,' said Tessa, in the hall. These days she kept a small hairbrush in her bag. She smelt of cigarettes, although she did not smoke. 'Part-time, of course. I told her I couldn't manage full-time, now that I've got Lizzie.' She brushed her hair in the hall mirror, replaced

the black velvet hair band. 'Do you see how dark I'm getting?' she asked. 'And I used to be a true blonde.' 'You're still
a blonde,' said Harriet. 'But you look a bit thinner. Do you
feed yourselves properly?' 'Oh, yes. We don't have much in
the evenings because we're not hungry—anyway, I don't
believe in too much food. Isn't it a bore, having to stay at
home in the evenings? I can't wait for Lizzie to be a bit older.
She'll go away to school, of course. St Mary's. She'll love it.
Anyway, I told Angie I'd give it a try. Ten to four, and it's
quite near. So if I could drop Lizzie off here first thing, before
I go to work . . . ? Marvellous. That way I needn't worry so
much. I'll know she's all right.'

She seemed to have decided—but to have decided a long
time ago, in one shrewd final assessment—that Harriet had
exhausted her potential, having done well for herself. She
had measured her friend's rise to comparative affluence and
had remained unimpressed, remembering too well their
childhood status, assuming that Harriet's relative security was
as much as she could expect, or indeed deserve. To exploit
this condition seemed to Tessa entirely natural, much as she
would demand a discount if she had a friend who worked in
a shop. She could be amiable enough with her child in this
way: any other dispensation would have had her raging with
frustration. Therefore it was in everyone's best interests that
Harriet should bear the brunt: in Tessa's opinion it made
sense all around. Freddie she did not concern herself with.
Freddie was Harriet's business. Good luck to her. She probably needed it.

Jack, in all this, remained elusive, but not entirely unac-
countable. Occasionally, and always unexpectedly, he came
home—home being England in general rather than Beaufort
Street in particular. He preferred, in fact, his own flat, where,
he said, he could sleep undisturbed. As he seemed always to
arrive in the middle of the night there could be no logical

objection to this. In any event he tended to regard Tessa as someone whom he had known in the past, and with whom he had no real connection in the present, apart from the little girl, of whom he appeared to be rather fond. All this Harriet learned from Tessa on mornings following the rare nights when Jack could be persuaded to stay for any length of time in Beaufort Street; on such mornings Tessa would arrive late with Lizzie, too late for the child to be taken to school, Dawn having been sent ahead with Imogen. For this reason further malfeasances would be added to Jack's list of misdemeanours, the gravest of which was that he seemed to prefer the company of his daughter to that of his wife. On such occasions Tessa had an awful allure, the mystique of the excitingly mistreated woman, frustrated, no doubt, but undeniably, enviably, aroused. Contact had been made with a man who was in some ways a complete fantasy: his very disdain for the ties of home and family made him seem legendary, not quite human, someone read about, some*thing* read about, as in a saga, or a poem, his brilliant looks—the tall thin body, the wary face, the penetrating gaze—conferring on him the status of a hero, haunting battle-fields, perpetually bringing the good news from Ghent to Aix . . . Once, to Harriet's astonishment, he called for Lizzie. The little girl rose slowly, as if from a sleep, at his appearance, moved towards him uncertainly, as if such a glorious destiny could not be vouchsafed to one as humble as herself.

'Say goodbye and thank you to Mrs Lytton,' he said, hoisting Lizzie on to his shoulders.

'Oh, she calls me Harriet, she knows me so well . . . Won't you stay for a drink? I'm sure my husband won't be long . . .' For it seemed vital to prolong the contact, to engage him, to divert him, he who must be diverted, yet what could she offer in the way of diversion apart from the sort of polite conversation that respectable matrons acquired in the course of their uninteresting days, anecdotes about the children, enquiries after Tessa, as if she had not seen her that morning . . . No, it was not to be thought of, the embarrassment was not to be borne. She was a dull woman, she knew, but now she wished to hide the fact, and hide it from this particular man. Suddenly the long journey she had accomplished from her own childhood to this position of safety, this comfortable place, seemed nugatory, worthless. Given a choice (but had there ever been a choice?) she would have chosen someone like Jack rather than someone like Freddie, one crowded hour of glorious life rather than the age without a name which her present life resembled. She was relieved when he turned to go, Lizzie on his shoulders; she could not have stood the strain of not pleasing him for much longer. She was interested to see that Freddie, encountered at the front door, seemed gratified by Jack's presence, although normally he lost no opportunity to condemn him. They had fallen into the dull habit of condemning exciting or scandalous people. And Immy, arrested by the sight of Lizzie on the glamorous stranger's shoulders, proved unexpectedly fractious when it was time for her to go to bed, and for the first time in her life refused to embrace her father, having discovered, in fact, that men can differ enormously, and that some are more attractive, more desirable, than others.

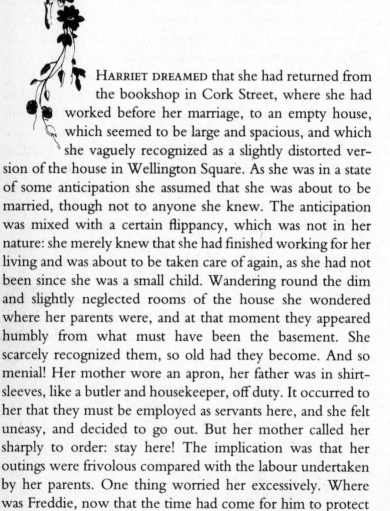

9

HARRIET DREAMED that she had returned from the bookshop in Cork Street, where she had worked before her marriage, to an empty house, which seemed to be large and spacious, and which she vaguely recognized as a slightly distorted version of the house in Wellington Square. As she was in a state of some anticipation she assumed that she was about to be married, though not to anyone she knew. The anticipation was mixed with a certain flippancy, which was not in her nature: she merely knew that she had finished working for her living and was about to be taken care of again, as she had not been since she was a small child. Wandering round the dim and slightly neglected rooms of the house she wondered where her parents were, and at that moment they appeared humbly from what must have been the basement. She scarcely recognized them, so old had they become. And so menial! Her mother wore an apron, her father was in shirt-sleeves, like a butler and housekeeper, off duty. It occurred to her that they must be employed as servants here, and she felt uneasy, and decided to go out. But her mother called her sharply to order: stay here! The implication was that her outings were frivolous compared with the labour undertaken by her parents. One thing worried her excessively. Where was Freddie, now that the time had come for him to protect her, to defend her? Where was her absent bridegroom? She somehow knew that Freddie had foreseen all her flippant and disloyal thoughts—for they were there somewhere, although they had not inspired her to any infidelity—and, stricken, had simply turned away, leaving her alone in a house which was empty except for parents who were now gaolers, and who could not be left because they had grown monstrously old.

When she awoke she wondered what on earth this could mean, since as far as she knew her parents were in good health, and an undoubted Freddie was lying in bed beside her. She felt uneasy, as if others might be able to understand the dream, which was obscure to her, or as if it might indicate trouble to come. But dreams, she knew, concerned themselves with the past and the present, with the unfinished business that prolonged itself from day to day. What concerned her was not her own adulterous frame of mind (which was so faint and so unfocused as to be almost innocent, a function of girlhood, even of virginity, although it required responsible adulthood to bring it into being), as Freddie's absence. This absence she effectively construed as deliberate disappearance, as if his heart were so broken that he had simply walked away. But why should Freddie's heart be broken? He was here, well enough, if a little tired, with his wife beside him, in his own house, which was as well run as she could manage with a small child—two small children—to look after. And the children too were doing well; Immy was never less than well, and Lizzie too was doing better now that her eyes were straightening out and her hair beginning to grow.

Of course she wished that they could get on better, for she always felt a slight anxiety when they were together, after school, an interval which seemed to bring out Lizzie's obstinacy and Immy's petulance. She could understand Immy's impatience with Lizzie: the child was cold, slow, prudent, resistant to the claims of others. Lizzie consented to be in this house only until she was old enough to do otherwise, ate her bread and butter simply in order to gain the strength she knew she would need, waited with grim patience for her mother to come and collect her, waited with tremulous but concealed hope for her father to reappear and bear her away in triumph, thus vindicating her entire existence. And her disappointment was so stoically controlled that it gave her the air of someone much older, and already a slightly difficult character. One could understand Immy's desire to challenge, tease, or even punish this child, who became maddeningly slow as Immy became excited; she even became slightly shrill, with frustration, when Lizzie sat down obstinately to read, her fingers in her ears, refusing to play with Immy, who would inevitably accuse her, cry, become over-excited, slap and even punch the smaller child until gathered into Harriet's arms and comforted. One could understand Immy very well, of course one could. What was more difficult to understand was Lizzie's dislike of Immy, which resembled the cold dislike of one woman for another. Lizzie, had she not had to struggle with the formless feelings of childhood and her ignorance of her own entitlements, would have felt contempt for the exquisite Immy, her tears and smiles, her scenes, her caprices. Already Immy was adept at imposing her whims, might or might not respond to her mother's blandishments, or her father's greeting. Sometimes, when Freddie came home in the evenings, she would pointedly ignore him, elaborately expressing lack of interest, be intent on dressing a doll, whom she would address in sharp and knowing terms, while Freddie slowly put down his briefcase, kissed Harriet, and with an air of fatigue sank down into his chair in the drawing-room. No amount of cajoling, then, would bring Immy out of her mood.

They were reluctant to chastise her, feeling that something as rigorous as natural selection was at work: if Immy despised

her father it was because he was old, plain, tired, because there
was a heaviness and a staleness about him which the child
found unappealing, even horrifying. There was justice in all
this. Yet the hurt she inflicted was disproportionate, and
sometimes Freddie became morose. Sometimes he left the
drawing-room and went upstairs to his study, preferring not
to remain in his daughter's presence and bear the burden of
her dislike. Of course, thought Harriet suddenly, in the middle of the day, when the dream came back to her, she has
broken Freddie's heart. That was why he would not stay with
me, even in the dream. The thought was so terrible to her that
she immediately suppressed it, but at the same time wondered
what she could do in order to beguile her daughter into a
better mood.

For Freddie was too old, she could see that, and too graceless to be accepted by the child as a worthy progenitor. And
Immy was too conscious of her status as a beauty and a prize
to allow herself to waste her attentions on so faded a figure.
Her mother she tolerated, retaining there a certain babyish-
ness: she would run to Harriet, nestle on her lap, lay her head
on Harriet's shoulder, and disappear into a dream of her own.
Immy, my Immy, Harriet would think, with a thrill of total
and exclusive ownership. She even felt pride when the child
did not reject her, felt at last worthy and valued, after the
well-behaved and disappointing years. She suffered for Freddie, but was gratified at being favoured, so gratified that she
made light to herself of her child's caprices, thinking with
pride that Immy would be prestigious as she grew older, and
would never have to acquiesce in the choices made by others
on her behalf. She was already exquisite, with a beauty of
bone and colouring which would not disappear with childhood or adolescence. Her small face was white, with only a
very faint flush of pink when she was excited or annoyed; her
eyes were dark, her hair—her most beautiful feature—dark

and silky, like her mother's. The very small mouth could
compress itself into a passion of refusal. 'You know who she
looks like?' said her grandmother. 'Why, me, of course.'
Merle and Hughie were 'up for the day', as they put it, 'to
take in a matinée', when what they really wanted to see was
Immy. The child accepted her grandparents, as if she were in
some way aware of their earlier liveliness and approved of it,
whereas what repelled her in her father was a certain resignation, a lack of virility. This, it seemed, she could not but
despise.

For Freddie disappointment struck early, as if the reactions
of a six-year-old, a seven-year-old, were the summation of a
lifetime's suspicions, as if the child had brought him to a
self-knowledge which he would rather have forgone. He
even begrudged his wife the caresses that came to her so
carelessly, while Hughie Blakemore, who always seemed so
like a child himself, appeared to have found a note of flirtatiousness which was a great success with Immy. I could never
flirt, thought Freddie, even with Harriet, even with Helen,
when I was so much younger. He was quite aware that he
must appear unattractive to the child. He was wise enough
not to reproach her: her mother, he thought, must do that,
although Harriet, he could see, was almost abject . . . And the
reaction was purely physical, which somehow made the
whole business more painful. He had his dignity, of course,
knew when to make himself scarce, knew too that he could
provide the child with certain resources which, when she had
grown older, would count for more than his appearance. I am
too old, he thought. And her mother is too indulgent; strange
how she does not see . . . The other child, Lizzie, kept away
from him too, but then Lizzie kept away from everyone.

When Dawn announced her departure there were tears on
both sides. 'Must you go?' begged Harriet.

'I've been here longer than I meant to,' said Dawn. 'I'll

never get home at this rate. And I want to spend more time in Europe.'

'There will always be a home for you here,' said Harriet, kissing the girl. 'You're like a daughter to me,' she heard herself saying, a remark on which she reflected with some surprise. Yes, she could be my daughter, and has always felt as if she might be. I am almost too old to be the mother of a little girl. 'But how shall I manage without Dawn?' she said to Freddie. 'Taking the children to school and collecting them every day—I don't know how I'm going to do it.'

She despised herself even as the words were out of her mouth, but Freddie took her seriously.

'She must go away to school,' he said. 'As soon as she is old enough. Lizzie's going, isn't she? They can go together. Immy needs to be disciplined; you spoil her too much. And she's getting boisterous—I don't like it.'

She thought there was some rancour in him which dictated this course of action, but was forced to see the wisdom of it. She sometimes got headaches these days, when the children were at loggerheads, sometimes longed to take an untroubled walk in the park, where a precocious spring had brought on the daffodils with the crocuses, and put thick green buds on the magnolias. She knew her indulgence was too extreme but could not forgo it: it was her secret passion, the only one she had ever indulged. She also knew that if Immy went away she would come to treasure that indulgence, and the idea did not displease her. On another level she knew that Immy's absence would allow Freddie's self-esteem to repair itself. This too might be necessary. Therefore the idea did not seem too extravagant to her. 'And we can take a decent holiday for once,' said Freddie. Immy's departure was fixed for a couple of years ahead, when she was ten: she longed for it. Lizzie, inscrutable, nodded when asked if she were looking forward to going away to school. There was no knowing what was in her mind.

'Am I a bad mother?' she asked Dawn, watching the girl pack. 'Am I bad for Immy? She seems to me so delightful, yet her teacher says she is disruptive. I can see that she's high-spirited, yet that's what I admire in her—her energy. I don't know where she gets it from. Freddie and I are, well, terribly ordinary.' She chose the word with care, loyally aligning herself with Freddie in this ordinariness of which she so carefully spoke. On reflection she believed it to be the case, although knowing that sometimes she harboured extravagant feelings, wistful imaginings, longings for experiences not in her peaceable domain. 'I have tried hard,' she said regretfully, as if taking the measure of what she had not achieved.

Obliquely, Dawn said, 'You should get out more. You're too tied to the house. Immy's okay. She needs a bit of discipline, that's all. Did you see the way she bossed that boy about, the one she brought home the other day?'

But Harriet had secretly admired Immy's imperiousness, a quality she herself had never possessed. It seemed as though Immy were developing the very gifts in which she herself was deficient, and, although she could see that this might cause a certain amount of disaffection, she thought that that very imperiousness might serve her daughter well in later life.

'I shall miss her awfully,' she went on, forcing herself to see a life, a house, without her daughter's presence to enliven them.

'You'll see enough of her in the holidays,' Dawn said. 'She needs more distractions. So do you, as a matter of fact. There's no need for you to stick around all day. Anyway, I'm off. Freddie's been awfully good—did he tell you?'

For an envelope had been passed over, with a substantial cheque inside it. Harriet had not witnessed this, leaving it to Freddie, whose suggestion it had been. The occasional generosity of her husband still impressed her.

A diversion was now decreed for her, however. More of an obligation than a diversion, she was beginning to think, so rooted had she become in general domesticity, in contemplation of her daughter's now foreshortened sojourn under her roof. The entity she now thought of as Mary-Pamela was to be in town—Mary and her husband home on extended leave, Pamela down on one of her visits to Harrods—and they were all to meet for one of those lunches which she thought of as a tradition, although they had necessarily been in abeyance while the children were small. 'My treat,' Mary had said, which made it more of an obligation. 'Why are you sighing?' asked Freddie. 'You used to enjoy being with them. As long as you don't bring them back here,' he added hastily. He had always distrusted her female friends, assuming, not incorrectly, that they indulged in scandalous confidences. His mistrust was automatic: he thought he knew more about women than his wife did.

For this occasion, half dreaded now that it had come about, Harriet dressed carefully, thinking she looked older than she should, and said as much to Dawn.

'That blue suits you,' said Dawn stoutly.

'Not too much?' she queried. 'I don't want to look overdressed. Mary was always very chic. Although Tessa always managed to look better, as if she'd taken no trouble, as if she didn't need to bother.'

Many worried glances were cast in the mirror before she took her gloves and opened the door. On an impulse she went back and left the gloves behind. Gloves were what matrons wore.

But the others looked older too, she saw with surprise. Seated at the table they eyed each other comprehensively and without indulgence. Mary was exquisite, certainly, although with a certain air of contrivance now, but Pamela's life in the country had given her a harsh flush. Tessa, by contrast, was pale, thin, abstracted and hectic by turns. Their husbands,

Harriet noted, they referred to unselfconsciously, with a certain indifference, as if they had written them off. Could have done better, they seemed to imply. Mary, composedly, admitted to having a lover.

'But how do you manage?' asked Pamela, who seemed affronted, not by the fact of Mary's having a lover so much as by the fact that, stuck on the farm, she found so little opportunity for having one herself.

'One can always manage if one wants to,' replied Mary, winking at Tessa. 'Anyway, be faithful to a man? Why should I? Why should any woman?'

This is exactly what Freddie was afraid of, thought Harriet, laying down her fork. She had a moment of lucidity, seeing them not as glamorous friends she had once envied but as harder and more practised than herself. Perhaps they are right, she thought, in a moment of exceptional discouragement. I cannot claim to be any better. I have often been bored by Freddie, although I have never done what seems to be the norm today. Perhaps the opportunity has simply never presented itself.

'How's Jack?' she asked, one thought leading to another.

'He's in London, actually,' said Tessa, who was not eating much either. 'He's at Judd Street. In fact I sent him off there. I've had some sort of bug. I didn't think he'd like to see me throwing up all the time.'

'Not pregnant, I hope?' queried Pamela.

Tessa smiled. 'Not much chance of that, is there?'

'You mean . . . ?'

'I mean he's hardly ever around, is he?' She yawned convulsively, and pushed her plate away. 'Excuse me for a minute, would you? I feel a bit queasy.'

There was a moment's silence after she had disappeared.

'Is she all right?' asked Harriet, appealing to the other two. 'She doesn't look it. I noticed it when she came in.'

'I thought you saw her all the time?'

'Well, no, not now that Lizzie's old enough to go home by herself. I haven't seen her for two or three weeks, as a matter of fact. But I'm sure she'd have told me if there were anything wrong.' She felt alarmed and at fault, as if her function, which she had once assumed so gladly, was to protect Tessa, who suddenly appeared to be without protection, almost fragile.

'She'll be okay, she's as tough as a horse. I'm going to have some of that apple tart, and blow the diet. Hattie? Come on, don't look so glum. I adore that suit, by the way.'

Tessa, looking pale, came back, sat down, and averted her eyes from the abandoned plates. She was a bad, greyish colour. Something is wrong, thought Harriet, with a stab of fear. Aloud she said, 'Do you want to go home? I'll take you, shall I? You probably ought to be in bed.'

The others looked up enquiringly. This was not how their lunches usually progressed.

'Perhaps I will,' said Tessa, forcing a smile. 'I'm so sorry. Too silly. Lovely to see you both.' Tears stood in her eyes. Harriet, with a feeling of distress which she knew or thought was quite disproportionate, guided her through the restaurant, a hand under her arm. Out in the air Tessa swayed a little. 'I've been awfully sick,' she said fretfully.

'Can you walk? The air might do you good. Take it slowly. It's not far.'

They walked slowly, heads down, along the road, which seemed endless, full of hooting cars and women with prams and shopping bags.

'I must have eaten something,' Tessa claimed, in the same fretful, almost querulous tone.

Strange, thought Harriet. I have never known her like this. Or has she altered and I not noticed it? In Beaufort Street, reached after a largely wordless, and to Harriet endless interval, in the course of which Tessa had bumped against her, as if no longer capable of steering her own course, she took charge of the key and inserted it thankfully into the door of the flat. 'Home at last,' she said.

'Oh, God,' cried Tessa, in naked panic, and ran for the bathroom.

Harriet waited outside the door, listening to the terrible sounds. A doctor, she thought; I must get a doctor. But when Tessa emerged she was calmer, very pale, very quiet, almost sad, distant.

'I don't need a doctor,' she said. 'I'm all right now. Only if you could have Lizzie tonight? I'd rather like to be on my own.'

'But you can't . . .'

'Yes, I can. I must.'

They looked at each other, as if what had taken place were too shameful, too distressing to be shared, or to be admitted to normal conversation, as if it must somehow be contained. They both sat in the room which continued to look careless, uninhabited. They said nothing. After a while Harriet took Tessa's hand and held it. Perhaps five minutes passed, perhaps ten. 'I'm all right now,' said Tessa finally. 'You'd better go. Tell Lizzie . . . Tell her I'm going out. Tell her I'm fine.' She gazed at the window, tears again in her eyes. 'Tell her I'm absolutely fine,' she said. 'She can come back tomorrow.'

'Should I ring Jack?' asked Harriet, knowing the answer.

'No, no, I'm all right. I'll go to bed. You go, Hattie. I'll call you tomorrow.'

'She's not going to sleep in my room, is she?' asked Immy, with an exaggerated expression of distaste.

'Of course she is. Don't be so rude. I hope you're not going to let Miss Wetherby hear you talking like that.'

She had already let Dawn's basement to a Miss Wetherby, an elderly, placid, slightly deaf woman who had been a nanny at a foreign embassy. Although past retiring age she had con-

sented to perform supervisory duties when necessary in return
for a token rent, which she could well afford on her pension.
She appeared to be satisfied with the arrangement, although
it was a little difficult to be sure of this. Miss Wetherby had
a certain authority, which showed in her absolute failure to
return winning or placatory smiles. When introduced to Imogen she had produced nothing more than a judicious look and
a dry outstretched hand. Yet she was kindly, and without
pretension: Harriet, paying a visit to the basement to see if
Miss Wetherby had everything she needed, had found herself
in a world of stored knitting patterns, tea cosies, and plastic
watering cans. 'So lovely to have a home of my own after all
those years abroad,' she murmured; contrary to most deaf
people she spoke very softly. 'I hope you won't mind baby-
sitting for us,' Harriet had said. 'It's only until she goes away
to school next year. And then in the school holidays, of
course.' Miss Wetherby inclined her good ear, which gave
her the air of a medium. 'I'm sure you'll get along,' Harriet
had added. She did not see how anyone could fail to get along
with so mild a person as Miss Wetherby. Yet the mildness was
deceptive. Imogen was slightly afraid of her, until she found
out that she could say things without Miss Wetherby over-
hearing them. 'I was just saying what a lovely day it was,' she
would explain, when Miss Wetherby's face turned in her
direction. Miss Wetherby, choosing to appear deceived, held
Imogen in check by allowing an unfavourable verdict to be
implied in her attitudes and movements: criticism was imma-
nent, never voiced. The level eyes, the pale conventual face,
the unhurried, slightly arthritic walk, although easily imitated,
nevertheless exacted a certain respect.

'Which yoghourt would you like, Lizzie? Pineapple or
apricot?'

For it seemed important to let the poor child have some
sort of a choice, although she was so stoical that it was hard

ever to detect disappointment. She had not asked where her mother was, but seemed to accept whatever conditions were decreed for her by others. Why was she so remote? There had been no major dereliction: her parents were unusual, but not delinquent. Was it that she needed more love than anyone had yet given her, and was too proud ever to demand it? In which case the road ahead of her was bleak, for few people gave too much affection, or more than they could spare from their closely guarded hoard, and the child had no pretty ways, of the sort that attract the indulgence of others. Her gaze was now normal, and indeed had become strangely uncompromising, not unlike Miss Wetherby's, but she was a pale little creature, thin, colourless, scrupulous, but not forthcoming. Her responses were obedient, no more. She seemed to be harbouring thoughts beyond her years. Her attitude to Imogen was now one of wariness; what had earlier seemed almost like contempt was circumscribed by caution. She accepted the fact that she must endure her company (for Immy would be the only person she knew when they went away to school, an event she anticipated with horror) while giving the impression that she was reserving her opinion. Harriet she submitted to, without a great deal of emotion. The one person she really liked was Miss Wetherby.

'You can watch television for half an hour after you've had your tea,' said Harriet. She did not normally allow this, but found herself unable to cope with them, slightly unwell. I must have the same thing that Tessa has, she thought. This effectively neutralized the more serious suspicion that Tessa was ill, and not only ill but in the grip of some strange withdrawal, which she could not penetrate. Why that withdrawal, which was almost silent? For a malaise which, however unpleasant, was surely routine, the sort of thing from which one had suffered as a child, and which returned as an odd reminder in later life? Was it because of the recalcitrant, the ever-troublesome Jack? Of course, she is upset; Jack has upset her, as usual. And a touch of food poisoning, no doubt; she was never very careful about what she ate. And the state of that flat . . . But I wish there were someone with her. This thought tormented her until she remembered that Jack was, after all, in town, as were her other friends. There was no need to think of herself as indispensable. She would go round in the morning. Or perhaps she would telephone first. Ridiculous to feel this apprehension. Nevertheless, when Freddie came home she embraced him ardently, surprising him. His eye dwelt on her appreciatively, as they sat over dinner. Oh no, that was not what I meant at all, she thought. Or did I? I no longer know: that is what I have come to. In Freddie's arms she trembled slightly, for many obscure reasons, and then fell, with deep gratitude, and almost as great perplexity, into sleep and dreaming.

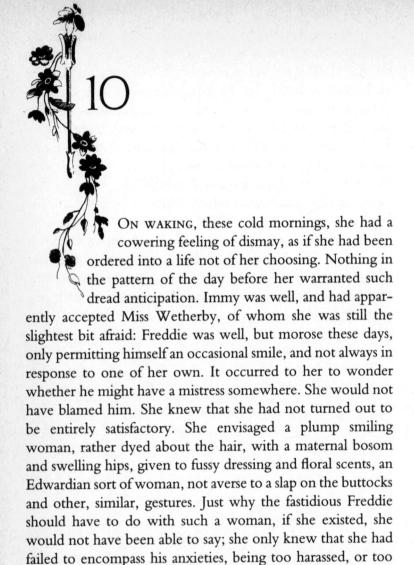

10

ON WAKING, these cold mornings, she had a
cowering feeling of dismay, as if she had been
ordered into a life not of her choosing. Nothing in
the pattern of the day before her warranted such
dread anticipation. Immy was well, and had apparently accepted Miss Wetherby, of whom she was still the
slightest bit afraid: Freddie was well, but morose these days,
only permitting himself an occasional smile, and not always in
response to one of her own. It occurred to her to wonder
whether he might have a mistress somewhere. She would not
have blamed him. She knew that she had not turned out to
be entirely satisfactory. She envisaged a plump smiling
woman, rather dyed about the hair, with a maternal bosom
and swelling hips, given to fussy dressing and floral scents, an
Edwardian sort of woman, not averse to a slap on the buttocks
and other, similar, gestures. Just why the fastidious Freddie
should have to do with such a woman, if she existed, she
would not have been able to say; she only knew that she had
failed to encompass his anxieties, being too harassed, or too
self-questioning herself. She had no idea what Freddie did
with his day. She only knew that he liked to lunch, alone, at
his club, perhaps joining a friend afterwards for a moment's
conversation. She supposed that the vulgar friendly woman of
her imagination could be fitted in some time after lunch, as

a *digestif,* after which he would be both relieved and gloomy, in the manner of well-meaning adulterous husbands, unable to take the thing lightly, yet determined not to take it at all seriously. She felt no animus against Freddie for this imaginary liaison—if it existed—but rather a certain guilt on her own behalf, not for alienating Freddie, but in fact for having always kept him at a distance, where she felt most comfortable with him, her own thoughts and sentiments—dissatisfactions, too—inviolate, and, she hoped, not perceived.

For if Freddie had a mistress, which was extremely unlikely, given his utterly predictable behaviour, the clumsiness of his occasional ardour, the lost look she sometimes saw in his eyes, the general prudence of his utterances, she would be the last person to accuse him. She knew that he thought her half-hearted, caring more for the child than she had ever done for himself, proud of and exasperated by the house and by her general respectability, tempted, perhaps unconsciously, by a freedom she had never known. Docile no longer, practical and competent, rather, preoccupied with the child and its well-being, only half attentive to himself. She knew this to be true, whether it had entered Freddie's mind or not. She felt the temptation of resentment hovering over him, although she was technically innocent. Why disaffection had entered her house she did not entirely know, but put it down to his acknowledgement of her complete lack of marital desire. She now found his overtures alarming, and sad. It was as if the birth of her daughter had restored her to virginity. Pinned down by his heavy body, she found herself gasping for air, and afterwards, when she was allowed to sleep, felt nothing but loneliness. After a rest, which always seemed too brief, she would stir awake with that sense of haplessness, even panic, as if the night had been impossibly short, too short to contain all the reflections she had reserved for those silent hours, in the hope of arriving at some resolution.

It was not resolution of conflict that she sought: there was no conflict. Simply some pointer to the way ahead, as if she had an exceptionally difficult problem to solve. Then she would get up and have her bath and dress, and the feeling would disperse. And once she had prepared the breakfast (missing Dawn on these occasions) and tried to subdue Immy in order to give Freddie a bit of peace, and usually failing, she was quite glad when they both left and she was really alone. Now that Dawn was gone, Freddie sometimes took Immy to school in his car; at other times Miss Wetherby officiated. Lizzie made her way independently, sometimes driven by Tessa, sometimes trudging on her own. They saw less of Lizzie these days. She was capable of going straight home on her own, and she preferred to. For a child of eight she was oddly mature.

My daughter is all I desire, thought Harriet, resting in the early afternoon, and yet somehow I desire more. For in this brief hour, on her sofa, she freed her imagination from its usual restraints and thought of another life, other lives. Lives lived in perpetual sunshine, not this meagre light, and, yes, that was it, just two of them. But here imagination let her down, for although she knew it was not Freddie at her side, she could not quite see her companion, or rather could not formulate him, since she was free to make him up. He bore a resemblance to Jack Peckham, but this was fortuitous, since the Jack Peckham character, the ruthless faceless lover, had been present in her thoughts before the real Jack Peckham had ever been encountered. She thought it strange that an obedient woman like herself should have fantasies of such strangeness and such intensity, yet she also knew that with such a partner she would no longer be obedient, but power-ful, irresistible, even. And all in that sunshine, somewhere far away, just the two of them, with no relatives, no friends, and no need of either. In these moods, in the half doze of early afternoon, she disposed of her present life, and substituted for it the life of the imagination, for which nothing in her experience or her reading had prepared her. Outwardly calm, but inwardly amazed at herself, she would rise, and see to her face, and go downstairs to prepare Immy's tea. Sometimes, very occasionally, Lizzie would turn up, without explanations. Harriet would scrutinize the child's face, to see if Jack were present there. Fortunately, there was no trace. This was a relief to her. It is not Jack I want, she thought. It is someone *like* Jack, but someone of my very own. That way there would be no guilt. For guilt she could not endure.

'How is Mummy?' she asked Lizzie, on one of the occasions when the child was present. 'I haven't seen her lately. And she seems to be out whenever I telephone.'

Lizzie observed her usual pause when directly addressed. 'All right,' she said finally.

'Can I wear your pearls?' interjected Immy.

'No, of course you can't. Besides, I am wearing them.'

'Yes, but you're old. You're too old to wear them.'

A beautiful child, more precious than life itself, Harriet reflected. But occasionally taxing.

'Perhaps Mummy and Daddy would like to come to dinner while Daddy is in London?' she went on. 'You could stay overnight, in Immy's room. Would you like that?'

Lizzie maintained a prudent silence.

'I wouldn't,' said Immy rudely.

The invitation was accepted, with some surprise, and—or did she imagine it—with a hint of something like amusement. Harriet found herself excited and daunted. To have Jack Peckham under her roof brought her dangerously near to fantasy, yet what could be more sedate, more bourgeois than an intimate dinner party in Wellington Square? On reflection, she decided against inviting any of Freddie's colleagues, sedate bourgeois persons like themselves, and although civilized and knowledgeable, elderly. She did not dare risk boring Jack. It occurred to her, while she was dressing, that Tessa knew something of her fascination with Jack, although she had always been careful, she thought, to hide it away, to reserve it for her most private moments. Slowly, as this sank in, she felt herself blush, put up her hand to shield her face. Then she resolutely turned to herself in the mirror, saw the mark on her jaw brilliantly infused with colour, and realized that she was a middle-aged woman, never very exciting, now positively dull, an old friend, and, she hoped, a good friend, worthy enough to take care of the children, to serve up a decent daube of beef, to observe (yes, that surely was permitted), but to observe in a spirit of detachment, as befitted an old friend, one who still valued the ties of friendship (overvalued them, perhaps) and would comport herself with dignity to the very end. The end of what, she wondered, then heard the doorbell ring, and hurried down the stairs.

On the bottom step she met Tessa, coming towards her. A rumble of talk indicated that Freddie had already taken Jack to the drawing-room. Tessa, with the light behind her, appeared darkened, crow-like, in chic but unbecoming black. One foot on a higher step, she looked up, and then Harriet saw her face, pale, with an unfamiliar pallor, drawn, tired. 'Oh, you're not well,' she said. Tessa looked at her with a certain weariness. 'Could I just use your bathroom?' she asked. 'Of course. Come up. I'll come with you. Use my bedroom as well, if you want to. Are you all right?'

'Of course I'm all right. How you fuss, Harriet.' She trailed past, a heavy musky scent following her, narrow ankles in fine black stockings turned slightly inwards.

Harriet. Not Hattie. Something guessed at, perhaps, more than suspected. Shame brought a high colour to her cheeks and inflamed the birthmark still further. Looking at herself in the glass, she thought, the game is up, and then, how absurd, how meretricious I have become. The flush subsided, leaving behind a resigned calm, and a slight but definite indignation. I have done nothing wrong, she reminded herself. In fact, I have done nothing at all. I have simply been here all the time, running when called to, waiting when not, always grateful for the slightest, most insignificant mark of attention. She felt a bewilderment: had it come to this, a tardy realization of past inadequacies on both sides? But surely there was always our friendship? More than twenty years . . . That is what counts, now that we are both middle-aged, and past the time when we might have been unreasonable? *Nothing has happened.* 'Of course,' she said lightly, 'I can see why you keep Jack to yourself. He really is most attractive.'

Tessa, applying lipstick, glanced at her sideways.

'Yes. I know.'

She then took from her bag a small compact filled with something which looked like gold dust, and applied it with a brush to cheeks which were already heavily coloured. Gradually a misty web was drawn over features which, Harriet saw, were thin, sharply defined. The mouth was once again, very slowly, painted brick red, almost brown. She looked amazing, but entirely absent, inhabited by some thought far from the surface of her mind.

'What is wrong?' asked Harriet quietly.

'Nothing more than a touch of indigestion. Eating at night doesn't really agree with me these days—too tired, I suppose. So don't be upset if I don't do justice to your excellent cooking. Shall we go down?'

Your excellent cooking? But she is behaving like a stranger, thought Harriet. And yet if anything were wrong she would surely have told me?

Dinner was less arduous than she had expected, but possibly more disconcerting. Tessa, true to her predictions, hardly touched her food, moved it expertly about her plate, and then left it. Freddie's prized Lynch-Bages was smilingly declined by her, but accepted with due appreciation by Jack, who, between courses, got up and roamed around the room, examining the books in the two fine pedimented bookcases. When he deigned to sit down, it was to place an arm on the back of Tessa's chair, to gaze searchingly into her face, as if oblivious of the other two. Harriet found it disturbing, ostentatious, this flouting of the rules of hospitality, of courtesy, of seemliness. She suspected that it was habitual, this exclusivity, that they met on this level, if on no other. But Freddie seemed to see nothing wrong, seemed, if anything, exhilarated, looked for once indulgently at Tessa's sharp and highly coloured face, hastened to pour Jack more wine.

'Shall we have coffee in the drawing-room?' asked Harriet, longing suddenly for the evening to be over.

'None for me,' said Tessa. 'Jack, I'm sure, would love some.'

'How long are you to be in London, Jack?' asked Harriet.

He stirred himself, seemed almost to yawn, then sat forward and nodded to Freddie, who hovered with a bottle of brandy.

'I go to Paris next month,' he said. He drank appreciatively, and then added, 'Intermittently.'

'Of course,' Harriet said, light dawning. 'Lizzie has inherited your way of speaking.'

He fixed her with his disconcerting eye. 'Which way is that?' he asked.

'Sparing,' she said. 'Laconic.' Just this side of rudeness, she thought. Aloud, she said, 'I see Lizzie's resemblance to you now.'

He cocked an eyebrow at her. 'We have to thank you for looking after Lizzie. You have been very good.'

So that is why you condescended to come this evening, she thought. Otherwise you might not have bothered.

'We love having her,' she said, very quietly.

He looked at her, as searchingly as she had seen him look at Tessa. She got up, removed empty coffee cups.

'We must go,' said Tessa, after a long abstracted pause. 'Jack has to go back to Judd Street. He's got a very early start in the morning.'

'Oh, I'll drop you off,' said Jack. 'I'll ring you tomorrow night.'

'Must you go? It's barely eleven . . .'

'Work in the morning,' said Tessa, with a smile that was almost a grimace. 'Can you tell Lizzie to come straight home after school?'

'Of course,' said Harriet, slightly bewildered. 'And when shall I see you? Shall we have lunch?'

'Oh, let's.' The reply was falsely enthusiastic; her eyes were on Jack. 'I'll ring you, shall I? Lovely evening, darling. Freddie, thank you so much.'

Harriet, with pity, saw Freddie struggle to his feet. He was now quite stout, his eyes rosy, looking forward, she could see, to his bed. 'You go up,' she said to him, as he closed the door. 'I'll just clear away down here. Don't stay awake for me.'

'What did you make of that?' she asked, removing her earrings, seeing him behind her in the glass, in maroon pyjamas, his glasses on a cord around his neck, one hand splayed on his book.

'I thought it went quite well. He's an interesting fellow. Rather glad they went early, though. Are you coming to bed? I think I'll turn out my light, if you don't mind.'

'Oh, don't wait for me,' she repeated. 'I don't feel tired. I think I'll read for a bit.'

She was in fact weary but alert, anxious to sort out her thoughts. She found herself vastly disappointed by what had taken place. That odd communion between Jack and Tessa, almost a seduction. Tessa's glamorous but bedizened appearance. Herself nowhere, an anxious handmaid. Freddie had drunk too much, something that must be watched. The extraordinary level of artificiality that had prevailed, as if there were secrets, not to be divulged. Secrets with an odd sexual connotation, or merely indicating a high degree of complicity. Herself excluded.

But surely, she thought, waking violently in the night, surely we are friends? I have known her for so long, all my adult life, the part of it that was not occupied by dreaming. I reached out to her from my childhood, and she summoned me, with a negligent hand, to join *her* friends. They were never really mine. Hard, I thought them, and noisy: pitiless. Tessa, however, was oddly loyal to me, though not always very interested. Perhaps I assumed too much eagerness . . . I remember a quickening of genuine interest only when I announced my engagement, and since my marriage—and hers—a change in her, to thoughtfulness, wistfulness, almost. But a return to her original authority when it appears to her to be indicated. Materially I raced ahead of her, although her money will always count for more than mine. But surely we were closer than all these sordid considerations might seem to imply? True friendship between women is rare, I know, but we were never disloyal. Until this evening I thought I knew everything about her, but suddenly there were secrets there, which plunged them both into abstraction. Really, they might have been anywhere. Not very polite to me, or to Freddie, come to that: odd, on the whole, that he was more indulgent than I was. He dislikes Tessa, always has, suspects her of pitying me for having to sleep with him, yet as far as I know she never has, is probably not sufficiently interested. Oh, this is awful, she thought with horror: the lucidity which comes unwanted, in the middle of the night. I might still be a schoolgirl, in the room at the back of the shop, feeling proud of having Tessa as a friend. Yet it hurts, that sudden distancing, even if I was a little deluded all these years. And now I am a middle-aged woman, and loneliness descends. I cannot bear my life if Freddie is to be my only friend.

But this thought, so suddenly and completely formulated, was so shocking that she renounced sleep, got quietly out of bed, put on slippers and dressing-gown, and went down to the kitchen to make tea. Glancing at the clock under the harsh white light, she saw that it was four-thirty. She unloaded the dishwasher, put away plates and cutlery, polished glasses, cancelling the rest of the night. Then she laid the table for breakfast, crept up the stairs, had a bath in Immy's bathroom, so as not to disturb Freddie, and appeared, brisk and smiling, with a cup of tea for him at six-thirty, trying not to notice the heavy slept-in smell of the room, or, when she pulled the curtains, the pearl-like drops of rain on windows still coated with a fine autumnal dust.

'It feels wintry,' she said. 'Wear your blue suit.' She shivered in the dank air, and thought, like Jane Eyre, no walk today.

She was brisk in the days that followed, arranged for Miss Wetherby to take Immy to school and collect her afterwards, and bought herself some new clothes, trying to create a more confident image of herself, entirely for her own benefit. She felt undeniably lonely, and although longing to see Tessa— with whom at last she felt equal in experience, and not all of it good—was uncertain of Tessa's willingness to engage with her in what now seemed like a fairly hollow friendship. She had been so cold, so distant . . . But she is ill, she thought, suddenly. Or she is pregnant, and for some reason doesn't want me to know. Again she came up against the loaded and wordless communion between the two of them, which threw such a painful light on her own marriage. There were no undertones between Freddie and herself. They communicated in rational speech on matters which could be discussed objectively. Information was exchanged, nothing more. The dimension of shared thoughts was lacking, always had been. At first she had welcomed this, thinking it made for openness. As indeed it had. It was Freddie's way of doing business, and had made him widely respected. She had adopted his manner of speaking out of a desire to please him, and now it was too late for intimacy to make inroads. Sometimes, in moments of affection, he caught her hand as she passed. On the surface, and indeed on the whole, they were moderately pleased with each other. But she knew she could not confide in him. And indeed what was there to confide, apart from various silent forms of dissatisfaction? And the occasional panic? Our old age will be like this, she thought. And I have perhaps been trained for it.

When Tessa telephoned it was to say that Mary was still in town. Did she want to join them for lunch?

'No,' she said, on an impulse. 'I'm rather busy at the moment. You go.'

She drilled herself out of her unsettled mood by going on long walks, and testing her reactions to solitude. She found it on the whole enlightening, blamed herself for excessive dependence on others. That has been my weakness, she thought, and it must go.

Tessa rang that evening, to say that Mary sent her love.

'Are you all right?' she found herself asking, in the teeth of her new resolution.

'I'm fine. Let's meet soon.'

'Of course, soon.' She put down the telephone, only partially reassured.

The days shortened, the nights lengthened, Freddie dozed regularly after dinner, and she could only be glad that Immy never saw him in this state, his waistcoat gaping, his glasses falling off his nose. She would wake him up in time to go to bed, for she rarely went up without him. Then they would read for an hour before switching off their lights. She read

Hard Times, and in her head heard the great cry, 'Alive!' And then, resolutely, turned off her light and composed herself for rest, if not for sleep.

One night, one freezing night, she drifted off into a doze, listening to the patter of the rain which might, by the morning, become snow, when she was jerked awake by the metallic echo of the telephone, its rings almost visible in the icy air. She sat up with beating heart. Again it rang, and this time she intercepted it.

'Hello?' she said urgently. 'Hello?'

There was a silence. Then a faint voice. 'Hattie.' Then another silence. 'Come to me,' said the voice, and the telephone clattered on to a table and went dead.

Shaking, she drew the nightgown from her body, a body that was already cringing with fear, found trousers and a sweater, and, distracted, picked up a torch, though this would not be necessary. Struggling into a raincoat, she put down the torch and picked up her keys, then, closing the front door behind her, ran up the deserted street until she reached Tessa's flat.

She found the door unlatched, heard noises coming from the bathroom. 'It's all right, darling,' she said, wiping the poor face. 'I won't leave you.' 'Ring Jack,' Tessa gasped. And, 'Don't wake Lizzie.' But as she got through to Jack, who was miraculously—and it was truly a miracle—at home, and told him to come at once, she turned, and saw Lizzie in the doorway. She dropped the telephone and tried to shepherd Lizzie back to her own room, but not before the child had seen her mother's empty bed, and the pillow stained with vomit.

Jack took charge after that. 'Time to go, Tess,' he said, picking her up in his arms, and kissing her on the mouth.

'Where are you taking her?' said Harriet, cradling Lizzie's head to her breast.

He turned without answering, and said over his shoulder,

'If you could just wait here till I get back? I don't want to leave Lizzie here on her own.'

'Don't worry, sweetheart,' she said to the child. 'Daddy is with her. She'll be all right. But I think we'd better get you dressed, hadn't we? In case Daddy wants you to come home with me.' She fondled the child, who seemed unresponsive. She looked past the cradling arms into the room, which was now empty.

An eternity passed, in which Harriet rocked the child, as though she were a baby again. They remained silent, anxious to make no sound in the silent flat. The sound of a key brought Jack back into the room.

'I should like you to tell me what is wrong,' she said, although by now she thought she knew the answer.

'She is dying, of course,' said Jack briefly, and her hands flew in horror to the child's shoulders, to steady her.

'How can you speak like that in front of Lizzie?'

He dropped to his knees and held Lizzie at arm's length.

'Your mother is dying, Lizzie. You knew that, didn't you? She is going to die, but you will have time to say goodbye to her. She is in bed, in the hospital. I will take you to see her tomorrow.'

'She is coming home with me,' Harriet protested.

'No,' he said, his face set in harsh lines. 'She is coming home with me. Pack a few things for her, would you?'

'But it's easier if she comes with me,' she insisted. 'She can stay with my daughter.'

He looked at her with a certain distaste.

'She can't stand your daughter,' he said.

'Oh, really . . .'

'She can miss school for a bit,' he went on. 'It's important that she miss none of *this*: she mustn't be cheated out of it.'

'Are you sure . . . ?'

'Oh, yes, Mrs Lytton. I'm quite sure.'

'You might call me Harriet,' she said furiously. 'After all, your daughter does.'

He ignored this. 'Come along, Lizzie,' he said. 'You've had a bad night so far. I'm going to take you home to Judd Street. You'll be staying there until we decide what's best for us all. Are you brave?'

She nodded, and took his hand.

'Go and wait for me outside, in the hall,' he said, giving her a little push.

'Unfortunately,' he said to Harriet, 'or fortunately, whichever way you look at it, she's in the same room that she had when Lizzie was born.'

'What is wrong?' she asked, her mouth dry.

'What does one usually die of these days?' he asked, it seemed to her with appalling negligence. 'It's in the liver. It will be quite quick.'

'You knew?' she whispered.

'She told me just before we came to dinner with you that evening. I found her . . . rather magnificent . . . There is no doubt, of course. But I think you guessed that there was something wrong.'

'Yes,' she said, bowing her head with sorrow, and wiping away bitter tears. 'Yes, I guessed there was something wrong. I shall never forgive myself.'

'Why not?' he said, picking Lizzie up and hoisting her to his shoulder. 'Most people do, whatever their shortcomings. I think you will forgive yourself, Mrs Lytton.' His dislike was obvious, shocking. 'And now, if you'll excuse us . . . You can find your own way home, I take it?'

She stood on the pavement, in the black night, and watched the car drive away, standing there until the sound had quite vanished, leaving behind an inhuman emptiness. Although she had seen them both get into the car, the image that stayed with her was of Jack, his child in his arms, striding away into the night, away from her, away from them all, for ever.

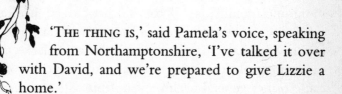

'The thing is,' said Pamela's voice, speaking from Northamptonshire, 'I've talked it over with David, and we're prepared to give Lizzie a home.'

'I don't know what plans Jack has made,' said Harriet. 'I haven't had a chance to discuss it with him. Anyway, isn't it a little too early to decide?'

She was lying on the sofa, battling with a headache, the result of grief and exhaustion, and also something else. Fear? That Lizzie might be taken away? That Jack might now disappear, all contact lost? Surely she could not be so unworthy as to be thinking of Jack, in these moments when reality appeared in its severest guise? At the funeral he had been accompanied by a small blonde woman, for whom she had felt an instant distaste, the distaste, she thought, of a respectable matron for a man flaunting his mistress, for a widower demonstrating that he had already made a convenient arrangement. This happened, she knew. She had had no doubt that the woman was his mistress, had probably been so for some time. What added to the distaste and the antagonism was the fact that the woman was not particularly attractive, no more attractive than Harriet herself. She had a small round tight face, round blue eyes, a meaningless all-purpose smile, shiny skin drawn over prominent cheekbones, an equally pronounced jaw, medium-length blonde hair. She had worn a navy blue coat, with a blue, yellow, and white scarf at the throat, navy tights, and navy court shoes: a conventional outfit, thought Harriet. She seemed, on the surface, a thoroughly conventional woman, neither young nor middle-aged, about thirty-five or so, with the kind of looks that would show no major deterioration. Lines would appear round the eyes, the skin would grow shinier over the cheekbones, the jaw become more pronounced, the mouth close more purposefully . . . What was her attraction? She had a confident air, beautiful legs and feet, an assurance of perfect health. Was that it? But she did not think that Jack was either so sentimental or so superstitious as to choose a woman because of her general health, even if his wife had died in the teeth of all reasonable expectations.

Besides, she thought, this woman had come into being before Tessa's last illness, summoned out of Jack's other life, where their imagination could not follow him. She must have been a secretary, or rather a superior sort of assistant, devoted, competent, level-headed, and ruthless, and therefore not unlike Jack himself, as he had recently revealed himself to be. This person—she could not bring herself to think of her as a girl—had had a settled air, betrayed no excitement, had no proprietory gestures, kept her hands by her sides. Nobody greeted her. This she ignored, assuming that her existence was at least as important as that of Tessa's broken parents, her stricken friends. Harriet, Mary, and Pamela had huddled together at the back of the crematorium, restored to childhood solidarity, aware of the process of separation. In the front row stood the Dodds, and on the other side of the aisle Jack and this woman. But was this not shockingly unorthodox? She had exchanged meaningful glances with her friends. The kindest thing was to suppose that Jack was so weakened by his ordeal that he needed the support of a friend, a friend whom none of them had had the chance to meet.

But Jack was neither weak nor weakened. He had been exemplary, had brought tears of admiration to Harriet's eyes, the only tears she had shed until the day of Tessa's death. And even then . . . Those three weeks in the hospital had been oddly serene, peaceable. They had sat there talking, their voices low. Pale sunshine briefly bloomed on the white bed. From time to time Tessa would turn her face to the window, and in those moments they would see her sorrow. Harriet and Jack had kept her company, although company was now irrelevant. She had passed beyond them, becoming recognizable as the woman they had known only when Lizzie came in, brought by Tessa's parents, with whom she was staying. At once the spectral look left Tessa's face, and for a while she was animated. The minute the door closed behind Lizzie she fell back exhausted. 'I don't want to go on,' she had once said. They had offered automatic words of comfort. The following day the nurse had remarked to Harriet, 'She says she doesn't want to eat or drink any more.' 'How long?' Harriet had asked. 'Perhaps a week,' said the nurse.

There was no need to say anything to Jack. He kept vigil, stern, wordless, not noticeably moved. She sometimes heard his heavy sighs, which were sighs of frustration as much as of endurance. The immobility was almost more than he could stand. When Tessa was put on a drip, when the oxygen cylinder was wheeled into the room, he moved nearer the bed, as if anxious to scrutinize these last days. Still Tessa turned her sorrowful eyes to the window, no longer able or willing to speak. Once she said, 'Lizzie?' but fell asleep before Harriet could reply, 'She'll be here soon.' The most intense silence prevailed. When the nurse came in to settle her for the night they left her, parting wordlessly at the hospital entrance. There was nothing left to say.

She died early one morning, when there was nobody there. Her mother, Jack, and Harriet, alerted by telephone, made their way instinctively to the room and stayed there for the better part of the day. Nobody seemed to think this strange. At some point Jack disappeared, went to Cadogan Mews, collected Lizzie, and took her in to see the dead Tessa. 'Lizzie has said goodbye,' he said, ushering the tearless child into the hospital room. Harriet had bent down and put her arms round the child, but, as always, she resisted. 'Take her home,' said Jack to Anne Dodd. 'I'll collect her later.' 'What have you decided about her?' Harriet asked, when Lizzie had gone. 'She could come and live with us. We should love to have her.' Belatedly, she saw how unpopular this might be. Her heart ached for Lizzie, so bleak, so composed. 'I haven't decided where she is to go,' said Jack. 'If we were staying in England we should have her, of course,' said Tessa's father, but he seemed too old, too bent under the weight of his grief to be able to tolerate a young life. 'Let me have her, Jack,' Harriet had said. 'She can go to France for the holidays. Wouldn't that be the best plan?' 'But then I should never see her,' he said. 'And she is my daughter. I'll let you know. You have been very kind,' he added, turning away.

Lizzie did not go to the funeral, the ugly flower-decked disposal at Golders Green. 'Where is Lizzie?' Pamela had hissed, but Harriet was forced to say that she did not know, had not seen Lizzie since that day in the hospital room. In any case this was no scene for a child to witness. And by that time she was distracted by Jack's companion, still mysterious, still without a name. After the service she had gone up to the Dodds and offered condolences. The colours on Anne Dodd's face had run, and a bubble of saliva bloomed at the corner of her mouth. 'So sad,' she gasped, 'so sad,' and let her husband guide her to the car. To Jack Harriet had said, 'Would you like to come back to the house? I'm sure you need some coffee.' He had merely replied, 'I'll ring you in a couple of days and let you know what I've decided. By the way, this is Elspeth Mackinnon.' The girl had bared tiny even teeth, but her expression was absent. Harriet had stood with Mary and Pamela among the terrible flowers, and watched them drive away. At this they exchanged looks which seemed oddly free of judgement, as if the ceremony had drained them of censure.

If they felt anything it was regret mingled with respect. They were growing old, Harriet thought. After the first shock of seeing Jack with another woman, the new alliance seemed entirely natural. They were suddenly very tired, with harsh involuntary shudders of cold and fatigue. The weather was immaculate, the first day of a new spring. The sun showed in cruel relief the lines on their faces, the recent passage of tears. 'Did you say coffee?' demanded Mary, almost querulously. 'Of course,' said Harriet. 'It's all ready. And sandwiches.' 'Curious how weak one feels,' observed Pamela, blowing her nose. 'You'll miss her, Hattie.' 'Yes,' said Harriet. 'I'll miss her.'

She had felt so close to them, the girls, as Freddie used to call them. They had spent the afternoon together, unwilling to part, in silence, mostly, lying back in chairs or on sofas, watching the light change and fade. At four o'clock she had made tea, which they drank gratefully. Reviving energy renewed their curiosity. 'Have you any idea who that woman was?' asked Pamela. 'A girlfriend,' Mary replied. 'Seizing the opportunity to go public. Rather cool of her, I thought. Had you any idea?' 'No,' said Harriet, daunted. 'No idea. Do you suppose Tessa knew?' 'I think she probably did,' said Mary. 'Or guessed. If so, she was immensely grown up about it. They both were, given the situation.'

'I never know these things,' confessed Harriet, who was beginning to feel intimations of a more normal emotion. The ease with which people make life bearable for themselves, she thought. The accomplishment . . . But she had not liked the girl, or woman, and now that the funeral was beginning to

recede she disliked—no, not disliked: distrusted—her all over
again. That air of competence, that glassy absent smile, which
seemed to proclaim them all as irrelevant, that air of having
a full timetable in reserve . . . It was as if Tessa's old friends
were already out of place in the new dispensation drawn up
by Elspeth Mackinnon. And what was to happen to Lizzie?
For surely there would be no room for Lizzie in whatever
arrangement Elspeth Mackinnon had in mind?

'I could have Lizzie,' she said aloud.

'Or she could come to us. I'll talk to David, and ring you.'

They kissed the air on either side of each other's face, then
smiled and hugged one another, rocking to and fro.

'Look after yourself. Take care,' they said, knowing that
they would not meet for a long time, if at all. With them, in
the suddenly empty room, went her youth, or what was left
of it. She bent to pick up cushions, found herself moving
slowly, heavily. I am tired, she thought vaguely. Well, it has
all been a strain. Sorrow waited in the background, waiting
for the night hours when she could give it her full attention.

Several bleak days followed, during which she felt a growing estrangement. She waited to hear what had been decided.
She felt it would be inappropriate for her to telephone the
Dodds, or Jack, that it would not be becoming to demand
accounts. Maybe she would be left out of the calculations
altogether. This did not surprise her: she felt listless, marginal.
She supposed she would now drop out of the picture. With
Tessa gone her early affections seemed to have disappeared;
the past appeared uninhabited. Now only Immy remained to
tie her to her present life. Even Immy, sensing her curious
mood, avoided her, preferring to spend time in Miss Wetherby's basement, eating toast and watching television. Freddie
was kind, respecting her grief, yet anxious for her to relin-
quish it and return to normal. He sensed detachment, even
disloyalty, was, at times like these, unsure of her. She herself

was outwardly calm, moved about the house as she normally
did, shopped, cooked, seemed self-possessed. Every afternoon, when the house was quiet, and the noises from the
street dropped to a monotone, she lay down on the sofa and
tried to think. Yet what she saw in her mind's eye was not the
important business of her own life, of Freddie's ageing, of
Immy's future, but Lizzie's tearless face. She does not love
me, came the sudden illumination. She has endured me, as
one of those burdens she has been forced to carry throughout
her uncomfortable childhood. If she came here she would
hate it, but continue to endure it. She is a stoic, more of a stoic
than I am, who can hardly bear . . . Banishing Lizzie's face she
thought of an empty room, with sunlight falling across a
creaseless bed, and herself preparing to lie down in that bed,
beautifully untroubled. So forceful was this image that she
recognized it as her deepest desire, akin to death, or to sleep—
it did not seem to matter which—and felt a yearning for it so
strong that she could almost feel the sun on her face, although
outside the window the weather was lightless and damp. The
false spring was over, it seemed. Only the mildness of the air
reminded her that it was late February. In the park the daffodils would be in bloom. She had no desire to see them; the
imaginary picture was more beguiling. If only I can hang on
until the summer, Harriet told herself, yet nothing threatened
her, weighed upon her. Only the unfinished business of Lizzie . . . But I am not her mother, she thought. Then memory
supplied her with the image of Elspeth Mackinnon, the tight,
patient, tolerant smile. Lizzie had not been at the funeral. Had
she met Elspeth? And if she had—and this must be faced—
would she prefer her to Harriet?

    She sat up. But surely Jack would not dream . . . ? And if
he did, could she prevent it? But this is unimaginable; the
child has suffered enough. And yet there was this curious
enmity between her and Immy. And Freddie would not be

happy to have another child in the house. Freddie. She had almost ceased to consider him, yet now she must. He was a generous man with money, but not with patience. Even Immy tired him; he looked forward to her going away to school. He was proud of her, but disappointed by the child's indifference to him. Her early raptures, when she was a tiny baby, and even up to the age of two, had cooled. Now she no longer turned to him, was sometimes tolerant of, sometimes irritated by, his clumsy overtures. This left a residue of bad feeling on both sides: something which must be watched. Immy, when a woman, would not bother with men like Freddie, thought Harriet. She would be capricious, demanding, as her beauty gave her the right to be. For she was beautiful, with her white skin and her dark hair, already slim and straight, not stocky and shapeless like other children of her age. I shall not discipline her, she thought. I shall let her have her way. Why should she make do, politely, with second best? For once women have been trained in the ways of politeness they can make disastrous mistakes. All those maidenly virtues were a way of selling the pass. I am not much of an example to her. She must be bold and fearless. Fortunately, she seems to know her own mind. Her lovely impatience . . . If there were to be a clash of wills between her daughter and her husband her daughter must win. For none but the brave deserve the fair. And none but the fair deserve the brave.

And Lizzie, in all this? Where would Lizzie be in ten years' time, when Immy was breaking hearts? Well, Lizzie would survive, she thought. Lizzie had toughness, stamina, qualities that had prepared her for the cruelty of the real world. She would have a sensible life. She was clever, thoughtful, loved her books. Books would be her companions. However, books contain terrible reminders. 'You know that you are recalled to life?' 'They tell me so.' 'I hope you care to live?'

'I can't say.' And there was the reality of her mother's empty bed, seen from the doorway of her bedroom, and the stained pillow. But childhood fades, she comforted herself, impatient now with grief. One grows up, grows older. One can do this at any age. Maybe Lizzie had made her gigantic leap into adulthood on that very night. Surely nothing would ever hurt her again as it had then. She would recover, might have done so already. There was something impenetrable about Lizzie: no one knew what she thought. She had not cried since she was very young, had learned, somehow, lessons of endurance. It would be unwise to bring her up with Immy, subject her to the suffering of being less beautiful, less endowed, less favoured. For Immy came first, and always would.

Lizzie would work, she thought painfully, and live a sensible life. Some children are born to lead sensible lives, others to folly and to joy. And there was no help for it; the die had already been cast. It was only the pale closed face that disturbed her, as it always had, the trudging resignation, the small empty hands. Let her go, she whispered to herself, already slightly frightened of the child. Life will take care of her. Or not, as the case might be. You are beyond anything I might offer you, Lizzie, she thought. And yet if you should want to come to me I should feel strangely rewarded. Like many difficult people, Lizzie had the capacity to bestow unexpected favours.

So that when Pamela telephoned, Lizzie's fate was still in the balance.

'She can come to us,' said the voice, restored to its normal briskness. 'She can grow up with the boys. You're in touch, I take it?'

'No,' she answered, sitting up, jerked out of her afternoon reverie. 'No,' she said. 'I haven't heard from Jack. Maybe he's taken her away somewhere, to get over it, you know.'

All this time, she realized, she had been waiting for the

moment when Jack would call. This was how she had remained so alarmingly calm. He would get in touch with her. She had only to wait for him.

'Well, I'd like to know,' the voice went on in her ear. 'It's time we got something settled.'

'It might be a good idea,' she conceded. 'But it's Jack's decision. And Lizzie's, of course. She must be allowed to choose.'

Pamela snorted. 'How much choice does she have?'

'That's what I don't know. Don't worry, I'll be in touch. As soon as I hear something.'

I am a bad friend, a bad wife, possibly a bad woman, she thought. My loyalties would vanish in an instant if there were sufficient advantage to be had, and by advantage I mean emotional advantage. Were it not for my Immy I might go away from here, from this pompous house, which is in every sense too big for me, and from Freddie, whom I would leave almost without regret. Why this sudden enlightenment? With Tessa's death part of my life finished, the part connected with early days, early memories, my unwitting struggle for a position of safety, my desire to compensate my parents for *their* struggle, and to set them free. And this is not madness but the sobriety of middle age talking. If Immy did not exist (my life, my joy) I might be tempted to go in search of that empty room, with the single shaft of sunlight across the undisturbed bed: I should stay there all day, and in the evening my window would bloom with mysterious light. I should know no one, merely pass my days dreaming. Yet the fact that in my thoughts the room is always empty must be significant. If my life is an empty room I must fill it before it is too late.

Jack appeared, suddenly, one evening as they were finishing dinner.

'Your servant let me in,' he said.

'I doubt if Miss Wetherby thinks of herself as a servant,' said

Harriet. 'And we should never dare to imagine such a thing. She is by way of being a nanny, although she is too deaf to be entirely effective. Fortunately, my daughter gets on with her . . .'

'Jack doesn't want to hear about Miss Wetherby,' said Freddie. 'By the way, did you ever find out her name?'

'Her name is Jean,' said Harriet. 'Jean Aileen, as it happens. Why on earth did you want to know that?'

'We are so sorry for what has happened,' said Freddie to Jack. 'My dear fellow, there are no words on these occasions.'

'Don't speak of it,' she interrupted. 'I cannot bear it yet. And Jack will have heard it all before, from so many people. What can I offer you, Jack? A drink? Coffee?'

Freddie, who thought his wife uncharacteristically voluble, suggested that Jack might not have eaten.

'Of course! What can I be thinking of? We had cold chicken and salad, Jack. And apple pie. Would that do?'

He considered this. 'I should like a chicken sandwich,' he said. '*And* apple pie. I am actually on my way to Paris. I can catch a later plane.'

'When will you be back?' she asked.

'Early next week, depending on how this interview goes.'

'What have you decided about the little girl?' asked Freddie, watching the white teeth sink into the bread.

'She's staying with my friend Elspeth Mackinnon,' he said briefly. 'I think it a good idea to leave her with Elspeth. A competent woman,' he alleged, as if no more need be said.

'Who is Elspeth?' asked Harriet, as vivaciously as she could manage. 'We saw her at the . . . You introduced us. Where does she live? Does Lizzie . . . ? I mean, will Lizzie be happy with her?'

'Elspeth is my assistant, my secretary, whatever you like to call her. She arranges my work, types my stuff. She has a largish house near Windsor. There is plenty of room for

Lizzie. And I can see her there, of course, whenever I want to.'

'What will happen to Judd Street? Will you give up your flat?' she asked, with sinking heart. She realized that plans had already been made, may have been long established.

'Oh, I shall keep the flat. I bought it years ago. Lizzie can have it when she's older, if she decides to work in London. This pie is excellent, by the way.'

She sat down slowly. 'Does this mean that we shan't see Lizzie again?'

'I dare say Elspeth will bring her to town in the holidays, for clothes and so on. I want her to have a fresh start. I want her to get away from all the old associations.'

'Poor Lizzie,' she said. 'Does she know she is being forced to make a fresh start? A fresh start sounds rather gruesome to me. Is she not to remember us at all?'

'Don't be so morbid,' said Freddie. 'I think Jack is right. A fresh start is what the girl needs. After all, she's going to school next year.'

'This year,' she corrected him.

'Already?' He looked startled.

'The children are leaving home,' she told him sadly. 'I somehow never foresaw it. Did you?'

'It will be quieter, certainly.'

'I think it so hard on children,' she went on, collecting dirty plates. 'There is so much for them to learn. And all that school, day after day. What if they are homesick? Will there be anyone to care for them?'

'Don't be so absurd, Harriet. Of course there will.'

'I enjoyed school,' said Jack, rolling a cigarette. 'I can't see that it did me any harm.'

'Has Elspeth children of her own?' she asked.

'No.'

'Then how can she look after Lizzie?'

'Lizzie will only be there in the holidays. Elspeth has a large family. Her mother has a place in Scotland. It will be a different life for her. A better one, I hope.'

'Well, of course, we hope so too,' said Freddie, glancing sharply at his wife. 'She can always visit us when she's in town.'

'Will I see her before she goes? To Elspeth, I mean?'

'She's already there,' he said mildly. 'We took her back there after the funeral. I came by this evening to ask if you would mind packing some clothes for her.'

'She had better have new ones,' Harriet said. 'I can't . . . I can't go to the flat just yet. I'll buy her some new clothes. And she left one or two things here. I'll bring them round next week. Round to Judd Street, I mean. When will you be back?'

'I'm sure Jack wouldn't mind picking them up,' said Freddie.

'Oh, it's no trouble,' she assured them both. 'I'm only sorry I shan't see her.' She was appalled at herself, mentioning the child in the same breath as arranging an assignation, if that was what it was. If Jack were a man of conscience, she thought, as he undoubtedly is not, even he would be slightly disconcerted. And if Freddie had any imagination, which he has not, he would be indignant. And if I were a decent woman I should feel ashamed, disgusted. As I am. And poor Lizzie, in all this. I shall buy her some decent clothes, as if I were buying them for Immy, and I shall simply leave them outside his door. There will be no need for me to see him at all.

'When will you be back from Paris?' she asked.

'Wednesday, at the latest.'

'Very well,' she said calmly. She said nothing more.

Later she was to wonder how they had all behaved so normally, while thoughts of insurrection came so near the surface. At that stage it was almost a dream, not yet an intention. She wanted only a meeting, some sort of exchange. She only wanted to know him, she thought. And Freddie sat there, unsuspecting. But what was there to suspect? Only a desire, that duty should have stifled, might yet vanquish, an unjustified desire for that one interview . . . It did not matter to her that he was completely indifferent. If the opportunity arose she would know how to deal with that. And of course, none of it need take place, she told herself. It is just that I should like something of my own, some memory that is entirely mine. She thought in terms of a conversation, one of those significant conversations that change everything. In the world's terms quite harmless. In terms of her own continued existence, almost a necessity.

12

As IF in collusion with her curious mood—which was one of daring, but a daring entirely unconnected with the idea of damage—the weather turned seductively mild, damp, sunny, profuse, spring-like. Drops of water sparkled on grass which was sprinkled with the pink strewn blossoms of cherry and prunus; magnolias, with their waxy purple and white buds, opened fatly on branches that were still black. Sometimes, in the late afternoon, a sudden sun chased a rainbow through dense grey clouds, and an unnatural Pre-Raphaelite intensity and radiance enveloped the evening landscape, before all the colours gradually dimmed, and she realized, with regret, that she must turn her thoughts homewards (though she had only been standing at the window) and resume her domestic duties.

She had two days like this, a Wednesday and a Thursday. On the Friday she thought she might go to Brighton, for she was restless, and the wider horizon of the sea beckoned: she wanted to walk until she was exhausted, for there could be no sensible thinking until this unforgiving energy was somehow converted to peaceful purposes. This is the best time, she thought, before any undertaking is possible; love is sometimes wasted on those who act on it. Like this, one has both ardour and innocence, and it is difficult to say which is the more precious. She only knew that she was bathed in a sort of gratitude, so that she looked at the jewel-like grass and the thick mauve fingers of the magnolia buds as if she had never seen anything of such splendour before in her dreamlike existence. All losses seemed cancelled: Tessa, Lizzie. The future, beyond the following Wednesday, was indistinct. On returning from taking Imogen to school, a task for which she suddenly volunteered, she met Miss Wetherby, prudently emerging from her basement into the sunny air. Miss Wetherby wore a raincoat and a hat shaped like a modified turban: she carried a shopping bag and turned her good ear to Harriet by way of greeting.

The dustiness of Miss Wetherby, her preparedness for rain, impressed Harriet as being emblematic of that age when nothing more than the daily round can be imagined, when desire is not even a memory. The idea made her feel boisterous, hilarious. Not for me, she thought, not for me. 'Shall I do your shopping for you?' she asked, unable to bear the sight of Miss Wetherby on this glorious day. 'I'm going out myself.' Miss Wetherby's pale lips moved, as they often did before words were allowed to escape from them. 'I like to get out,' she said. 'But I should get out more often if I had a little dog.' This hint had been dropped on more than one occasion. 'If she had a dog she'd be out all the time,' Freddie had said. 'Just when we might need her. And anyway, I don't want a dog in the house.'

Freddie could thus legitimately be blamed for Miss Wetherby's unpartnered state, yet in some ways, Harriet reflected, she was the ideal dog owner, placid, regular, uncommunicative. Was it not unkind to deprive her of what might be a natural companion? These days she walked with a stick, although she was apparently quite healthy in other respects. She was getting old; her usefulness was diminishing. Yet the very fact of her age gave her a claim to greater indulgence. Harriet began to see that she could never be dislodged from the basement she loved so much. After consultation with Freddie she had suppressed the rent. 'We are in *your* debt,' she had said. 'And Freddie insists on your having a salary.' Miss Wetherby had been delighted. And Imogen seemed to get on with her, the two of them enjoying a comfortable mutual independence. Apart from her ghostly air of contentment it was difficult to know exactly what Miss Wetherby thought. Harriet always felt humble, and a little uneasy, in her company.

Today, however, she was in a generous mood. 'Perhaps when Immy goes to school,' she smiled. 'We could talk about the dog then. I'll have another word with my husband.' Miss Wetherby's pale lips moved, prior to another pronouncement. 'If you would,' she eventually said. 'You see, I shall miss the child so much.' Harriet felt ashamed: she had not taken this factor into account. 'You shall have a dog,' she promised rashly. 'As long as you keep it downstairs.' Miss Wetherby smiled, her unexpectedly fine teeth glistening in the sun. 'We shall both miss her,' she said. 'I dread the day. But you have all been very kind.' She really does love Immy, thought Harriet. How could I refuse her anything?

With Imogen away, how would life be? Her thoughts were reckless, unfocused, as thoughts of liberty always are. The idea of a future which might consist of personal gratification seemed audacious beyond the bounds of belief. For one brought up in the ways of docility, as she had been, such thoughts had not previously presented themselves: unawakened, she had had no quarrel with her own peace of mind, although tacitly recognizing its limitations. Now she felt reborn, simply from the power of her own expectation. This had very little to do with Jack himself, although without him the transition might never have taken place. She simply knew that for once she was acting on her own volition, and the sensation was almost fulfilment in itself. For what could Jack add to this? Jack dwindled in importance; his own thoughts were as nothing to her. She had read an answering calculation in his eye, nothing more. In a sense she was willing to make do with that, for anything more might add weight, depth, to something so delightfully immaterial that she experienced it rather like a degree of painless intoxication. And part of her wished to retain the status of an honest woman, or at least, she thought, in a moment of true honesty, of an honest dissimulator. To have all she had *and* this would be almost enough, she reckoned. To have anything more would put her in the wrong. This wrong was a nebulous condition, unexamined. Freddie would be wronged, undoubtedly. But when she thought of Freddie it was only in terms of the most disagreeable aspects of Freddie, his restrictions, his suspicions, his stoutness, the horn of his fingernails. In comparison with Freddie she felt scandalously young. No, to be in the wrong would have to do with her daughter, whom she might never yearningly contemplate, with the same degree of love, again. Love would have become subterfuge. To be diminished in Immy's eyes, even if Immy never knew anything about any imagined misdemeanours, would be something from which her mother might not recover. Therefore the mood alone, the amorous mood, would have to suffice. There remained the question of the visit to Judd Street, a now almost unwelcome reminder of present realities. I shall leave the bags outside the door, she thought, or simply hand them in. There will be no need—or time—for anything more. And as if in repentance she bought Lizzie three Viyella dresses, two pairs of jeans, some cream-coloured tights, and a red jacket. Shoes made her hesitate; she was unsure of the size. Elspeth can buy her the shoes, she thought.

Later in the day, when the light finally faded, and with it her ferocious energy, her mood became darker. It was physiological, she consoled herself, something to do with low blood sugar. At this time she saw herself as a restless dissatisfied woman, dissatisfied because of that very innocence that had seemed her safeguard, and likely to be frustrated through the very timidity of her desires. It is all very well to be innocent, she thought, but I sacrificed true innocence long ago. Since meeting Jack I have made do with a facsimile, whether I knew it or not. It seemed real enough at the time, but secretly I wanted more. Perhaps most women did. Perhaps most women had unfulfilled life left in them, and sought a way to use it. But these thoughts were stale, and she dismissed them impatiently. In this mood of distaste, which always coincided with the early evening and the fading of the light, she knew that she had a choice, and that to deny that choice, or the possibility of choice, would be fatal. She did not doubt—she had never doubted—that the burden of responsibility was hers. The fabled lover, the imagined love affair, must be subsumed into one encounter, and that one encounter, which she still could not entirely envisage, must do duty for the life of adultery which she knew she desired. She judged herself quite coldly as a foolish woman, despised herself for being weak, but recognized the decision as ineluctable. Quite simply, the desire remained. But the desire, she knew, must also remain unsatisfied.

'Do you want to come to Brighton with me tomorrow?' she asked Immy. 'You can miss school for a day. It's nearly the end of term anyway.'

'We have painting tomorrow,' said Immy. 'And my dancing class after school.'

'Oh, of course. You don't want to see Granny and Grandpa, then?'

'Where has Lizzie gone?' asked Immy, her cheeks unusually flushed, her attention to her drawing redoubled.

'Lizzie has gone to stay with a friend of her father's. You

knew that. I told you. Why, do you miss her? You'll see her at school in the autumn, you know.'

Immy slid down from her chair, and carried her drawing off to show to Miss Wetherby.

'I don't miss her,' she said. 'I don't care where she is.'

But Harriet paid little attention to this, struck as she was by the sight of the new moon, glimpsed unluckily through the window. Later she was to see that moment of bad luck as emblematic of all her indecisiveness.

'You can have dinner with us tonight,' she called after Immy. 'Would you like that?' There was no answer. She had not really expected any.

The seduction fantasy, or what she later came to think of as the seduction fantasy, took hold again the next morning, as the train was pulling out of Victoria. The seduction fantasy was, in itself, extremely seductive. It enabled her to bask in a glow of possibilities, imagined endings, which brought colour to her cheeks, but permitted her to remain on the safe side of experience. All it needed, she thought, was an element of imaginative daring, the knowledge that the situation was already adumbrated but could be controlled at will, like the switching of channels on a television set. Outwardly a pleasant-looking middle-aged woman, still youthfully slim, with dark hair that showed no signs of grey, she was inwardly luxurious, ruminating adventure. It was perhaps significant that the adventure was limited to one incident, which might not even take place.

Sun, shining through dusty windows, illuminated her seat. The southern suburbs of London struck her as poignantly homely, beautifully unassertive. Back gardens, narrow strips of poor soil, with clothes-lines and sheds, boasted a few late daffodils, a flowering tree. Briefly she imagined herself in one of those little houses, the French windows of her sitting-room open on to that small private space, sitting with a cup of tea, listening to a serial on the radio. A careful humble retreat from the outside world: something she no longer had. For she was marked now, both by affluence and by dissatisfaction, both conditions absolutely foreign to her. She felt homesick for the shop, for the back room, and her father humming as he made the tea. He pulls me back, she thought; had he been stronger I might have left home more easily. I should have left home anyway, but I should not have felt this homesickness. Whether I like it or not, I have kept true to those early experiences. They seemed sweet now, pitiable, filled with the pathos of a home long gone. I am more like him than I realized, she thought with some surprise. Everything else has been a madness. One room would have sufficed. But then she would never have had Immy, and it was almost worth living as she did—for she hated it, she now realized—to have had her daughter, the daughter who was so marvellously unlike herself, who was bold, beautiful, fearless, and who would take what she wanted without a second's hesitation.

In her mind her parents and her daughter belonged to two disparate lives. The link between them—herself—she could no longer get into any kind of perspective. Her daughter seemed to her to possess a spirit which she had come by as if by magic: certainly she had not inherited it from her mother or her father. Freddie, corpulent and cautious, might never have been young, while Harriet's famed docility had not only kept her from harm but had precluded curiosity, experimentation. She had learned nothing but contentment in obedience, whereas Immy had been audacious, unafraid, even as a baby. Rough, sometimes, and laying claim to privileges without waiting for them to be handed down, and always, in every mood, beautiful. She seemed made of finer materials than those who had produced and nurtured her, like a princess in a fairy tale, bearing witness to money, and to that slow social ascent made so painfully by her anxious mother. She had an assurance which was entirely natural; in this, did she but know it, she resembled her father in his professional capacity. Otherwise, no features, no trick of expression, could link her with her parents, or, despite fond comparisons, with her grandparents. In character too she was different, impatient, voracious, easily roused to anger. Yet these not notably attractive characteristics possessed a certain virtue, for it was understood that Immy demanded only the best, was impatient only with the second best, required from life only what she saw it could deliver, was not fearful, shy, self-effacing, knew, with some scorn, how meekness could conceal a certain holy vanity, preferred vanity unadorned and unashamed, was in fact shameless.

What perplexed Harriet was the task of guiding such a daughter through life, when she, her mother, was so uncertain. For this reason she wagered everything on Immy's turbulent nature, hoping that this might lead her forward to a life which would be, in the world's terms, successful. She suddenly had no use for success of any other kind. Let the meek inherit the earth, if that was what they so desired (yet it seemed out of character): she could see that the really astute contented themselves with the kingdoms of this world.

She saw Merle and Hughie before they saw her. They were sitting on their little balcony, gazing out to sea. Although she had not told them she was coming, they looked expectant, unoccupied, ready for diversion, any diversion. She waved. 'Mother! Father!' All at once they sprang into vivid life, stood up, conferred excitedly, waved back. Bored, she thought; they were monumentally bored with their peaceful existence, their labour-saving retreat. Brighton was not the West End. Whatever local hostelries they frequented were not Ciro's or the Café de Paris. They probably even missed the war, which to them had been a time of youth, extravagance, and occasional frenzy. Her mother, she saw, was dressed as if for a morning's shopping in Bond Street, in a navy suit, with a striped silk blouse; her father, by contrast, seemed designed for a day in the country, in cavalry twill trousers, and a greenish tweed jacket. What courage they still possessed, if only to turn themselves out so spectacularly for a day of purposeless inactivity! Humbled, she hastened into the building, noting that the carpet in the entrance needed cleaning, and that the cream stucco of the walls had collected a bloom of grime. The door of the flat was already open, her mother's arms were spread wide, her father's delighted face radiated disbelief. 'Hattie! Is anything wrong? You didn't tell us you were coming. Is everything all right?' She embraced them both, presented her mother with the armful of narcissi she had bought outside the station, and said, 'Let me look at you. Of course everything's all right. I just felt I wanted to see you. Are you all right?' Unexpectedly she felt her eyes fill with tears. She was both glad to see them and sorrowful that they could supply no pointers to her adult life. Parents are only good as parents at a certain stage of their children's lives, she reflected. Merle and Hughie were probably quite admirable when I was a child of ten. I found them companionable then. They were never harsh, or unreasonable, never took themselves very seriously as parents. But when lightweights grow old they are glad to lay aside burdens which threaten to grow too heavy. They abandoned the task quite thankfully when I married. Now we meet on uncertain terms, with little enough to say to each other. And yet there is that tug, that one moment of instinctive joy, that radiant instant of recognition, as if only the three of us belong together, as if there is no room, and never has been, for anyone else.

She did not doubt that Merle and Hughie recalled with perfect clarity and with unexpected nostalgia that little room behind the shop, and the rain lashing against the windows, and the doughnut on the cracked plate ready for Harriet's tea.

Probably they now, with hindsight, viewed her marriage with the same regret as she herself did, but said nothing, even to each other, antagonized secretly by its lack of beauty. For they themselves were still beautiful, designed for a more beautiful life than the one in which they found themselves becalmed. She saw that they were more stoical, had more depth, than she had ever perceived. They dressed up, they went out, they befriended strangers, they made do with second- or third-rate distractions, and they were entirely loyal to each other, so loyal that they never confessed to disappointment, even in their moments of closeness. They had enormous pride, and their pride was on the whole justified. They did not envy their daughter: they pitied her. They preferred their flat, with its cold white windows and its rakish accoutrements, to Harriet's solemn house, with its nurseries and its studies, its basement and attic floors. They felt, though this was never acknowledged between them, that they had given her away. Therefore, any gesture that she made towards them, even of the peculiar subdued love which they all felt but kept modestly out of sight, was greeted with incredulity, with joy, as if all their mistakes were cancelled, all their calculations forgotten, and the past resurrected with all its sadness removed: a moment of unity for which they felt unbounded gratitude.

Hughie insisted on making coffee. 'But I've come to take you out to lunch,' she told them. 'I thought we'd go to the Grand.' 'Oh, let Daddy do it. Yes, do, darling. And find some of those nice biscuits.' They sat dazed with pleasure, the pleasure of recognition.

'You look marvellous, Mother. How do you do it?'

Her mother preened slightly. 'We keep up our standards, dear. It's so important when you get older. My mother—your grandmother, whom you never knew—insisted on that. "No slippers outside the bedroom, Merle. Always think of your husband looking at you." Of course, after a day in the shop

I did give way a bit, didn't I? But there's no excuse now.
And,' she added sadly, 'we have all the time in the world.'

At that point Hughie came back with a loaded tray. The
usual assortment of cups, she saw, a glass plate of biscuits—a
profusion of biscuits—and the inevitable buttered toast,
which she obediently ate. Her parents sipped coffee, their
faces thoughtful with pleasure, a pleasure to be savoured both
now and later. Little rituals like this must make up their day,
she thought.

'Do you eat properly?' she asked.

Her mother eyed her with sudden hauteur, as if she had
overstepped the bounds of propriety.

'Of course we do! What a question! As a matter of fact
Daddy is very good in the kitchen. He even went to classes
this winter.' She looked at him with love and pride. Harriet
noted that the tremor in his hands, which she remembered
from childhood, was almost gone, only noticeable in the
exaggerated care with which he stacked plates and cups.

'Well,' said her mother with feigned reluctance, indifference. 'If we're going to the Grand I'd better see to my face,
I suppose.'

'You look fine, Mother. You don't need anything.'

Again that look of hauteur, that slight resumption of for-
mality. Of course, she feared patronage, as if her daughter
might so forget herself as to offer advice, refer to a discreet
financial arrangement. She was in many ways a superior
woman, Harriet thought, and thought so again when her
mother reappeared freshly powdered, in an aura of scent. In
the background she could hear her father vigorously brushing
his jacket.

The next few hours were very pleasant. Their reception at
the Grand was triumphant. 'Oh, they know us here,' said
Merle. Waiters hovered around them with excessive zeal.
Hughie offered little jokes, timidly, as if fearing to offend her.

The head waiter came over to see if everything was to their liking. 'Very nice, thank you, Carlos. By the way, I don't think you've met our daughter, have you? From London.' Carlos inclined his head graciously. 'Delighted to meet you, Madam. Everything all right, Sir? Madam?' 'We'll have coffee in the lounge,' said Merle. They beamed with pride and gratification.

In the lounge ('I don't think you've met our daughter') they all felt that the visit had been an unexpected success. But now they were anxious for her to leave, so that they could savour it to the full. She recognized this, and did not press them. 'I'll walk a little,' she assured them. 'Don't come to the station. It's been a lovely visit. I'll do this again, shall I? When Immy goes to school I'll have plenty of time.' They exchanged a sad look, as if in acknowledgement of time passing. That was the only reference to her other life. Otherwise she did not speak of her daughter, or of her husband. The day, the sunny day, belonged to the three of them. She thought they were in fine form. Nevertheless, she turned and waved until they were out of sight, as if she might never see them again.

Her mood, when she left them, was curiously diminished. It was as if remembrance of things past had cancelled the earlier excitement. Now she felt only distaste for the feeling of recklessness to which she had only that morning so willingly surrendered. It was as if she would be betraying them if she acted out of character, and even to fantasize an erotic episode—now vague in her mind, almost irretrievable—was a lapse from everything, notably good taste. Whatever she was or had become was unlikely to change. Evening sun lay beneficently on the back gardens of the suburban houses. Now she longed to be inside one of them, with a clear conscience, preparing for the return of the breadwinner. Quiet ways, simple thoughts, seemed to her utterly desirable. And yet she knew that she had somehow put herself beyond their reach. Freddie, Immy, Miss Wetherby, possibly even Jack, awaited her with varying degrees of impatience or indifference. They appeared unimaginably complicated, as indeed they were. Marriage, the married state, *her* married state, presented incalculable difficulties. How, then, could she ever have contemplated adultery?

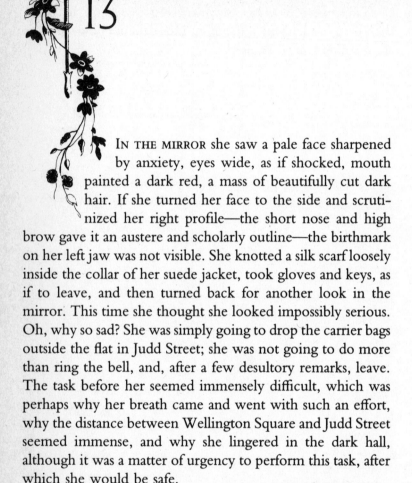

13

IN THE MIRROR she saw a pale face sharpened by anxiety, eyes wide, as if shocked, mouth painted a dark red, a mass of beautifully cut dark hair. If she turned her face to the side and scrutinized her right profile—the short nose and high brow gave it an austere and scholarly outline—the birthmark on her left jaw was not visible. She knotted a silk scarf loosely inside the collar of her suede jacket, took gloves and keys, as if to leave, and then turned back for another look in the mirror. This time she thought she looked impossibly serious. Oh, why so sad? She was simply going to drop the carrier bags outside the flat in Judd Street; she was not going to do more than ring the bell, and, after a few desultory remarks, leave. The task before her seemed immensely difficult, which was perhaps why her breath came and went with such an effort, why the distance between Wellington Square and Judd Street seemed immense, and why she lingered in the dark hall, although it was a matter of urgency to perform this task, after which she would be safe.

Her reluctance to leave the house was so severe that it amounted to a kind of dread. She knew, without knowing exactly what she knew, that she faced the greatest challenge of her life, that she was in danger, not of succumbing to Jack—even supposing that he wanted her, or had ever wanted

her—but of succumbing to self-knowledge, which she had
now successfully kept at bay for half a lifetime. And now it
was here, exposing her in all her venality. Technically innocent, as she had always been—but only technically—she
strove, in the dark hall, her gloves clutched in her hand, for
a memory of times when she had known herself to be candid,
transparent, and could summon up nothing more substantial
than a picture of herself on her way home from the bookshop
in Cork Street. Sometimes she had stopped for a cup of
coffee, eager to prolong the adventure of independence;
sometimes she had opened the novel that was always in her
bag. Sometimes she read, in the bright café; outside, the
peaceful home-going crowds, the fading daylight, a rising
evening excitement. At home, she knew, this peace would be
lost. Therefore the journey was a respite, one she thought she
was allowed. After that all would be spoiled.

And what shabbiness, what uncertainty since then! Lying at
Freddie's side, alternately amused and repelled by his touch,
silently conjuring up a lover who did not have a name, and
in the daytime hiding that unawakened body in expensive
clothes, and being gentle and gracious to friends who were
ruthless enough or sensible enough to have discovered life for
themselves, and who saw through her disguise with casual
cruelty, and pitied her. Thus everything had been false, everything except the birth of her daughter, which had freed
her momentarily from frightened acquiescence, made her
calm and strong, and a little more selfish, but not quite
enough. Thus are lives lost, through what must be despair at
knowing oneself too weak to deal with the dangers, the
choices. And only the memory of those few brief moments of
permitted freedom, in a café in New Burlington Street, a
book on the table in front of her, with the clear conscience
of one who had done a good day's work—only that memory
now appeared to be free from any kind of adult stain. The

image was almost virginal, or at least pre-pubertal, for virginity had never been truly surrendered. The heaviness which she now felt, turning her gloves in her hand, loosening the scarf at her throat, as if she were oppressed, must also date from those days, when she had known, instinctively, that her path must be one of obedience, because obedience was the discipline in which she excelled. And was there not also an adolescent fear, prolonged well beyond the age of adolescence? And how could she, having at last seen all this in perspective, ever live with it again?

She wanted to leave the house before Freddie returned, for to compare Freddie with Jack in the space of an hour seemed to her too cruel, both to Freddie and to herself. She wrote a note: 'Gone round to Judd Street with Lizzie's things. Back in time for dinner.' She realized that she could have gone earlier, when there was less chance of seeing Jack. Or was there more? She had no idea of how he spent his working day, whether he went to an office, or whether he still came back to the flat in the evenings. Maybe he simply went off to Windsor and Elspeth Mackinnon. It was all, somehow, irrelevant. What mattered more was that she should once again have the freedom of the evening, that moment when the street lights came on, and the workers lined up at the bus stops, virtuous, tired, and harmless after their honest day, with the prospect of home to comfort them. What mattered now, and perhaps for the first time, was not to be part of that population, which she could never now rejoin, but to leave home, simply to leave home, and to go out into the night with ardour and desire, no matter how impure those qualities were.

She knew that she would never again have a clear conscience. Innocence would no longer protect her from her thoughts. She saw herself putting the plastic bags down on to what she saw as the cracked black and white tiles of the floor

of the Judd Street building, saw her hand reach out to a brass
bell push, saw a green-painted door slowly open, saw herself
hand in the bags, and retreat. Intact, and guilty. For the
invasion of her mind by uncensored thoughts and unwelcome
images was total; her mind, she knew, would remain subject
to those thoughts and images for a very long time, until the
slow death of the body released her from their dominance.
She knew that she had always been guilty of not loving her
husband, but had somehow not considered her lack of love to
be a grave error or a culpable fault; now she saw how absent-
mindedly she had given her affection, and how insulting this
behaviour must have seemed. The first intimation of guilt had
been to wonder—but idly—whether Freddie had had a mistress, and to sympathize with his imagined need. Now they
were locked together for the rest of their lives, and her bad
faith must be her punishment. For she saw, drearily, that there
was to be no going back, or forward. The revelation of that
moment coincided with the beginnings of a headache, which
she could ill afford.

   She bestirred herself, went down to the basement, where
Miss Wetherby and Imogen were watching television. It was
cosy down there: she would have liked to linger. Imogen sat
on the floor, on several shabby cushions, in front of Miss
Wetherby's brown velvet sofa. The curtains were comfort-
ingly drawn, although it was not yet dark, and the lights were
low.

   'We've had our tea, Mother,' said Miss Wetherby, who
only addressed Harriet in this manner in Imogen's presence.
Harriet suspected far more conspiratorial exchanges between
the two of them when she was not there, something far more
idle and natural than she was ever permitted. It occurred to
her that Miss Wetherby was a little uneasy with her, just as she
was occasionally uneasy with Miss Wetherby. And how to
avoid being addressed as 'Mother'? When she encountered

Miss Wetherby at the top of the stairs, or at the front door, the woman seemed quite composed and dignified, yet it was clear that she found Imogen an easier conversational proposition. Or perhaps the child was more genuinely lovable, crude, and, yes, it must be said, cruel as she was. She had the careless cruelty of the natural beauty, of those favoured by fortune. Already she had outdistanced them, had a sureness denied to either of her parents. Only with Miss Wetherby did she behave like a child, consent to be treated like a child. After initial hostility she now took Miss Wetherby for granted, someone with whom no pretence was necessary. And there were deplorable indulgences, Harriet knew, orgies of crisps, toast, thickly buttered bread, terrible unhealthy foods that she was not allowed upstairs. Imogen was not greatly interested in these treats, and was certainly not interested in the fact that her presence permitted Miss Wetherby to recreate the atmosphere of a nursery which she had long outgrown. She liked Miss Wetherby's television, which was larger than the one her parents had; she liked being silently handed a Mars Bar while she was watching; she knew she could, and would, stop visiting Miss Wetherby the minute she found something more interesting to do.

'I'm going out for half an hour,' said Harriet. 'Will you see that she gets to bed? She can stay up and say hello to her father, and then she must go to bed. But of course I shall be back by then. I just thought . . . In case I am delayed. But there's no reason why I should be.'

She found herself addressing their rigid profiles, and felt irritation.

'An apple would be better for you, Immy, than that chocolate. You'll get spots, and then you'll be the first to complain. You can watch this programme, and then I'd like you both to come upstairs. Miss Wetherby can give you your bath. I want you in bed by the time I come home.'

She later thought that if Immy had asked her where she was going she would have accomplished her errand in all simplicity, have come home, greeted Freddie, kissed her daughter, all with a semblance of ease. But Immy was indifferent, uninterested, did not remove her eyes from the screen. 'She does love this programme,' said Miss Wetherby, by way of an excuse. 'It's her favourite.'

'I'll see you later, then,' said Harriet, heavy-hearted, all her indecisions restored.

On the way out she felt a ladder springing in her stocking, which seemed to seal her fate. No one would want her now, she who was never less than immaculate. She suppressed a desire to run upstairs again and change, walked steadily out of the front door, realized she had completely forgotten the carrier bags with Lizzie's things, the very pretext for her visit, saw that time was getting on, and that Freddie would soon be home, rushed back into the hall, and finally sat in the car, her heart beating uncomfortably fast. If it was to be like this the battle was lost even before it had been engaged.

The evening was blue, mild, conducive to dreaming, but with an acid edge to sharpen desire. It was April, traditionally the cruellest month. The soiled petals of almond blossom lay in drifts in gutters; trees opened clenched buds to release tentative leaves. All of this—and the bushes thrusting greenly at her through the railings—was a backdrop to the marvellous electric bustle of the city, the queue outside the cinema, the doors of pubs opening and closing, the slow surge of buses, the clashing trolleys at the entrance to the supermarket. She realized how seldom she was out in the evening, and yet it was the time she loved the best, most of all when she was alone. She drove, with a pleasurable coolness from the open window fanning her cheek. At the same time she longed for summer, for intense heat, when tensions are released, and energies renewed.

She mounted the stairs at Judd Street calmly, saw, also calmly, that the floor was indeed paved with dirty black and white tiles, but that the door was brown, thickly varnished, with a few blistered bubbles where the job had been hastily finished. Calmly she rang the doorbell. The door opened instantly.

'Hello, Jack,' she said, almost indifferently. 'I didn't expect to find you here. I've brought Lizzie's things.'

He stood back and ushered her in. 'You must let me know how much I owe you,' he said.

'You owe me nothing.'

She felt that she had made some sort of statement, unconnected with matters of material exchange. At the same time she followed him into the flat, glancing, without much curiosity, at the dingy cream walls, the desk and the typewriter, the terribly large sofa. At the window hung incongruously dainty and expensive curtains, the work, she thought, of some Elspeth Mackinnon or other, an attempt to introduce a feminine touch, a reminder of the donor.

'I like your curtains,' she said, aware that there was nothing much else to admire.

He took the bags from her and put them behind him on a chair.

'You won't forget to give them to her? With my love, of course.'

'With your love,' he said gravely. She thought he must be laughing at her; there was, perhaps, a hint of amusement in the way he looked at her. At the same time his movements were slow, as if this transaction might be expected to take a long while.

Her cheeks burned; she had no idea how to behave, for she supposed a seduction was about to take place, or rather a mock seduction, in which she would be cast for the lesser role.

'You find me ridiculous, don't you?' Her voice was still calm, but now desolate.

'I find you interesting.'

'Oh, I am not very interesting. I dare say there have to be women like me, but we don't arouse much interest.'

'You could be mistaken.'

After that there was a silence.

'Well,' she said. 'I had better be getting back. I'm sure you have work to do.'

'I'd rather you stayed,' he said, moving away from her. His tone was as indifferent as her own.

'I must get back for dinner. My husband will be home.'

'Ah, yes. Walter.'

'Freddie.'

'Freddie,' he agreed.

When he kissed her she knew that her whole physical life, the life of the senses, had been dormant until this moment. When they disengaged they looked at each other, in silence.

'Do you do this all the time?'

'Not all the time, no. You could stay, you know.'

'Why should I?'

'Possibly because you want to. And because I might want you to.'

'You?' There was no answer. 'I have to leave, you see. You do see, don't you?'

'I should expect nothing less of you.'

'Oh, don't be so . . . so *rude,*' she said angrily. They both smiled.

'Goodbye, Jack,' she said, holding out her hand. He kissed her again. There was no doubt now about her response.

'That's better,' he said. 'I loathe soulful women, with consciences.'

'Goodbye, Jack,' she repeated.

'I suppose you want to talk,' he said. 'About your conscience. Dear Mrs Lytton. Shall we sit down?' He gestured towards the sofa.

He feels it too, she thought. 'You know my name,' she said. 'Why don't you use it?'

'I could only use it in different circumstances.'

'Then that will never be. I must go. Shall I ever see you again?'

'Only you can say that.'

'And yet I am so uninteresting,' she marvelled.

'You have managed to make yourself so, certainly.'

'Goodbye,' she said for a third time. And then again, 'Goodbye.'

'Goodbye, Mrs Lytton,' he said politely. At the door he kissed her again.

'Ah, Jack.'

'Goodbye. Harriet.'

Outside, in the street, without knowing how she had got down the stairs, she put her hand to her burning cheek. The mark on her jaw, to which she had not given a thought, was now forgotten, obliterated. She sat in the car, watching the clock tick away the minutes. Finally she drove off, back to Wellington Square, and Freddie. She knew that she would never see Jack again, and yet felt strangely fulfilled. So that is what it is all about, she thought. They were right, those others. At the same time she was amused, tolerant, as if now permitted to see the world in a different light, as one of the successful, the secret, the admitted. Admitted to what? To that place at the centre, which all seek to reach. She was less uninteresting to herself now. Whatever life had to offer her, or rather to deny her, she could meet it on equal terms. She loved him, of course, and had always done so, but, fearful and correct, had hidden from the truth. And by running away from him she had preserved him in her mind, where he belonged, where no one could discover him. Regret would

come later, in the years ahead. In her imagination he would
always be there, and they would accomplish those acts, so
many of them, which she had refused to limit to one isolated
opportunity, hurried and probably spoiled, which was what
she had been offered. For the moment it was enough. She
thought her refusal had probably been wise. She was not yet
sorry for it.

There was no one she could tell about this. The only
person she could have confided in was Tessa, and the impossibility of this, on every conceivable level of reality, jolted her
at last into shame, crimsoned her cheeks, brought tears to her
eyes. Love had brought her to a state of perfidy, which was
what she had always feared. This abortive passion, this adventure, which would have endeared her to her friends, been the
passport to their affections, enabled her at last to meet them
on equal terms, must remain hidden, shameful. The curious
fact was that she herself felt no shame, although she was
overwhelmingly aware that she had fallen from openness into
concealment. In this situation she felt the onset of a belated
sense of the world's realities. And also a stricken irradiated
bemused wonder, as at the ending of one state of consciousness and the beginning of another. Her husband, her friends,
even her daughter, now appeared to her at one remove, as if
she had known them in another life. Estranged, absorbed, she
felt as yet no sense of infidelity to her husband. What pain she
felt was for Tessa, all unknowing, in the grave. She saw once
more that rapt and lonely profile on the pillow, in the hospital
bed. And Lizzie, she thought, wincing. The crime is all
against Lizzie, no one else. Too many crimes had been com-
mitted against her already. She saw the lonely trudging little
figure, burdened with too much reflection, and now out of
her reach in Elspeth Mackinnon's house in Windsor. Living,
forced to live, with her father's mistress. She supposed that
Jack and this woman would marry, eventually, after a discreet

interval. But this thought, and the thought of Lizzie, so re-
duced her own part in Jack's life that she preferred to dwell
on it no further. And she was late, very late, and Freddie
would be waiting.

She smelt cigarette smoke as she went up the stairs to the
drawing-room. It was unlike him to smoke before dinner: he
must be hungry and exasperated. She glanced at her watch:
eight-fifteen, and they usually ate at seven-thirty.

'Where on earth have you been?' he demanded.

'I told you. I took Lizzie's things round to Judd Street. I'm
sorry I've kept you waiting. Dinner won't take a minute. It's
cold salmon. Unless you'd like some soup? Watercress soup?'

She was aware that she was overdoing her solicitude, was
conscious of a rather specious animation. But how was she to
behave? How did one behave in such a situation? They were
not sufficiently friendly to discuss intimate matters, and she
thought that even in the most sophisticated circles one did not
discuss one's potential adultery with one's husband. All she
could achieve in the circumstances was a hostessy flutter. This
she despised, but could not hit on a natural attitude. She
longed to go up to her bedroom. She had applied more
lipstick in the car, but had a suspicion that she had applied it
unevenly.

'You've laddered your stocking,' he observed. 'And your
hair is untidy. No, don't go up now: I'm extremely hungry,
and anyway I want to talk to you.'

She sat opposite him with lowered eyes, every inch a
hypocrite. So this was what love in middle age led to, she
thought: was it worth it? She doubted, in that instant,
whether she possessed the strength, the will, to go on with it,
and then reflected that there was nothing to go on with, no
continuation, no arrangement to meet Jack again, no real
desire to calculate how much was possible. He was to remain
in the realm of secrets, where he would be safe from prying

eyes. She would guard her secret, and if the resulting insincer-
ity was the price she had to pay then she would pay it. Maybe
I am taking it all too seriously, she thought, suddenly tired.
Her head ached with tension; she longed to go to bed.

'So I've decided to leave in the summer,' Freddie was
saying. 'Thirty-five years—not a bad record with the same
group. I could stay on, but I think they secretly think I'm a
bit too old.'

'You'll miss the office,' she said, alarmed.

'I'm getting on, Harriet. I've earned my time off. Of
course, it'll take a bit of getting used to. But there's golf. And
I thought we might travel a bit, when Imogen goes to school.
I may go back as a consultant, if I find the time hangs heavy,
but I doubt it. My seat on the board won't change; there'll be
the usual meetings. But I want a break, and now's the time
to take one, or make one, or whatever one does with a break.'

He got up, went to a side table, and poured himself a glass
of brandy. He lifted the decanter with an enquiring gesture,
but she shook her head, conscious of her headache.

'And I've invited George Godfrey to dinner. You might
ring Muriel in the morning.'

The Godfreys, whom she disliked, without exactly knowing why. Was it their appearance? He was corpulent, red-
faced, overripe, carrying his stomach complacently before
him, sitting down to a meal with barely disguised pleasure.
And his wife, similarly ill-defined about the waist, dignified
above it, with her diamond earrings and her iron-grey curls,
all spreading knees and support stockings below. They were
in their seventies, rather grand, invited everywhere. They
were in fact a mild-mannered couple, devoted to the opera,
but they went out so much that everything they said was of
a public nature. He offered a stream of anecdotes; she was
largely silent, except for the isolated discreet remark, endors-
ing whatever it was that her husband was proclaiming on her

behalf. Freddie's friends: the husband was a business associate. She felt a weariness at the prospect, as if entertaining these two old people put her automatically into their camp. She knew that Freddie felt at home with them, felt comfortable with that age group, liked the illusion of himself as a comparative youngster in their midst. But Harriet, watching George Godfrey wiping his rather large mouth, watching his wife's thin lips closing primly over a cheese biscuit, felt as if she were being buried alive. On previous occasions she had made Immy an excuse, had left the table briefly, and hurried up the stairs, for a respite. But now Immy was too old, and she herself must behave like a respectable, even an ageing, matron.

'I thought we might join them on a cruise next winter,' she heard Freddie saying.

'I'd rather the two of us were on our own,' she replied prudently, at which he brightened, and looked at her with interest.

'Don't drink any more,' she begged, getting up to clear the table. He caught at her hand as she took his plate. 'Freddie,' she warned. 'You'll make me drop something.' She was aware of a nasty and factitious flirtatiousness in her manner, when what she felt was a sudden blind panic. To be with him in that bedroom, to smell the brandy on his breath, to watch him undress, was, she thought, more than she could tolerate. It would be the surest sign of divine punishment if the evening were to end like this.

'I'm going up in a minute,' she told him. 'I've got a terrible headache. Don't disturb me when you come to bed—I'm going to take a sleeping pill.'

'You won't need one if I come up with you.'

He used sex as a threat, always had, as if the anticipation of pleasure had to make her shrink with fear. He liked to dominate in these circumstances, although he was too timid to put his desires into action. He enjoyed seeing her discomfiture, not suspecting that it was embarrassment. She wondered how she could have stood him for so long. And yet he was very kind, she thought, with a sinking heart.

'Oh,' she said, standing in the middle of the bedroom. 'I really have got a terrible head. I think I must call it a day, Freddie.'

'I have just the thing for headaches,' he said, taking off his jacket. 'Come here. Let me show you.'

She smelled his breath, felt his weight, turned her head stiffly aside, her mouth smeared with his saliva. A tear trickled on to the pillow. There were no words for the thoughts in her head, and no ear into which she could speak them. She felt a loneliness beyond measure, and before sleep descended, thought, I have no friends.

From a distance she heard Freddie say, 'You're not much good at this, are you?'

14

AFTER THAT the dark days started, culminating in that darkest day of all, from which there never was, and never would be, any remission. In her psychic vision, the uncorrupted, unalterable vision that finally makes sense of the past, she saw them all as condemned from that time on. But this conviction was gradual, perhaps resisted. With the memory of Jack still fresh in her mind she was for a short time able to shrug off all annoyances. In the light of Jack Freddie dwindled into a person of no importance. She felt extravagant, ebullient, desirous of another life. But that other life, she was later to reflect, was not the life of a mature woman, let alone of a woman obsessed by a man, but the life of a girl, even a rather silly girl, one who was light on her feet, and read fashion magazines, and wore inexpensive clothes, and had no ties. She had no idea how this feckless image had taken hold of her, for she had never been feckless, and rather despised those who were. It was just that the image of a girl, stepping lightly down the street on her way to work, without encumbrances, seemed to her so attractive that she returned to it with pleasure throughout the day, as she did her conscientious shopping, and took Freddie's heavy suit to the cleaners, and waited in for the plumber.

Outside, in the mild air, women like herself, growing a

little tired as time went by, pursued a life so devoid of frivolity that she wondered how they—and she—could bear it. She felt herself on the brink of an indiscretion which she perceived as merely mischievous, as if she were indeed that young girl, who did not have to think of matters like constancy and fidelity. All she had to do, she thought, was to pick up the telephone, or get into the car, and she could have her heart's desire, for that was what it was. She toyed with this delicious possibility for perhaps two or even three days. And yet she made no move, seeing herself as that unencumbered girl, for whom there were as yet no decisions to be made, stepping lightly through her world, favoured by the indulgent glances of her elders.

Later, much later, she thought that she must have been imagining Immy's life rather than her own. Yet she could not deny a certain beguiling hopefulness in her imaginings which had nothing to do with her daughter. For Immy was an aristocrat, straight-nosed, straight-backed, largely unconfiding. Her early flirtatiousness had entirely disappeared; she was self-contained, extraordinarily so for a child of nine. She appeared to find her parents uninteresting, for which neither of them blamed her; she was too beautiful for them to feel anything but humility in her presence. She left the table as soon as she could, running up to her bedroom to practise her recorder. Miss Wetherby she now found too old and too dull, much to Miss Wetherby's disappointment. But Miss Wetherby was experienced with children, experienced enough to let Immy go. In the face of Miss Wetherby's resumed impassivity Harriet persuaded Freddie to relax his ban on having a dog in the house, albeit in the basement. Soon Rex, a small wire-haired terrier, accompanied Miss Wetherby on her surprisingly active walks round Battersea Park. Imogen remained unimpressed by the dog, and unattracted by it. She was developing a kind of scorn for her surroundings. 'Growing up,' said

Freddie, who no longer kissed her anywhere but on the top of her glossy black head. They felt a little apologetic when she was with them, aware of a timidity to which she was a stranger. So the light feckless girl of Harriet's imagination was not her daughter, who sometimes seemed quite angry, but herself, her embryonic self, who might have existed in another life, but who had got married and settled down.

This fantasy, these ephemeral feelings, receded gradually like a tide on a silent beach, leaving behind a cold residue which was equally tenacious, for it enveloped her for the rest of her life. She thought at first that the weather might have something to do with it. From greenness, promise, mild days, and soft skies it veered to frost at night, and a colourless mist which lasted until midday. Nor did these mists hold the promise of fine weather: they persisted keenly, damply, covering the sun with a grey haze, subduing bird-song. She began to doubt the existence of spring in this prolongation of winter, although the lilac and the may were in bloom and the chestnut candles had turned from green to white. 'It will all be wasted,' she thought. 'It is no longer relevant.' In this new damp greyness she began to doubt the memory of that evening in Judd Street, probably the most significant of her life. She had exhausted it with reflection; it no longer yielded anything when she summoned it up. Then she knew that it had been inadequate, that it had no status as an amorous encounter. No doubt it had been a form of politeness, the sort of compliment that a cynic like Jack might pay to a prude like herself. She blushed with shame, although she knew that if he were to make the slightest sign she would go to him. But she was not brave enough, or perhaps not foolish enough, to make the first move.

When the blush, and the successive blushes, faded, she felt a chill that sent her to her bedroom for an extra sweater. That was when she had that curious episode of being unable to get warm. Freddie had been quite alarmed by her pallor, and by her apparently insatiable desire for sleep. On the pretext of her indisposition she slept voraciously, going up almost as soon as they had finished dinner, spending afternoons under a rug on the sofa. Her descent into sleep was voluptuous, as though it were all she had ever craved. She awoke trying to retain the fragments of a dream, or even a memory: for instance, what had the shops on either side of her mother's shop in William Street been called? Where precisely had she bought the cakes for tea, when Mr Latif was due? The persistence of these memories horrified her, as did the sight, when she awoke, of the thick cream linen curtains and the thick white carpet of the bedroom she shared with Freddie. He was very kind to her at this time, thinking that she was upset at the prospect of their daughter going away to school. 'It is your age,' he said. It was undoubtedly a crisis of some kind, but in fact it only lasted for a month or two. She tried to treat it like a physical illness, was not above using it as an excuse for her desire for sleep. Freddie, convinced that she was undergoing a process common to all women, left her alone, for which she was grateful. The coldness, the sleepiness, and the gratitude persisted; even when recovered she retained a memory of disorder.

They had a family holiday that year, the last before Imogen went away to school. They took a house on the Devon coast, near Salcombe. 'Do you want Lizzie to come?' she had asked. 'Lizzie's not my friend any more,' said Immy, tossing her head. 'Sophie and Alexandra are my friends. Anyway, I don't like Lizzie. Are we going to a hotel? I'd rather go to a hotel.' 'We are going to a very nice house,' said Harriet patiently. She managed not to say, And do be nice to your father. He has a great shock coming to him. It is called retirement. She knew that Freddie would be bored with no office to go to, knew that he disliked the house in the daytime, disliked it even more now that he could hear the distant bark of the dog, had suggested that they have dinner earlier, could be heard making hearty telephone calls. Yet the holiday had been a success, she thought. They had felt happier away from London, at least she and Freddie had; Immy had been bored, except when they took her out to dinner. The weather had been perfect, a succession of hot cloudless days, and the doors of the drawing-room opened on to a patio, where Freddie sat in a short-sleeved shirt and a panama hat reading P. D. James. She wore a cotton dress and sandals, and did her shopping first thing in the morning. Then she took Immy to the beach, and read *What Maisie Knew*. They ate sparingly at lunch, and, in deference to Immy, dressed up in the evening and had dinner at the hotel. 'And how is Madam this evening?' asked the waiter with a flourish of napkin. 'Very well, thank you,' said Immy distantly, fingering the necklace of corals which Freddie had found for her in a local jeweller's. She had, at those moments, an entirely adult air.

She thought that they had been contented on that last holiday. The idea of going back to London had terrified her. At night, after Immy had gone to bed, she and Freddie had stood wordlessly in the little garden, Freddie with his arm round her waist. Then she knew that he too was reluctant to leave this place, and to face a future without work, without Immy. In bed he did not touch her, occasionally gave a kind of groan. 'I am too old,' he once said, into the darkness of the night. So that is to be the end of it, she thought, and it is all I have ever known. She felt sorry for them both, sorry for their daughter, who would have to deal with lightless parents when she herself was on the verge of so many discoveries. She would get no help from them, and must therefore encounter no hindrance from them either, must not endure the humiliation, the tastelessness of prohibitions, warnings. Yet Harriet longed for her daughter to marry young, and happily, to go away from them to a better life, not a worse one. They would do what they could for her, acknowledging their deficiencies. It was all that they could do, for the young now had the upper hand. They were both conventional people; perhaps convention was what they had in common. It may even have been all they had in common. Immy would have her year abroad, if she wanted it (but she seemed to take no interest in her future), and then they would prepare the upstairs flat for her; she would have her own friends, and no obligations. But how would they endure the long days without her? She was sometimes bad-tempered in their company, as if they were a heavy burden for a child with such high standards of beauty. Her beauty had already staked many claims. She was effortless with the opposite sex, already commanded the attention of the twelve-year-old French twins staying at the hotel. She was shedding childishness rapidly, too rapidly. Already she found this peaceful holiday dull, was bored with the beach. At fourteen she would be a woman, while her mother was still a girl. 'Can't we go out somewhere?' she fretted every morning. 'It is too beautiful a day to spend in the car,' Harriet would reply. But Freddie could not quite hide his disappointment.

Late in the warm dark nights she found that she missed Tessa painfully, and on waking she yearned for her. The house had wide sunny windows, which reminded her of the flat in Beaufort Street, and the afternoons they had spent there before the children were born. She missed a female friend, who would be all compassion, all competence. This too she saw as an illusion, for Tessa had been brooding and sometimes impatient. But female friendship, these days too often turned into some kind of ideology, was what she craved, something to soothe her unreliable heart, and she saw that that was what they had both wanted, and even Mary and Pamela as well, some vision of safety in a cruel world, some haven, once they had outgrown mothers and fathers, who, in her case at least, had proved insufficient. Tessa had been strong, wayward but strong. And she had been right, entirely right, in forcing Jack to marry her—it was indeed a proof of her strength—for Jack would have passed on, not unaffected, but unregarding, irresponsible. Suddenly the image of Jack was diminished by the memory of Tessa, of Tessa's lonely face on her hospital pillow. She longed to have her back, to assure her of her own loyalty. She longed, once more, to protect Tessa, although she had never been in a position to do so, had in fact been the weaker of the two. Tessa, until she was cut down, had wrestled with life, and her defeat was cruelly out of character. Now Harriet could see that they had susceptibilities in common, and longed to tell Tessa as much. She thought that if she could see Tessa now, there would be no lies or silences between them. Tessa, having experienced death, would forgive her friend's ultimate foolishness, for there is little time for foolishness this side of the grave. That flower-decked horror at Golders Green . . . And no Lizzie. But where was Lizzie now? Did she belong entirely to the past, and to her uncertain future? Lizzie, as always, registered as an absence, an unknown, passed over by the likes of Imogen. Sometimes Harriet yearned to be with Tessa, childless again. Yet Immy came first, must come first, and it was for Immy that she persevered in what had become a difficult and lonely life. Even Freddie, she saw, was lonely. But Freddie was lonely because he knew that his daughter did not love him. This added another silence to all the others.

The return to London was as bad as both she and Freddie had privately believed it would be, and was further darkened by the prospect of Immy's departure. The child was now restless, demanding to go out, yet all that Harriet could devise was met with an elaborate show of disappointment. She kicked her way round Peter Jones, waiting for her school uniform to be assembled, and had to be mollified with a milk shake in the restaurant. This was not entirely to her liking either. Harriet could see that her daughter had it in her to be one of those rich proud beautiful women who seem to be composed of superior materials to the ordinary model. She felt a sudden chill of estrangement as she contemplated the brooding face, and it was with a curious misgiving that she compared it with the childish hand clasping the spoon. 'My darling girl,' she said gently. 'We shall miss you very much. You won't forget us, will you?' She despised herself for this appeal, but felt in that instant so denuded that it might have been she who was leaving home, and going away from all that was familiar. Leaving home! Even the thought of it made her weak, yet she had not particularly minded leaving home herself, had in a sense volunteered to go. And yet ever since she had longed to get back there, not in any geographical sense, but symbolically, had felt a yearning, a heaviness, an aching sense of loss on summer evenings, had never felt like the rich woman she was supposed to resemble, had never believed herself to be a suitable or even a credible consort for a wealthy man, had longed for old simple ways, for her little walnut bed, the rain beating against the windows of the back room, the cracked willow pattern plate, and the cup and saucer which did not match it. Were they happy, she thought, suddenly and painfully, those childish parents, in comparison with whom her daughter was infinitely more worldly? Did the day drag for them, did they, with a sigh, contemplate the empty noisy sky outside their windows, the traffic, the raucous gulls? Was the day empty for them until the light faded, and they had their baths, and with a languid air, as if the day had exhausted them, prepared themselves for their public appearance, in hotel lounge or bar, aware that they were too old to be frivolous, and never, in any case, fond of drink?

It was with the greatest difficulty that she pulled her mind back to this hot morning in the present, the sun flashing off the plate glass window of Peter Jones, the plastic bags collapsed at her feet. 'I think we should go down to Brighton,' she said. 'Granny and Grandpa will want to see you before you go away.' She hated the sound of the words, and their long echo, but could not see how to avoid them. Immy appeared unmoved. 'I don't want to go to Brighton,' she said. 'There's nothing to do there. And they don't see me anyway.'

'Well, then,' said Harriet firmly. 'They must come and see us. Remind me to ring them when we get home.'

She would book a table for tea at the Ritz, she thought: they would love that. It seemed more important to provide pleasures for her parents than for her daughter, who was so disdainful. Oh, darling, she thought, please be a good girl, a loving girl, one with tender feelings, and a long memory. I know that you think us both inadequate, your father and I, and have no time for that pathetic couple, your grandparents, but it is important that you keep the faith, or memories will come back suddenly, unannounced, when you are far advanced into another life. You are our miraculous child, unhoped for, more beautiful than we had ever dreamed you would be. You have the advantage of us there. But you take for granted what is only temporary. It is necessary for you to develop a loving heart, in which, at the moment, you appear to be a little deficient. It is not your fault, or rather it is not your fault yet, but one day it may be. Then she saw the little hand clutching the foamy spoon, and felt her own heart nearly break. 'We shall miss you,' she said, having received no answer to her earlier question. 'We must see that you have a good time before you go.'

At home she telephoned her parents, who agreed, with apparent carelessness, that they might have a day free towards the end of the week, that they could just manage lunch at Wellington Square, that tea at the Ritz might be fitted in. And then, on impulse, she dialled Directory Enquiries, and asked for a number for Mackinnon in Old Windsor—she had the address from a postcard which Lizzie had been instructed to send her, thanking her for her new clothes. Soon a crystalline Home Counties voice answered. 'Miss Mackinnon? This is Harriet Lytton. My daughter is a friend of Lizzie's.'

The voice expressed polite interest, but held forth no promise of further exchange.

'I was wondering if Lizzie would like a day in London, before going off to school? With us, I mean. I should like the children to have something nice . . . The ballet, I thought. My husband can always get a box at Covent Garden.'

There was no answer.

'*Swan Lake,*' she said, rather more decisively.

A throat was cleared at the other end. 'Well, of course, it's very kind of you . . .'

This signified neither yes nor no: how did Jack put up with this woman?

'I'd be very grateful if you could make arrangements to bring Lizzie to London,' she said firmly. 'She can stay the night here. She is quite used to us.'

'She can come up by herself,' said the voice. 'She is used to that too.'

'On the train?' said Harriet, horrified. 'At her age?'

'Oh, yes.'

'Then shall we say Saturday week? She can stay the night, and I'll bring her back the following day.'

'Oh, there'll be no need for that. For her to stay the night, I mean. I shall be driving up to Judd Street later that afternoon. If you put her into a taxi she can join me there.'

'Will her father be at home?' asked Harriet at last.

'I'm not sure. He's being posted to Berlin at any moment.'

'In that case won't you come to us for a drink?'

'No, I don't think so, thanks. Just put Lizzie into a cab; she'll be all right.'

Such rudeness, she thought, putting down the receiver;

intolerable. I have never been as rude as that in my life, although I may have wanted to be. And I have no reason to be polite to her either. Ah, I am out of my depth here, and everywhere else too, it seems. It occurred to her that Elspeth Mackinnon disliked her for exactly the same reason that she disliked Elspeth Mackinnon: she had been discovered. Oh, to hell with it, she thought; and it is now too late to cancel the arrangement. I should never have spoken to her. But then Lizzie would have been deprived of her treat, and I do so want her to enjoy it. Freddie must come too: a Saturday matinée, and they can drink fruit juice in the Crush Bar. Except that Immy would demand champagne. Oh, let her have it, if that's what she wants. There was so little time left for her to enjoy herself, although it was clear that she regarded school as more of a treat than anything else that might be planned for her. Otherness was what Immy wanted. Unlike her mother, she had no fear.

For her parents she made a cheese soufflé, with a green salad, and caramelized oranges to follow. 'We don't normally eat lunch,' said her mother, picking up her fork with every sign of reluctance. She was nervous, Harriet saw, intimidated by the size of the dining-room and its heavy appointments, all inherited from Freddie's parents. 'We usually have a sandwich in the kitchen.' She took tiny mouthfuls of the delicious concoction until it cooled, when she pushed it aside and lit a cigarette. Hughie ate cheerfully, greedily, fork clattering slightly against the side of his plate. 'Don't give him any more,' warned Merle. 'He'll only get indigestion.'

'And where's our precious girl?' asked Hughie, impervious.

'She's downstairs with Miss Wetherby,' said Harriet. 'I wanted you to myself for a few minutes.'

In fact she had wanted to protect her father and his tremulous hands, their quiver now restored by his increasing age, from the child's sharp gaze. Her parents looked much older, she thought, were now sadly too old to be bright young things. And becoming timorous, perhaps. But still, she had to admit, expertly turned out. Her mother had dressed for the Ritz before leaving home, in a bright blue silk print dress, with three rows of cultured pearls. Her father wore a grey suit. They looked more than presentable; from the back they looked remarkable. Only full-face did the eagerness, the longing show, in their naked eyes, as they waited for Immy to join them. Both now seemed to be afflicted with a degree of agitation.

But the afternoon was a success, practically a triumph. 'It was smashing, Mummy, ace. We saw —' and the name of a rock star of whom even Harriet had heard.

'And did you thank Granny and Grandpa properly?' she said.

Her parents, now fully recovered from their earlier timidity, and restored by the friendly impersonality of the hotel world, their world, held out loving arms. After Immy had embraced them—and Hughie had tried to lift her, but had found her too heavy—they stood, flushed with pleasure in the child and with pride in each other. 'A lovely day,' they assured Harriet. 'Just a little bit tired now, dear. We must be getting home.' And, '*Au revoir,* darling,' they waved from the taxi. Immy, at the drawing-room window, waved back.

And the ballet tomorrow, thought Harriet, going thankfully to bed. And then, next week, she will be gone.

The sight of Lizzie, at the front door, was so familiar that Harriet did not for a moment recognize what made her look so different. At last she saw what it was: Lizzie was wearing a dress. It was a Laura Ashley creation, with a sash and a lace collar, above which her serious face appeared too old. Or perhaps the dress was too young for her. In any event it was ill chosen. She gazed impassively at Harriet, her personal effects in a small pouch on a long strap over her shoulder. 'Hello, darling,' said Harriet. 'How lovely to see you. Did you get here all right? Well, of course you did. Lunch is nearly ready. Do you want to go up and see Immy?' She saw the child nearly wrecked on the dilemma of whether or not to tell a polite lie, saw that for her a lie would be an impossibility, decided to rescue her. 'Would you like to come into the kitchen and help me with the fruit salad?'

Lizzie, relieved, swallowed. 'Yes, thank you,' she said.

'Well, Lizzie,' said Freddie, putting down his paper. 'Good to see you. All right, are you?'

'Yes, thank you,' she said once more.

He waited attentively for something further to be said, then, when it was obvious that silence was to prevail, took up his paper again. Even Lizzie disappointed him.

The ballet had an alarming effect on both children. Freddie did things well: the box was much appreciated, as were the orange juice and the champagne. Leaning over the velvet rim, animosity temporarily forgotten, they were almost disappointed when the house lights dimmed and the music started. After that they were lost to reason. She tried to explain the story to them, but they waved her away. In the first and second intervals they were too busy trying to stem Immy's tears to bother much about Lizzie. Harriet smiled at Freddie, who was wiping away a tear of his own. 'Harriet,' said Lizzie hoarsely, plucking at Harriet's sleeve. 'Will they get married? Will the prince marry the swan?'

'Oh, yes, Lizzie,' she said, strangely moved by the urgency of the enquiry. 'It will all end happily. You'll see.'

Miss Wetherby too had had a good afternoon. Miss Wetherby had prepared a tea of anchovy toast, cress sandwiches, and walnut cake, but they were too drained to eat much, or to talk. Freddie took a visibly tired Lizzie back to Judd Street, while Harriet put Immy to bed.

'Can we go again?' she asked her mother.

'Whenever you come home. You and Lizzie.'

Some days after this she was passed by a man in a car, travelling very fast. She saw a hand raised from the wheel in some sort of greeting. She thought it might have been Jack, but could not be sure. In her mind's eye the gesture repeated itself for several days, but there was no way in which she could imagine a suitable answering gesture from herself. This worried her excessively: her lack of response. It was only the pain of Immy's departure that put an end to her preoccupation.

15

BUT *Swan Lake* does not end happily. It ends nobly, affectingly, upliftingly, as befits a tragedy. It ends, above all, appropriately. This matter of the ending—of a suitable ending—was to preoccupy Lizzie for some time. The resolution of the matter would, she knew, afford her a measure of relief. But of all this Harriet saw no sign, for on leaving the theatre her thoughts were all of Immy; in comparison Lizzie seemed to dematerialize, to vanish into thin air, as if her presence were merely notional. Harriet, when she looked round for Lizzie, saw merely the unchanged and unchanging face of Lizzie, small, white, impassive, saw the unapproachable reserve, saw the same stoic tolerance, which extended to the unbecoming flowered dress, and the journey to Wellington Square uncomplainingly endured by train and cab. Had she thought to ascertain that the child had been accompanied? The cab had driven off, and she had forgotten to enquire. But Lizzie had survived her journey, whatever it had been like. Lizzie, she thought, had even enjoyed the ballet.

Lizzie's uncharacteristic emotion at the end of Act II had certainly been expressed, but expressed so minimally in comparison with Immy's lovely tears, perhaps an alteration in the timbre of her voice, and her two hands clenched into fists, as Odile, in black, deployed her dazzling, her irresistible seductions.

In fact Odile's variations had proved an intolerable ordeal for Lizzie. She could not have said why she was so frightened and repelled by the dangerous figure, and its assumptions of triumph, of victory. To see virtue so easily discarded, and the prince so easily beguiled, brought a feeling of sickness to her throat, and yet she could not have explained why. Only when the prince and Odette were reunited in the beauty of their apotheosis did she release the breath she had been holding. Stumbling after the others down the stairs and into the car she was still distressed, not quite reassured. Immy, for all her tears, was fully recovered. This simply served, once again, to reinforce her knowledge that she and Immy were constructed out of different material, and were bound to be strangers to one another. It was not simply that Imogen was loved, whereas she, Lizzie, was not. In her mind Imogen was like Odile, who can simulate passion without feeling. Her excesses, her carelessness, and what Lizzie perceived as ruthlessness were alien, frightening. Even Harriet, of whom she was cautiously fond, seemed dazzled by her, as the prince had been by Odile. This diminished Harriet in Lizzie's eyes.

Her quarrel was with appearances, attitudes, when she knew herself to be dedicated to seriousness. She was inclined to mistrust first, only later to accept. Her life had been all caution, wariness, withholding. Her lonely courage was of no advantage to her, since it merely prepared her for more loneliness and the need for further courage. Going away to school was for her one more ordeal, yet as far as she could see school would be no worse than the holidays, when she would be transported to Scotland and more strangers, or put on the plane to France to stay with her grandparents at Ramatuelle, where she was a not altogether welcome reminder of her dead mother. Blinking in the fresh air of Bow Street, Lizzie wished momentarily that Freddie might adopt her. But then that would mean seeing more of Immy, so that was no solution either. There was, she felt, no solution to anything. In her childish perception most outcomes, when not tragic, were uncomfortable. She looked askance at Immy, and at Immy's insistence on being happy, or being made happy. This made Immy seem a lightweight, yet none the less demanding, for all the frivolousness of her nature. Altogether Immy was a painful subject, doubly painful now that the character of Odile had been shown to her. Lizzie could not have been said to have been reassured by her contact with art, since art casts so critical a light on life itself.

None of this was she able to articulate, so that Harriet did not know, was never to know, how profoundly she had been affected. Harriet remembered Imogen's tears, and felt tears in her own eyes at the thought of them. And she was to be parted from her for long years: how and why had she brought this about? It was true that Imogen was high-spirited and capricious, perhaps inclined to be disobedient. It was true that her vivid face was too often clouded with disappointment at what they had hoped was a modest treat. 'Your favourite, darling,' Harriet would say, serving her a pear enrobed in chocolate as a dessert. 'I don't like it any more,' would be the reply. Anything to avoid that look of disappointment, Harriet would think, although Freddie was less indulgent. It was Freddie who had insisted on the school, although the child was so young. 'Let her go,' he warned, 'or she will be bored stiff.'

To Freddie, Imogen was somewhat alarming, since she resembled no one so much as Helen, his first wife, and sometimes, on waking, he had a moment of panic, wondering to whom he was really married. He saw in Immy some of that recklessness, that ruthlessness which Helen had mobilized in order to taunt him: he saw, in her childish eyes, a scorn that was unfriendly. He remembered Helen's jibes, and knew that his daughter would be sexually unmanageable. He longed for her to be gone for a while, so that he could recover some

peace with Harriet, whose dark head he saw bent docilely
over the Cash's name tapes. An additional worry was that he
did not feel quite well. The panic, on waking, was com-
pounded by a dizziness; once he had nearly fallen on his way
to the bathroom. 'What is it?' Harriet had called. 'Nothing.
Go to sleep. It's early,' he had called back, but he had sat on
the edge of the bath, sweating, until the attack, or whatever
it was, had passed. Blood pressure, he told himself later in the
day: must have a check-up. But while believing in all sincerity
in the existence, the reality, of high blood pressure, he
thought his trouble was caused by a vague unhappiness, by
retirement, by his wife's indifference, by the more than indifference of his daughter. He was careful enough not to approach the child, never to show her his dreadful eagerness to
hear a loving word. He would be the provider in the background, and as such he would achieve some value in her eyes.
The day would come when they would be brought together
by Imogen's material needs. Then he would deploy his resources. Until that time, he thought, he might just manage.
But it put a strain on him, and he did not want to see her for
a while.

They drove Imogen to school: she ran off without a backward glance. Harriet, trembling, got back into the car, and
presently wiped her eyes. 'This has got to stop,' said Freddie,
getting in beside her. 'She dominates your life. You think
about her far too much. She's happy, she's healthy, thank
God, she's intelligent—and she's bored, Harriet, that's what
you don't realize. She's bored with your concern, and with
your fussing. Let her go! She'll go sooner or later, I can tell
you that for nothing. Our place is in the background now.
She'll never want for anything, I promise you that. Neither
will you, if anything happens to me.'

She turned to him in alarm. 'Are you not well?' she asked,
with genuine concern.

'I'm getting on. I have to think of these things.'

'Don't die, Freddie,' she said, weeping again. 'I couldn't bear life without you. I know I'm tiresome, and not quite what you hoped, but I do value and respect our life together. I am so fond of you,' she said, slightly surprised. 'You are an ideal husband, you know.'

'Perhaps I shouldn't have married you,' he sighed. 'I was too old. It wasn't fair.'

'But you see I was too young. I should always have been too young. I am a foolish woman, Freddie, not much good to you. My life comes out of books and dreams, like a girl's. And I go to bed too early. I sometimes think I should never have married because I need too much sleep.'

He laughed, and after a while so did she.

'You are more of a child than your daughter is,' he said. 'Strange how ready she is for life, while you still hang back.'

I hang back because I am waiting for a sign, she thought, and you must never know. And yet I should have made a rotten mistress. It was never on the cards, or at least it may have been on the cards but it was never a reality. I am Freddie's wife, whether I like it or not; cautious, fearful women like myself are no good for anything else. She felt a nausea, a hollowness, and yawned nervously. 'Could we stop for tea somewhere?' she asked. 'I feel quite exhausted.'

He glanced at her. 'It means going in to Oxford,' he said. 'But I could do with a break myself. A real break. A holiday. I've been having these dizzy spells. Oh, nothing to worry about: at my age I must expect something or other.'

'You've been feeling unwell, and you've said nothing?' She was appalled.

'Now don't fly into a panic. You do it all the time. That's why I didn't tell you. Immy is quite right, you know, to resist you when you're like that.'

'Does she resist me?' asked Harriet. 'Is that what she does?'

He sighed again. Immy, always Immy.

'I was talking to Sanders, at the club. You don't know him. He was troubled by the same thing a couple of years back. Somebody recommended this clinic in Switzerland, near Geneva. He went there for a month, and he's been perfectly all right ever since.'

'I don't think I could go away for a month,' said Harriet. 'Not until I know Immy is settled. You'd better see Mordaunt. It's pointless to think of some foreign clinic that nobody knows anything about, when you're not even sure what's wrong with you. There are clinics here too, you know. Health farms. It's probably what they call executive stress, one of the many diseases of Western civilization.'

She was chattering, because she was now very frightened. If Freddie left her on her own she would die. She knew that now, ineluctably. And if Freddie left her alone with Imogen how would she sustain that immense demanding appetite for life, so immeasurably greater than her own, and bring it to fulfilment, happiness, success? Anything she desires, she thought, I would give her. But I can't quite do it on my own. And Freddie? For a moment she felt his loneliness, and saw that it corresponded to her own. She put a hand on his arm. 'Dear, it is not too late.'

'Tea always cheers me up,' she said later, as they resumed their journey.

'I noticed you made a meal of it.'

He was restored to something like good humour, now that he had weaned her away from her daughter and told her of his troubles. He knew from experience that he had not made a particularly deep impression, that Harriet's thoughts were still with Imogen, that she dreaded the return to the empty house. Nevertheless he felt mildly appeased. What he had experienced as a dreadful secret (for he had been seriously alarmed) was no longer entirely his responsibility. The shared confidence was to him significant, more significant in his mind than his daughter's absence, for he had begun to notice in himself an antagonism that answered her own. He loved her dearly, as ardently as any rejected lover, yet he could not admire her as her mother so foolishly did. He saw a cruelty there which left him with grave doubts, saw, as Harriet failed to see, that Imogen found them both boring and unsatisfactory and that this characteristic was not merely a childish indifference to their failed lives but an active condemnation. Although he himself thought Harriet beautiful he knew that his daughter, except for some rare moments of favour, or of regression, found her timid and dull, fatally lacking in the kind of smart aggressive attractiveness that the young find admirable. Although without much sympathy or liking for Merle and Hughie Blakemore, whom he contrived never to see, he dreaded the day when he would have to defend them against Imogen's snobbishness. They had given her too much, had spent too much time loving her, marvelling at that beauty and independence, which in themselves seemed such reassuring qualities, as if their stewardship alone had been responsible for that superior viability. Now he saw that they should have corrected, admonished, chastised, while the child was still young enough to mourn their displeasure. And if she had had to court their continued favour, what harm would have been done? Better a few misgivings, a little reserve, that the queenliness that Immy had never ceased to exhibit.

He himself was both afraid of and in awe of her physical fearlessness; awkward and clumsy himself, it was many years since he had been able to run up the stairs, or even to take them two at a time. As a boy he had fumbled catches, been overweight, slow to move, badly co-ordinated even then. As a businessman of almost national standing he had moved with more majesty, but inwardly he was still humiliated. His *gravitas,* he knew, was nothing more than a disguise. This flaw in his physical make-up made him ludicrously susceptible to beauty in both women and men; he viewed them as if they were objects of virtù, paintings or sculptures, with the devotion of an amateur, eternally unqualified to take a detached view. To be the father of so beautiful a child—That black hair! That white skin!—had afflicted him with awe, and for some years, until she was about seven, he had felt that he did not possess the right even to criticize her. Now that she was older he was not so sure. He saw the woman she was going to be emerge, take shape: saw that she would be contemptuous, lawless, indifferent to another's hurt. He feared for his wife's soft heart, the heart which he himself was unable to reach. He felt sorry for her, unawakened as he knew her to be. He sighed and covered her hand with one of his own. It seemed to him at that moment that he would have to stay well in order to protect her. He had succeeded in worrying her, but only slightly. The rest he would have to take care of himself.

To Harriet the house echoed with emptiness. Even Freddie was affected by it and went out to his club every morning, walking there after breakfast as she had instructed him, mindful of his health. She had no idea what he did there, presumed that he read the papers, ordered coffee, found like-minded company, joined somebody for lunch. She similarly had no idea what he did in the afternoons, and it occurred to her to wonder, yet again, whether he found company of another sort. In fact he visited the art galleries around St James's, went to the Royal Academy, aware that he cut a solitary figure, mildly melancholy, too humbled to be discontented. Harriet merely noted that he had nothing to tell her when he came home, after being out all day, and she assumed, rather sadly, that his life was a secret that both eluded and excluded her, that it was too late for confidences of an intimate nature, and that all they could do was observe the formalities of their relationship, and occasionally keep each other company.

If she had hoped for more from this period of their lives, with their daughter absent, and lost to pursuits which left them far behind, she submitted with a fairly good grace to her new loneliness, even grateful for the solitude which she re-membered from years long past, when she was growing up and trying to make sense of certain anomalies: her father's empty eyes and perpetual cheerfulness, Mr Latif's hand on her mother's breast, that same mother's bad temper and dis-comfiture, her own deliberate lack of understanding. That innocence of hers, so willed, so excessive! And sustained throughout the years of adolescence, when Tessa, and Mary and Pamela, would look at her slyly, and then exchange their secrets and giggle, confident that she would always misunder-stand them. Harriet, in her empty drawing-room, her morn-ing duties discharged, the house silent in the absence of Miss Wetherby and her dog, absent, as was Freddie, on exercises of their own, thought back with distaste on her life, which now seemed to have been lost through inanition. Suddenly there was nothing for her to do. Freddie ate lunch out, so she made do with a sandwich. She could have taken a long walk, for in the early days of her marriage she had keenly regretted her lost liberty, but now that she was older she preferred to stay indoors and look out of the window. There was little to see in the quiet square; few people passed, and if she saw anyone she knew she retreated instinctively. Sometimes she thought of Tessa, sometimes of Jack. She realized now, at last, with sad conviction, that love of the one precluded the other, that the thrust of her own history allied her with Tessa. Jack had been merely the lure that she was bound, by the terms of her own nature, to resist. He remained unchanged in her mind, unaltered by time. In her imaginings he was always about to return, as if, at any moment, she might see him cross the square and come towards her. She was aware of the crassness of this fantasy, its out-of-date romanticism, its unfor-

givable timidity. She would shake herself free of it then, make
a cup of tea, settle down with a book. *Madame,* she read,
permettez-moi de vous dire que j'adore votre courage . . . When the
light faded, as it seemed to more quickly now, winter and
summer, she would get up and pull the curtains. Freddie,
crossing the square, would see her lifted arm and wave back.

When Immy came home in the holidays she was already a
stranger; taller, more boisterous, shrugging off their questions,
demanding a television in her bedroom, suffering only Miss
Wetherby's adoring attentions. They came to know her
moods, her restlessness, her boredom, were obliged to apolo-
gize for their lack of amenities, a house in the country, a ski
chalet to which she might invite her new friends. 'But darling,' Harriet said. 'You have a very nice house in town. Why
don't you invite your friends here? I'm sure they'd be delighted. There's plenty of room for them to stay. Why don't
you invite Henrietta? Or Arabella?' The names were invariably decorative, belonging, or seeming to belong, to Restora-
tion comedy. 'Actually, Henrietta has asked me to stay with
her people in Somerset.'

'Then Daddy and I must meet her first,' said Harriet firmly.
'And I must speak to her parents.'

This was successfully negotiated, although Harriet was not
much reassured by Henrietta's mother, who called at Wellington Square with her daughter before going on to Harrods.
Tall, glamorous, a compulsive talker, Lady Aldridge's eyes
wandered expertly round the room while expressing un-
reserved enthusiasm at the prospect of having Imogen to stay.
Harriet wished that Freddie were there, to put a damper on
Jane Aldridge's boundless and meaningless euphoria. Harriet
wondered if the woman drank, or if she were already drunk:
the eyes from time to time flashed desperation.

'I'm afraid we're rather selfish,' she said firmly. 'I'm sure
Immy would love to come to you, but her father sees so little

of her . . . Perhaps next year. But we should love to have Henrietta. There is so much for them to do in London—my husband can always get a box at Covent Garden.' At that moment she thought of Lizzie. Why, she said to herself, with some surprise, I had quite forgotten her.

Imogen was furious, of course, but then she so often was. 'It is dull for her,' said Harriet to Freddie, by way of excuse. Nothing came of the invitation to Henrietta; perhaps it had not been offered. One day, coming home with her shopping, Harriet saw a very young man getting out of a car and advancing towards her front door.

'Can I help you?' she called. 'I'm Harriet Lytton.'

He swept off the tweed cap he had been wearing; she had time to appreciate a handsome brown face, dark eyes set a little too close together.

'Hello,' he said. 'Julian Aldridge. Henrietta's brother. I believe you met my mother. Is Immy around?'

He was perhaps nineteen, at the most twenty.

'She's not in,' said Harriet thankfully. 'Can I ask her to telephone you?'

'Not to worry,' he replied. 'I just thought she might like to come for a drive.'

'Daddy and I would much rather you met your friends here,' she told a predictably angry Imogen. 'Anyway, he's much too old for you.'

'I'm nearly fifteen,' shouted Immy.

'You are fourteen and a half,' Harriet replied. 'If you are so anxious to see your friends why not invite them to dinner?'

'Oh, you don't understand,' was the predictable reply.

'If you are determined to grow up so fast at least you might behave in a more grown-up fashion. You were positively rude to Daddy last night.'

It was as much as she ever managed to say. She found herself indignant on Freddie's behalf, fearful of an explosion

of wrath from him. Imogen disregarded him, was careless of
his basic reserve. Every month she trailed a slight feral odour,
which he found distasteful. Harriet too found it distasteful,
but could think of no suitable comment. In any event she
knew that the girl's negligence was in part deliberate. She
seemed to want to antagonize. Harriet found herself occasionally intimidated, even frightened, as she might have been
by a bully at school, when she herself was a girl.

She was all the more reassured to come home one afternoon and find Lizzie standing on the front doorstep.

'Lizzie! What a lovely surprise! Does Immy know you're
here?'

'There's no one in,' said Lizzie cautiously.

'But, my dear child, you must come and have some tea,'
insisted Harriet. 'Immy will be home soon, and Freddie said
he'd come back early too. Why on earth didn't you let me
know you were in London?'

'I can't stay,' said Lizzie. 'I've got to get back to Windsor.'

'Freddie will drive you back. At least . . .'

'I've got my return ticket.'

'Well, he can take you to Waterloo. Tea first.'

She surveyed the girl, who had grown taller and filled out
a little, but retained the air of childishness that she had had on
the occasion of the visit to the ballet. The face was still pale,
impassive, the straw-coloured hair hung limply: only the
eyes, now fully recovered from the astigmatism that had afflicted them as a child, were beautiful, a dark blue, further
darkened by thoughtfulness and secrecy. She wore jeans and
a denim jacket, into the pockets of which her clenched fists
were thrust. As far as Harriet could see she was unlike Imogen
in every respect, and once more she appreciated her daughter's beauty, her vividness. Not only could she see no resemblance to Immy, she could detect no trace of either Tessa or

Jack in that closed white face. Jack's daughter, she thought, but the idea was without resonance.

'Well, Lizzie,' said Freddie. 'What are you going to do with yourself? Later on, I mean.'

'I'm going to be a writer,' said Lizzie, laying her slice of bread and butter down on her plate. She had always been a poor eater.

'Jolly good,' said Freddie tolerantly. 'And how will you go about it? You'll go to university, I suppose?'

'Oh, I shan't start until I'm old. Until I'm forty.'

Freddie laughed, and Lizzie blushed painfully.

'I think that's very wise,' said Harriet. 'You'll have to travel a lot, and get experience, and so on.'

'Not really,' said Lizzie, her blush fading. 'I shall get it all out of my head.'

'I don't want to go to university,' Immy interrupted. 'I'm not going to do any more exams. I'm going to go to work. I'm going to be a stockbroker. A millionaire.'

'And how will you go about that?' asked Freddie, Lizzie's career already forgotten.

'You'll help me, won't you, Daddy? Get me a job, I mean. In one of your firms.'

It was Freddie's turn to blush, this time with pleasure. It was to be as he had anticipated, his own worldliness at the service of his daughter. 'We'll see what we can do,' he said. 'Mind you, you'll have to work.'

'Oh, I'll work all right.'

'And I can have the upstairs flat ready for you as soon as you want it,' Harriet put in eagerly. 'How does that sound, darling?'

'Smashing,' said Immy, who at last exhibited something like enthusiasm.

'Would you like to show Lizzie the flat?'

'I'm afraid I have to go now,' said Lizzie, sliding down from her chair.

She was quite childish in some ways, Harriet saw. Still that residual envy of Immy, yet combined with a reluctance to complain that was truly admirable. Still that inability to dissemble. Lizzie could not lie, and was therefore graceless.

'You must come again,' said Harriet kindly. 'We are always pleased to see you. And Immy too. You must have so much to talk about.'

But Immy was already out of the door. Her exuberance was so blissful to them that they could not bear to curtail it.

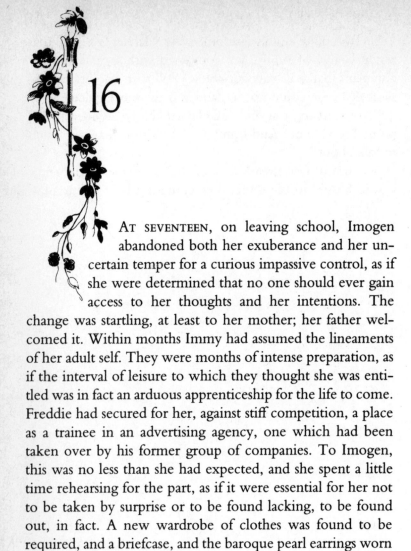

16

AT SEVENTEEN, on leaving school, Imogen abandoned both her exuberance and her uncertain temper for a curious impassive control, as if she were determined that no one should ever gain access to her thoughts and her intentions. The change was startling, at least to her mother; her father welcomed it. Within months Immy had assumed the lineaments of her adult self. They were months of intense preparation, as if the interval of leisure to which they thought she was entitled was in fact an arduous apprenticeship for the life to come. Freddie had secured for her, against stiff competition, a place as a trainee in an advertising agency, one which had been taken over by his former group of companies. To Imogen, this was no less than she had expected, and she spent a little time rehearsing for the part, as if it were essential for her not to be taken by surprise or to be found lacking, to be found out, in fact. A new wardrobe of clothes was found to be required, and a briefcase, and the baroque pearl earrings worn by young businesswomen in the television commercials she watched: she liked the gesture of removing one to answer the telephone. Harriet, aware that her daughter's tastes were both expensive and inclined to be meretricious, found this touching, so touching that for the first time that she could remember she longed for Immy to grow older, to gain experience, and to become wise in the ways of this harsh world. At the

same time she longed for her to be safe, to be protected, and
to stay at home with them for ever, instead of for the few
weeks of summer and autumn before she started taking the
bus every day, with her briefcase, and an expression composed in equal parts of gravity and scorn, the expression of a
survivor and a winner in those battles she read about in the
fat paperback novels she favoured, and which constituted
worldly wisdom in her understanding, an understanding both
advanced and curiously narrow for a girl of her age. But
behind her beautiful nun-like face, composed and severe,
who knew what intelligence was forming?

They saw little of her. She had moved into the upstairs flat,
occasionally ate dinner with them, but more frequently preferred to join her friends in various wine bars and restaurants.
It was clear that her home meant little to her apart from the
fact that it was agreeable and extremely well situated. She
liked the flat because it gave her the freedom to practise a way
of life that seemed glamorous to her: black coffee and grape-
fruit for breakfast, although she had no need to lose weight,
and a glass of white wine and the television news in the
evening before going out to drink more with her friends.
Julian Aldridge was a frequent caller, was indeed already accepted as her accredited suitor by her mother, although there
were others of whom her mother knew nothing. Harriet had
insisted that Julian come to dinner, although she had already
heard him rushing upstairs to the flat on more than one
occasion. The dinner was thought of as a staggering imposi-
tion by both Julian and Imogen, who raced upstairs as soon
as it was over. Loud music covered what was happening up
there: Harriet preferred not to know, shrinking from the idea
of kisses, embraces, although in her mind they remained
perfectly harmless.

'You could ask any of your friends, you know, darling.
Until you know how to cook.'

'Actually, we prefer to eat out.'

'But it is nice for them to see you at home. And you have the flat if you want to be quiet.'

Imogen said nothing, which encouraged Harriet to think that her suggestion was being considered. But nothing came of it, and they got used to hearing her feet on the stairs and the door being banged shut behind her.

'We see so little of her,' Harriet remarked sadly to Freddie.

'We shall see even less of her when she starts work. Where did you go today? Sloane Street? Bond Street? You're not buying her a trousseau you know. Most of them wear jeans, these days.'

'Can you see Immy in jeans?' asked Harriet scornfully.

For at that time, at seventeen, at eighteen, Imogen was beautiful, in a way that spoke of devoted nurture, spotless, unmarked, glossier and more finished than those around her. Her black hair was tied back with a velvet bow, and the face thus exposed was flawless in its symmetry, still pale, still very slightly flushed only in moments of exceptional exertion. She wore her expensive clothes immaculately, conscious of luxury, extravagance, and appreciative of them. It was easy to admire her, less easy to understand her. To her parents she was as phenomenal in this new withdrawn mood as she had been as an obstreperous child; they saw her as touchingly grown up, although she possessed a steeliness which was foreign to both of them. Harriet wished for more of her company, but had to be content with shopping expeditions; fine clothes were a solace to them both, and it did indeed seem as if Imogen were being bought a trousseau. One day, seated in Harrods restaurant, Harriet said, out of the same guilty compulsion from which she had always suffered, 'Why don't you get in touch with Lizzie?'

'I told you. She's working.'

'Working? I thought she was going to Oxford.'

'She's working in a bookshop until she goes up. I suppose she hasn't got any money,' said Immy indifferently.

'I think it would be nice if you telephoned her, darling. I
feel she hasn't got many friends. It must be lonely for her
sometimes. Where is she living now?'

Immy shrugged. 'Judd Street, I imagine. She always said
she was anxious to be on her own. At school, I mean. Always
sneaking off with a book. Things like that. Most of my friends
thought she was pretty crazy.'

'Get in touch, darling. Remember she has had quite a hard
life in many ways.'

Immy assumed an expression of pain, and laid the back of
her hand to her forehead—a silly gesture, Harriet thought, in
an unguarded moment. To make up for what she perceived
as a disloyal thought she added, 'And now, if you really want
that pink sweater I'll buy it for you. It can be a present, until
you start earning your own money. Pink was always your
colour.'

To Imogen her mother, in this indulgent mood, was exas-
perating. She felt sorry for her, sorry for her restricted life
with a man as unattractive as her father, but she also felt
contempt for the choice that had been made, the fate to
which she had consented. She herself had nothing but pity for
those who settled for marriage, seeing it as a kind of willed
imbecility, more indecent, in its sacrificial aspects, than any
amount of concubinage. The thought of her parents' bedroom produced a shudder of disgust, as if even the act of
ageing bodies undressing together was indecent. Her father
she avoided whenever possible: she perceived him as gross,
was shudderingly aware of the heat of his heavy body, the
redness of his face after half a bottle of wine. Mentally she
divorced herself from her father, as she had done, instinctively, when she was a growing child. This time the decision
was final, on grounds of aesthetic inadequacy. It did not
matter to her that she hurt him, for she regarded him as
someone who deserved the hurt. There was anger in this
reaction; she dared him to come near her, so that she could

repulse him. She was also a little afraid of him, thinking him so alien that if he were to approach her she might feel a horror that contained its own helplessness. In order to avoid being kissed by him she had taken to wiggling her fingers vaguely in his direction. Freddie sat monumentally at the dinner table, inwardly slumped in disappointment. Harriet claimed a kiss, apologetically.

'Don't mind her,' she said to Freddie. 'It's her age. Young girls tend to shy away from men; they become terribly aware of their own bodies. It's a kind of modesty, really.'

Freddie said nothing, aware of Julian Aldridge's entrance into the house, and Immy's languid welcome.

'Julian,' he called out. 'I want you out of the house by eleven.'

'Oh, right,' said a startled Julian, miming incomprehension for Immy's benefit. He had as little intention of marrying anyone as Immy had; a hearty distaste for convention, and an enquiring disposition, had united them since they had first met some five years earlier.

'Freddie!' Harriet had reproached him. 'Don't spoil things for her. You will make her self-conscious.'

'I would have her a little more self-conscious than she actually is,' he grumbled. 'I don't like the way she's behaving. Always running upstairs with that boy. Merchant banker, my foot. Aren't you worried?'

'What you don't realize is that Immy is very fastidious. She is too fastidious to get herself into trouble; perish the thought, although that is what you are really thinking, I know. They only play records up there, or watch television. Perhaps smoke a cigarette. I think it shows great trust that she can entertain him under our roof. It's not as if there were any-thing nefarious going on. Immy would never dream . . .'

'Just remember that it's my roof,' said Freddie. 'I'm entitled to make the rules.'

He thought Harriet foolish, as did her daughter. To Immy Harriet had the foolishness that only came with sexual innocence, an idea which she found deplorable. She was fond of her mother, in a vague impatient fashion, tolerated her kisses and her indulgences, both equally embarrassing, and looked forward to a time when she would no longer have to bother about her, about either of her parents. This time seemed very slow in coming. In the meantime she exerted herself to be as neutral as possible, judging it unwise and unnecessary for them to see the extent of her own emancipation. It was as much as she could do not to fly into a rage in their presence, so clumsy and inept did she judge them to be. Her flight to the upstairs flat with Julian was as much to escape their gracelessness, the physical evidence of their bodies, as a desire to be with Julian, an attractive boy whom she had earmarked for the reserve, being already active on various other fronts, and entertaining other speculations. Julian was devoted. Devotion made her irritable, slowed her down, forced her to respond in words, other than instinctively, as she preferred. Julian was beginning to bore her, but he was her own kind. He too avoided his parents. His mother drank; his father preferred to be out or away for most of the time. From such indignities he too escaped, seeing in Imogen something clean, unspotted, intact, with whom he could enjoy interludes of communication which he must learn not to spoil with too many words. Imogen, he had noticed, turned fretful when he tried to talk to her, explain his work, his reactions to the day's news, his ideas for their future (which, whether he knew it or not, included marriage). She would shrug her shoulders, pour another glass of wine, and drink it thoughtfully, ignoring him. He loved her, but was a little frightened of her. But this was exactly what she intended.

At work, severe, with her briefcase, she learned quickly. Removing her earring she made several telephone calls, including one to Lizzie. 'If anyone asks I'm with you this weekend.'

'Are you?' asked Lizzie, startled.

'No, of course not.'

'Then I don't want anything to do with it.'

Immy replaced the telephone without comment. Such a prig, she thought. Do her good to tell a lie now and again. Just like everyone else.

'So nice that you're seeing something of Lizzie,' said Harriet. 'I always hoped that the two of you would become close friends. Not that we want to interfere in any way, darling, you know that.'

Her own state of mind was not always clear to her these days. She mourned the absence of her daughter from the house yet rejoiced to see her a citizen of the world, as she proudly thought of it, and waved to her each morning as she went off to work, although Immy rarely turned and waved back. She was aware of having too little to do, and at the same time felt increasingly tired. She saw few people, her life too occupied with thoughts of her daughter to afford much room for anyone else. She was vaguely aware of Miss Wetherby, lonely in her basement since Immy no longer needed her or sought her undemanding company; at least Miss Wetherby had the dog, she comforted herself. Freddie, she thought, seemed better, although she had never taken his indisposition seriously. She felt, above all, middle-aged, and was surprised that middle age was so problematic. She had thought of it as a time when the discomforts of youth resolved themselves, a blessed interval before the more acute discomforts of old age declared themselves. Wandering about the house in the empty afternoons, she was surprised by an amorphous longing, and a desire which she quickly banished from her mind, thinking it indecent that she should be subject to such feelings when she had a young daughter in the house. Desire, she was aware, was appropriate only to girls of Immy's age, although, through weakness or selfishness, she was aware of a hope that Immy would remain untroubled until the ideal marriage partner came along. And even then . . . She did not care to contemplate the matter of her daughter's sexuality, aware that the whole subject was taboo, as it had always been in her own case. And yet I suffered, she thought, as she must not. At least Immy seemed happy with Julian, although she changed the subject whenever Harriet tried to elicit what she felt for him. 'I thought you might want to talk about him,' she had once ventured, only to be told, 'There's nothing to talk about. We're friends, that's all. Don't *fuss*, Mother.' For she was Mother now, demoted, and, she felt, warned to keep her distance.

Lizzie, at her bookshop, inserting paperbacks into bags and handling change, determined to keep out of the way of all the Lyttons. She liked Harriet, a misguided woman, as she saw it, although kindly disposed, hardly noticed Freddie, to whom, however, she remained indebted for the afternoon at Covent Garden, high spot in a dreary childhood, and regarded Immy as dangerous. The danger stemmed from Immy's lawlessness, which posed a general threat to her view of the world which she strove to make benign. She was not aware of loneliness so much as of endeavour: her future career as a writer, of which there was as yet no sign, would, she thought, in time validate her entire existence. Until then she would adopt—had already adopted—a regime which would steel her against rejection and disappointment. She ate a sandwich at lunchtime with her friend Cameron, an out-of-work actor also putting in time in the bookshop. Cameron was small, neat, and dynamic, and had a burning faith in Art, which embarrassed her. Apart from that he was self-centred, companionable, and appeared to find her unexceptional. She was grateful for this, listened to him gravely, nodded from time to time, and reck-

oned that once she went up to Oxford she need never see him
again. This seemed to her the best way, the safest way; friends
were a burden for which she had neither the time nor the
inclination. Her own silence, her own solitude seemed to her
entirely preferable. It was with relief that she entered the
empty flat in the evenings; after eating her yoghourt and her
apple she was free to read or to write in her diary. She had
very little to confide to it, since her nature was neither expansive nor introspective. This posed a problem for some time,
for without self-consciousness she was aware that her material
was bound to be thin. Neither religion nor art kept her
company; she read with horror that Flaubert, in the throes of
Mme Bovary's death scene, vomited twice. She vowed to
herself never to allow such encroachment. She had a vision of
a writer's life as clean, economical, controlled. The lack of a
subject bothered her until she remembered that she did not
need to think about this matter until she was forty. In the
meantime she composed a list of aphorisms and quotations,
inscribing them in her diary in her beautiful italic hand.
These, she felt, would guide her on her way. Aphorisms were
hard, concise, unemotional. She liked their tonic effect, since
they had to do with a stoical view of the world. She trained
herself to be cynical although she still missed her mother, of
whom she thought with pain and terror.

Her life was frequently a burden to her, and only a residual
curiosity kept anguish at bay. By concentrating on the me-
chanics of the day, plotting her way from one hour to the
next, eating, in so far as was possible, the same food at the
same time, she managed to outwit an anxiety which had been
in place for as long as she could remember. She supposed that
this was due to her rootlessness; she had no conviction that a
place was reserved for her in this world, lacked benevolent
elders from whom she might have inherited some kind of
grace or endowment, some indulgence, some love. She had

been wary since earliest childhood, eternally on the lookout for danger, or for threats to an existence which she strove to make as circumscribed as possible, as if only by being inconspicuous would she be allowed to continue. Her one hope was to make her father proud of her, yet she knew that this was a romantic notion to which she must never confess. Her father, quite simply, was absent, eternally abroad; if he thought of her at all, as she supposed that he must do from time to time, it would be with a passing fond amusement. From him she had learned to keep her own counsel, for to embarrass him, or to be faulty in his eyes, would be unthinkable. She feared his disfavour, feared even to risk his disfavour, since she had seen the expression of distaste setting like a mask on his face when Elspeth abandoned her hard-won equanimity and began to plead with him, to accuse, to become tearful, to let her voice wander and become plangent . . . The horrors of those scenes had been a warning, as had Elspeth's fugues. Waiting too long for Jack to fly in, sitting up too late, and then almost deliberately drinking too much whisky . . . And when he did finally arrive, tired, it was to be met with a list of grievances: he was selfish, thoughtless, an opportunist; he made use of her; she had given up so much for him; and of course he should marry her, should have married her long ago. Lizzie, sitting up in bed, put her hands over her ears at this point. In her horror of scenes and demands she resembled her father.

His approval was measured, not lavish. 'Lizzie has strength of purpose,' he had once said, and this remark had been an encouragement to her on many a lightless day. With her strength of purpose—acknowledged, and therefore an undoubted attribute—she might eventually find a place of her own, which she envisaged in a far distant country, where she might go about her business in peace, with no ugly eager voices to disturb her.

As a child she had been cautiously grateful to Elspeth for providing meals—which she remembered from her other life as being unreliable, irregular—and clothes, although these were haphazardly chosen. Money did not appear to be in short supply: there was a kind of housekeeper, a Miss Friel, who cooked lunch and prepared dinner, but who did not appear to like children. Any question Lizzie had asked her, while Elspeth was locked away in her study, typing, was met with the words, 'Haven't you got any homework?' The house was largely silent in the daytime, apart from the noise of the typewriter, and there were strict orders that Elspeth was not to be disturbed. It was out of the question to bring home a friend, and anyway there were no friends, no one to whom Lizzie could entrust her life. In the evenings they watched television, and then there was bed, which she learned to enjoy. In bed she could be herself, without the need to court anyone's favour. With Elspeth she was on neutral, fairly silent terms, aware that although she was cared for, in a distant fashion, she was only of value as a hostage to whom her father was bound to return. The holidays were an ordeal. The house in Scotland was full of relations, with whom she never got on on any terms at all; guests came and went and she was supposed to look after herself, which she quickly learned to do. She did the same at Ramatuelle, where she spent the long summer break, and this was better, although there was no one for her to talk to except Donatien, the gardener, and his wife, Marie. In this way she improved her French, which was good. Her grandparents remained strangers, uneasy with her; she was aware of being an unwelcome reminder of something they would rather not think about. There was relief all round when they took her to the airport, and for half an hour she felt some kind of family solidarity. But really the only one she acknowledged as any sort of intimate was her father, and he was never there.

On the rare occasions when he was at home between assignments there was a sense of anticipatory excitement. When the car drew up outside the house she would be shut firmly in the drawing-room while Elspeth, her neat blonde face flushed, would greet him in the hall. Voices would reach her, but these too were unreliable, since her father seemed humorous or impatient and Elspeth too questing, too yearning. Dinner that evening would be briefly jovial, and then the two of them would disappear. She was aware that her father did not love Elspeth, and vowed at this time never to feel for a man what he was reluctant to feel for her, aware too that Elspeth counted on an eventual marriage, although this now seemed out of the question. Then he would inexplicably go out again, or perhaps simply go to the television studio, and Elspeth, giving way to the frustration · which plagued her, would start drinking. She deliberately drank more than was good for her, which gave rise to a ragged uneven voice; Lizzie escaped to bed. Later, when her father returned, there was a scene of sorts, which she was careful never to witness. The next day she would leave the house early: there were never enquiries as to where she was going. She was aware that she was sensible, and that both Jack and Elspeth knew this. They had no fear for her, and so she had little for herself. Her loneliness she put down to boredom and idleness. Only her books gave her comfort.

She would catch the train to London, and had done so from an early age. Windsor had no charms for her; London was her real home. She would spend the day walking, and thus got to know the city well. When she was tired she would go to the National Gallery, and sit on one of the benches. She found a coffee bar in St Martin's Lane where she could have a sandwich. Nobody asked her her business; London was beautifully anonymous. Occasionally there would be a visit to Judd Street, which she marked out as her future home. When she was old enough she would live there. In the meantime there was school and the proximity of Imogen Lytton, whom she took pains to avoid. This was not difficult; Imogen had a horde of scornful friends, and Lizzie, in her turn, was avoided. She avoided, too, the kindly overtures of Imogen's mother, whom she perceived as well-meaning. She had early got into the habit of relying on no one; adults were broken reeds, too conscious of their own concerns to assist her in the immense unburdening which she felt, sometimes, as necessary. Somehow this would have to take place. Yet since no one was apparently interested she hit on the idea of becoming a writer, of finally having a voice which no one could ignore. Unfortunately she did not quite see how this was to come about, since concealment was bred into her. She looked forward to the day when she would be able to tell the truth at all times, for truthfulness was her uncomfortable companion. Her solitary days in London were her stratagem for not having to reassure her father that everything was all right, when she was aware of so many anomalies: the drinking, the raised wandering voice, her father's answering burst of impatience, her own loneliness. She knew that he knew all this, but shrank from the task of burdening him further. Therefore she fell into the habit of taciturnity, which she instinctively knew he would appreciate.

At last her long apprenticeship was coming to an end. When she left school she announced that she was going to live at Judd Street. This brought few objections: she would be leaving home in any case to go to Oxford. The job in the bookshop brought her a little money, which she spent on two new pairs of jeans, a transistor radio, and food, which was meagre because it did not sufficiently interest her. Sometimes in the evening Cameron would call and take her out for a long walk, occasions on which he would talk and she would remain largely silent. He was kind, in an abstracted way, about invitations to the theatre, but she preferred not to accept, since Art, which threatened and appalled, might disturb her careful solitude. The telephone call from Imogen had upset her, since it adumbrated treachery, a fabrication not of her own making. She felt free, as she supposed her father must feel. She preferred to sleep on the couch in his study, with his car rug as a cover. Sometimes, on the couch, with friendly sleep on the horizon, and the radio for company, she was cautiously happy. Her happiness came from her conviction that she would now survive. The past, which she preferred to leave unexamined, receded. At times like these she thought that with the aid of her own specially fashioned resources she might make something of her life. Its beginnings had been problematic, disappointing. But now that she had got rid of everyone she might go on to better things.

17

A LIFETIME of inactivity had kept Hughie Blakemore in perfect physical condition. Slim, straight, if a little dry and jerky in his movements, he sat on the edge of a hard chair, his eyes, empty of guile, shining with the pleasure of providing tea for his daughter and her husband, and, perhaps, with the greater pleasure of registering the fact that his contemporary and one-time companion, Freddie Lytton, was an old man, heavy, inert, and possibly a bad colour. Harriet, glancing from her husband to her father, understood very well what the latter was thinking, and did not begrudge him his moment of pride. It was a feeling shared by Merle, proud, certainly, but also exhausted by this acme of healthy manhood, with his eternal unnatural youth, whom she had saved from possible dereliction and who had confined her life within crushing limits for as long as she could remember. The need to look after this fossilized boy, so agreeably good-natured, so loving, so submissive, had deprived her of the life she might have had as a mother, a grandmother. In both of these roles she had been largely absent, wishing for her daughter only viability, durability, financial security, and seeing in her granddaughter the fulfilment of these wishes, and the great changes they wrought on the human personality.

Harriet, she saw, had only reached the halfway mark of

ter, persisting, amazed her. Could she not see that she was bored? Or had she a secret? Merle, an adept at keeping secrets, thought not. Whatever had once, momentarily, brought a look of beauty to her daughter's face had vanished, to be replaced by this premature calm. It was as if she had sacrificed whatever it was that had brought her to life. She is a fool, poor girl, thought her mother. I did the same, but I loved my husband, whereas Harriet never loved Freddie. At least Hughie repaid my efforts. We have not done too badly. He is a dear old boy now, whereas once he was a dear young one. Simply, he missed out on maturity, so that I never had the satisfaction of relying on a man's strength, a man's judgement. But he has done me proud, or I have done him proud: it no longer matters. He is more than presentable, so much so that women of my age envy me. And he sleeps like a child in our grand bed, and will never again be wakened by me. I could have done better, she thought, lighting a fresh cigarette, but I loved him. Still do, for that matter.

But Freddie! Who could be proud of Freddie, once so impressive in his incarnation as a captain of industry, but now so defeated, retired and unsought-after? There was no need, surely, to slump so in the wide armchair, head forward, legs apart. Did he not know how unwieldy he looked? Did Harriet not see this? And if she saw it why did she permit it? A man needed to be knocked into shape: almost any woman could manage this. But not Harriet, apparently; all Harriet cared about now was her daughter. Yet Merle, who had so little maternal feeling, could see that Imogen had already outgrown her mother, that she possessed all the calculation that her mother so signally lacked, as if the evolutionary process, so slow in Harriet, had suddenly speeded up, providing Imogen with a full quota of adult thoughts and feelings, had turned her into a keeper of secrets. Merle felt a different sadness when she contemplated Imogen, whom in fact they

such a development; she was unfledged, expensive to look ,
confident in matters of manners and appearance, but st
timid, and, her mother saw, physically unawakened. For th
fact Merle blamed herself; her husband, poor darling, was no
worth blaming. His curious innocence exonerated him from
all adult feelings. They had been ardent lovers once; in their
little flat in Soho they had sometimes stayed in bed all day.
The image of their rumpled bed, and the curtainless window,
and the smell of coffee from the café downstairs came back to
her sometimes, but not in the way of real memory, rather as
something she might have seen in a film, long ago. More
vivid were the images of Hughie, back from the war, his eyes
empty, or restored to contentment, at home in the small back
room of the shop, supervising the making of the tea. Memory, real memory, that brought a grimace to the lips, was Mr
Latif, and his urgent and expert hands. She did not blame
herself for the decision to escape at all costs, which somehow
also involved the decision to sacrifice Harriet, although this
last was a painful matter. She had found that her grief for her
daughter, who had somehow been denied her real life, could
be mitigated by anger, so that now she managed to feel
genuine indignation when she saw in Harriet's eyes something of the same benevolence that emanated, like continuous
good weather in a boring climate, from her husband.

A woman had no business to look so empty of calculation,
when she should be busy thinking, planning ahead. A woman
of Harriet's age should not be spending time with her husband and her elderly parents when she could be in bed with
a lover. A woman, if she had any pride, should have preserved
that husband in better condition, or discarded him altogether.
Merle had never much liked Freddie Lytton, although she
had always seen him for what he was: a solid prospect, a sad
man humiliated by his first wife, and in many ways an ideal
husband for her docile daughter. The docility of that daugh-

rarely saw. The girl was not interested in them, could not, moreover, be trusted to safeguard Hughie's feelings when he laid before her the offering of his simple treats. At least Harriet had kept her sweet nature. Merle was not sure that Imogen had ever had a particularly good character. When she was a child her naughtiness had promised a kind of worldly success, allied as it was then to prettiness of a grand order. When that prettiness became beauty, and the girl had returned home from that school of hers, with different friends and ambitions, Merle could see what her character now contained was courage, boldness, ardour, and also something inordinate, to which she had no access, all disguised by a perfect mask, so pure that it was almost without expression.

Merle, who mourned the child she had been, did not know quite what to make of Imogen, was not quite sure that she liked the girl, although she approved of her, and in her heart loved her, but loved her as though she were already lost to them. If there were a choice between cultivating Imogen's confidences—for she did not doubt that much was concealed from Harriet—and preserving Hughie, who never left her side, she knew that Hughie must prevail. In his monstrous innocence he had always prevailed. Therefore Imogen, to a certain extent, must be renounced. All she could do now was to send her something pretty to wear on her birthday, something expensive, almost too expensive for their budget. But Imogen had an unerring eye for quality, would lay aside something not quite up to her standard with a moue of distaste. This her grandmother had once caught sight of out of the corner of her eye, and had vowed never to be the cause of it again. She still burned when she thought of it, she whose taste had never been in any doubt. But she supposed the girl was right, in her way. Simply, she had preferred her as a baby, had kept all her baby photographs, for fortunately Hughie was good with a camera. Sometimes, when Hughie was having a rest, she went through these, almost secretly, to see if there was any trace in that baby face of her own child, Harriet, whom she had not loved at that age. Harriet's birthmark was no longer shocking, was almost concealed, was less important than it had been. And Imogen had been flawless. There was in fact no trace of Harriet there. And later on, apart from a brief resemblance to herself at the same age, there was no trace of any of them. She longed to ask Harriet whether Imogen was happy, but somehow happiness was too banal a concept to attach to Imogen in her present state. She was cool, sensible, ambitious: a new order of womanhood. Happiness was for the credible, the soft-hearted, the hopeful. Harriet had been all of those things. In truth she had changed very little. She was a good girl, a good daughter, and no doubt a good wife. But she should have had a chance to transcend her situation. Had she really so little spirit?

Harriet in fact no longer thought of her life as promising, and indeed this reunion, with her husband and her parents, all the same age, seemed to prove that nothing had changed. Part of her felt peaceful at the thought of this. Yet another part deviated wildly. One day, very soon, she thought, when Imogen was a few months older, twenty-one, say, and no longer in danger from either of her parents, she would contact Jack Peckham again. That she had not already done this surprised her, and yet she knew that she could wait. Indeed she avoided any mention of his name, any invitation to his daughter: she no longer wished her contact with him, if it ever came again, to be mediated. There would be no Lizzie, no Elspeth Mackinnon; there would simply be a calm claiming of her due. That she was so calm in anticipation of this she attributed to what she had seen in his face on the evening of her visit to Judd Street. Rightly or wrongly (and if wrongly what did it matter?) she thought that he would be there when the time came. What would happen then she did not know, although she had imagined it many times. In that moment, perhaps in that one episode, there would be no husband, no children, hers or his, no former wife, no present mistress: she willed it so and knew that she could make it happen. That her thinking was magical, fantastic, did not concern her; she knew that in this mood she could bring about the impossible. And the grand adventure of a lifetime, for which she had waited so long, would faultlessly engage her and be completed, perhaps in that one episode, after which she could grow old resignedly, having done her duty to husband, parents, daughter. For she knew that with Jack Peckham she would loosen the ties which had so burdened her (and still did, still did), and with this sudden daring would rediscover her marvellous solitude, so that after being with him she would find that the others had retreated a little from her, had merely become figures in her landscape, instead of energumens whose needs were her duties.

If Jack and she were to come together (her mind fought shy of thinking in specific terms, of using specific words) she would no longer be so strenuously connected to her world; her dependents would, equally magically, have ceased to intrude upon her, and would have, at last, to take care of themselves. She would no longer feel anything for them, would smile at them, feel affection for them, hand over discreet sums of money, as she always had done, but would no longer be at their disposition. Service she could offer, but she would no longer be subservient. She would no longer be tormented by her love for her daughter, whom she would, simply, love. Jack would bring all this about, had begun the process of detaching her from her husband, might now finish it. She had no thought of flight or of desertion. She would continue to be Mrs Lytton, but she would have been mysteriously enabled to continue her life with a freedom so far denied her. In this way she thought the waiting easy. The conviction grew in her that Jack knew all about this, and that he was waiting too. What had been started, so long ago, would then be completed, and completed in more than one sense, for she might renounce him on the same occasion. For he had given no sign . . . And in any event she must return to Imogen. But it would all be understood between them; there would be no injury, only a sense of what was right, what was fitting. No one would suffer. It would merely be a question of activating something that had been too long dormant, and of putting it to rest.

This thought kept her benign; this, and the memory of Jack Peckham's face, which for a short time had been as naked as her own. He might not remember, but she would remind him. What she had seen of his expression stayed with her; no matter that time had passed. It had passed for both of them; they were both older now, both mature, and, more important, there was no ghost of Tessa hovering between them. It had been decent to wait; she owed them that. She knew nothing of his life, which she somehow suspected had been indifferently domesticated; he roamed about the world, and seemed happy to do so. Sometimes she caught a glimpse of him, reporting from Washington, when Freddie was watching the early news; he looked older, she thought, standing in front of the White House, sometimes in the snow; he looked cold. When Immy was safely gathered in by somebody else (Julian?) she would contact the BBC and say she had to get in touch with him; could they tell her when he was next due in London? This tactic was also hazy in her mind but partook of the same ease as the rest of the adventure. There was nothing criminal about making a simple enquiry. He was still, as far as she knew, unmarried, for she thought that there would have been an announcement if any marriage had taken place. He might even have got in touch himself, or Lizzie would have done so. She avoided the thought of Lizzie, for

the girl must be spared knowledge of this. Perhaps she should
see her, find out how she was. Yet she could not quite admit
Lizzie to her thoughts of Jack, and Jack was now more important. And in any event the dream, if that was what it was, had
become so pervasive that Lizzie was almost irrelevant. Almost, but not quite. In another mood, her ordinary daytime
mood, the one which usually claimed her attention, she wondered how Lizzie was getting on. Fortunately Imogen saw a
lot of her, or said she did. Details were hard to come by.
Imogen was elusive, went straight up to the flat in the evening, usually went straight out again. What she did, whom
she saw, they no longer knew. They took a pride in not
questioning her.

Freddie, supine in his chair, listening without comment to
the pleasing inconsequential rumble of Hughie Blakemore's
voice, was thinking that if he were on his own (and the
thought occurred to him more frequently these days) he
might prefer to live in a decent hotel, with room service,
somewhere warm. He was over seventy: time, he thought, to
retire in earnest. Sometimes the thought of his wife, his
daughter, his house, weighed on him like a burden. He did
not feel well. He felt dizzy in the mornings, and despite the
life he led these days his blood pressure remained high. He
had been glad of Harriet's suggestion that they travel to
Brighton by train, for he did not think he was up to driving
the car, had not done so for some time. He was even glad of
Hughie Blakemore's company, his agreeable voice, his undemanding presence. This was new, he thought, a measure of
his vulnerability, or infirmity. Merle he had never much
liked, suspecting that she was a calculating woman who had
masterminded his present entanglement. And yet he had
loved Harriet, still did, but had always known that she regarded him as someone who had graciously offered to take
care of her, an offer she had been unable to refuse, and for

which she was grateful. But half measures were no longer enough for him: he was conscious of a lack in his life, and blamed his present feebleness on various deprivations of a sensory order. These extended to sunlight, fruitfulness, warmth, the abundant warmth of a different climate. He was not as soulless as most people thought him; he had read his Colette, had dreamed of meals with friends on Provençal terraces, beneath the shadow of a fig tree. Instead he was making do with the pale brittle sunlight of an April day in England, and although the Blakemores kept their windows shut he was aware of an acid wind, had felt it when they left the train, dreaded going out into it again.

He was nearly comfortable in this unpretentious flat, which had cost him something to maintain: that was a surprise. He felt his horizons shrinking: all on one floor, close carpeted, highly convenient—it was the next best thing to a hotel suite. Yet it was the suite he really wanted, with a vista, and nobody else to bother him.

That was the problem, of course: Harriet would hardly understand if he took a holiday on his own, although she was so preoccupied with her daughter that he felt he hardly mattered. This was unfair, he knew: she was, and had always tried to be, an excellent wife. It was not her fault that she lacked certain qualities. With a father like that she had grown up in ignorance of what men were really like. And yet he was fond in a way of old Blakemore, who persisted in remaining so young, was able to reminisce with him about service days, was reminded that he had once been young himself. That was now Blakemore's charm: he bore witness to a state of youth which had long departed. He felt that if only the women would go away somewhere he might very well sit for another hour with Hughie, remembering, appreciating the other man's harmlessness. In any event he felt unable to move, having eaten two slices of a fruit cake made by Blakemore

himself, who now attended cookery classes. Strange: he had
always been so dashing. Harriet had shaken her head and
looked disapproving, but he had felt a sudden burst of anger
at being treated like a child, and had taken a second slice from
the proffered plate. Now he felt heavy, vaguely uncomfortable, as he so often did these days. Food was not the problem:
Harriet fed him carefully, and he could usually digest anything. But he could not drink as he used to. Sometimes, in the
evenings, he felt a fluttering in his left eyelid which he did not
seem able to control, and in the morning, after the atrocious
moment of coming back to consciousness, and the dizziness
that afflicted him when he sat up in bed, there was always a
bad half hour in the bathroom, where he bathed with increasing caution. Freshened with cologne his face looked momentarily better; he was always reassured by the sight of himself
fully dressed. But his days were empty; pleasant, but empty.
The walk to the club, the morning papers, coffee, and then
that lonely hour before lunch, which he would fill by wandering round St James's, looking at the odd picture. He felt
humble in art galleries, although the young girls at the desk
were hospitable and kind (and indifferent), and sometimes he
was alone there for the space of twenty minutes or even
longer. Dutch pictures were best, when he could find them.
For a month he had studied a large flower-piece of improba-
ble profusion, on a dark ground. He thought the picture
sinister, for in the foreground there was a split fruit, a peach
or a nectarine, and on the lip of the fruit a fly, breeding
corruption. He realized that the picture was meant to remind
him of his own decay, and felt chastened. This was not a
feeling he welcomed, although he acknowledged that it was
appropriate. But he found the picture's impassivity reassuring,
in a bleak way. There is no escape, the artist had meant to say:
our substance is being consumed.

After this he tried to find something a bit lighter. An

Impressionist would have gone down well, but there were few to be had in commercial galleries; he wandered to Wildenstein's and looked thoughtfully at Marquet and Manguin. Then, glancing at his watch, he saw with relief that it was half-past twelve, and turned back to St James's Street, and lunch. There was usually someone to talk to around that time, and the afternoons were not too bad. It was only when he set out for home that a sadness began to descend. He could never quite understand this. It had something to do with the fact that attention was always turned away from him, so that he stood hapless, in his own drawing-room, while Harriet, and even Miss Wetherby, busied themselves upstairs in Imogen's flat. When Imogen was there, which was rarely, he felt positively ignored. The women were not technically at fault, were simply active in the ways in which they were programmed to be active, and yet he was uneasy with them. Hence the desire for, the dream of, the hotel terrace in the sun, and a short post-prandial stroll to buy *The Times*. One read the English papers so much more thoroughly when one was abroad, which was where he now ardently wished to be.

Nobody liked the spectacle of Freddie heaving himself from his chair. Freddie felt it himself, but he was so used to being considered graceless by his daughter that he was almost philosophical, more philosophical than the Blakemores, who looked on in frank dismay. Old Hughie had the decency to offer him a hand, which he refused. What worried him more than his loss of vigour was the fluttering in his left eyelid which had started up again, although he had had nothing to drink, nothing having been on offer. He saw Merle Blakemore studying him: a tiresome woman, whom nothing escaped. He was, once more, glad that they were going home by train. The effort of securing a taxi bothered him slightly, until dear old Hughie darted down the stairs: from the balcony they saw him standing in the road, gesticulating, and then his face turned up towards them, and his hand beckoned them down. Harriet kissed her mother; he could only manage a grunted, 'Goodbye, my dear.' With Hughie he shook hands. Hughie, like himself, must surely be glad of a little masculine company from time to time? How did he manage? And yet he looked fit, happy. Perhaps slightly thin in the face. Ah, they were all growing old. That Dutch master had got it right.

They travelled home in silence, both tired. Harriet tired easily these days, although her dreamy expression indicated not fatigue so much as absence. Sometimes he hardly knew her, although they slept in the same bed every night, while she sometimes seemed to return to him from a great distance. He yawned; for once he would be glad to get home.

'Is Immy in this evening?' he asked.

'Darling, you know I never ask her.'

He sighed. He had never become reconciled to what he considered his daughter's fecklessness. He loved her, but did not entirely trust her, whereas her mother's trust was absolute. He wondered how Harriet could be so blind to the expression of concealment which Imogen habitually wore for her benefit. He knew that blank classic look, so very different from her childhood exuberance: a shutter drawn down on her real feelings, her real intentions. What did Imogen intend? What did she think, or do? He doubted whether her affections were secure, or sometimes, in dread moments, whether she had any deep affections at all. She was engaging, certainly, but with her ostentatious politeness and her brief smiles she no longer seemed to belong to them, if indeed she ever had. He suspected her of a fund of sexual knowledge, used coolly, deliberately. This he must keep to himself: Harriet must never know. Harriet, in fact, would look bewildered if he ever touched on the subject. To Harriet, as he well knew, sex was but a half-open book. He sighed, feeling the beginnings of a pain below his ribs. How could he blame his daughter for not resembling her mother? Yet he preferred women to be virtuous: it became them better. His daughter's secret life unsettled him, not only because he was her father but because the very idea was unseemly. Although he knew virtually nothing about Imogen's friends, he imagined them all with the same affectless masks as she herself habitually wore. That boy, Julian, however, seemed to be more deeply engaged. He sighed again. He did not like the idea of Julian as his daughter's lover, but since he was almost sure that Imogen was secretive about her other affairs he could not help hoping that Julian would not get too badly hurt.

'I shan't want anything to eat tonight,' he said. 'I've got a touch of indigestion.'

She turned her head to him slowly. After a moment her expression cleared. 'You ate too much,' she said. 'You must be more careful.'

He ignored this. 'It stays light in the evenings now. I might take a walk when we get back.' Suddenly he wanted to be alone with his thoughts, which seemed so treacherous when he was in the presence of his wife.

She glanced at him, more vaguely. 'There is vegetable soup if you want it,' she said.

'I won't be long,' he assured her. He could not wait to be out in the air, instead of imprisoned in this train, with his wife whom he loved and occasionally hated for not returning his love. Abroad! He thought. Abroad!

After calling up to Immy, and getting, as she expected, no reply, Harriet looked at herself searchingly in her bedroom mirror. She had matured late, was even now young in appearance, her hair still dark, her skin unlined. Tentatively she touched the mark; in truth it no longer bothered her. All she could discern in the glass was an expression of anxiety which widened her eyes, yet she was impatient rather than anxious, for the day of her return to Jack, which she saw now with an hallucinatory clarity. The fantasy, if that was what it was, had a sharpness that was surely indicative of something more substantial than imagination. She thought that it was indicative of the life to come, and felt her skin becoming warm at the thought that in a very short time, perhaps a month or two, she would see Jack again. She might even leave home. She laughed. That she, a respectable woman, could contemplate leaving her husband, and the daughter she adored, was unthinkable, yet she thought it. Immediately the laughter faded. It was ultimately impossible, she saw that. She would stay. But nothing, and no one, would stand in the way of her return to Jack, however soon she had to say goodbye to him. Maybe, if all went well, he would wait for her. Maybe he would be a friend, to whom she could turn, for moments of sweetness, in a life that would become more arid. For she knew that however illusory, however transitory it proved to be, she must have love in her life, before the darkness set in. She moved to the bed, tired now. Her thoughts had exhausted her.

The following morning Freddie, getting up with his usual feeling of dread, straightened himself with an effort, and fell heavily, pulling the bedclothes with him as he went down. The next thing he knew was Harriet's frightened face hovering above him. She was in her nightdress. 'You'll catch cold,' he tried to say, but found himself unable to speak.

The doctor, jovial and expansive, a professional optimist, was reasonable and full of explanations. 'He should be back to normal within forty-eight hours,' he said. 'One might have a minor stroke without knowing it. Quite common, you know.' At your age, was what he did not quite manage to conceal.

'Don't let Immy see me,' were the next words that Freddie managed to say. He was aware of his drooping left eyelid, and the rigidity at the left side of his mouth. These gradually diminished as the day went on, a long day, spent in bed, very frightened. To stay in bed meant to succumb: this he knew he must not do.

'How are you feeling?' asked Harriet, kneeling by the bed in what he recognized as a shaft of late sunlight.

'Better.'

They longed to believe it. But his speech had improved, and the mouth had slightly relaxed, and later that evening he managed to get up and walk to the bathroom.

She got into bed with him, to keep him company.

'I never liked Mordaunt,' he said.

'Everyone says he's an excellent doctor. But actually, no, I don't like him either.'

'When I'm better,' he said heavily, 'I might try that clinic Sanders told me about. That Swiss place. Stay there for a bit.' He saw something of his original image, only this time the Mediterranean was replaced by a mountain range. 'You don't need to come,' he said, and a tear rolled down his cheek.

She looked with pity at his sad and mottled face.

'Of course I'll come,' she said. 'As if I'd ever leave you.'

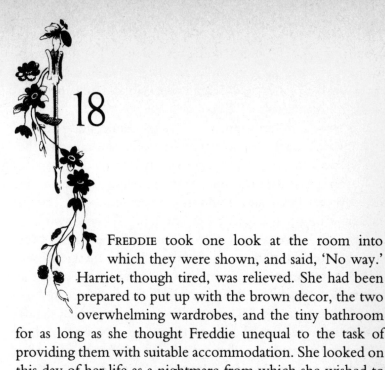

18

FREDDIE took one look at the room into which they were shown, and said, 'No way.' Harriet, though tired, was relieved. She had been prepared to put up with the brown decor, the two overwhelming wardrobes, and the tiny bathroom for as long as she thought Freddie unequal to the task of providing them with suitable accommodation. She looked on this day of her life as a nightmare from which she wished to be released by a profound sleep. It did not much matter to her where she slept: everywhere was exile. She had been patient, she thought, and sensible. She had obtained from Mordaunt a list of clinics in the Lausanne area, and also an introductory letter, Freddie's friend having proved disappointing in the matter of directions to and exact location of the place that had saved his life. 'I couldn't tell you the way,' he said. 'We were driving, from Geneva. I'd know it again, of course. You could ask around. It's called l'Alpe Fleurie.' Mordaunt had been polite but dubious. 'Everything in Switzerland is called l'Alpe Fleurie,' he had said. 'You're as likely to find yourself in a restaurant or a children's home as in a clinic. You'd be better off somewhere else. As a matter of fact my partner— Strang, you know—has made a study of clinics and spas. I'll give you a list.' Harriet had taken it with a sinking heart, seeing them posting from clinic to clinic for month after

month, perhaps for years. Mordaunt had saved them. 'Lecoudray is very highly thought of,' he had said. 'Specializes in
arterial cases. Got his own clinic near Montreux. I met him
once, at a conference. I'll give you a letter.'

But they had come, first, to Nyon, for no good reason
other than Freddie had thought he might stumble on the
clinic from which Sanders had so signally benefited. It was the
hotel room that decided him. Anger at being cheated of his
vision of balconies and woodsmoke had restored a certain
vigour. 'Bring that bag, Harriet,' he said. 'I'll go down and
order a taxi.' 'Are we going to Montreux?' she asked. 'Not
directly,' he said, with some cunning, for the mirage of the
perfect hotel was still vivid in his mind, and he knew that it
had to be somewhere undiscovered, far from urban life.
Dazed, she sat in the back of the taxi, watching small stands
of trees give way to fields of yellow rape. Nyon was left
behind, forgotten, cancelled. So, in due course, were Rolle
(Hôtel Regina) and Morges (Hôtel du Mont Blanc). 'Freddie,
I am very tired,' she said, watching a red sun descend slowly
into the grey waters of the lake, as they speeded past. 'Lausanne, *vous connaissez?*' asked the driver, who was now far
from home. Without waiting for an answer he unloaded their
bags in front of the Beau Rivage, casually mentioned an
enormous sum of money, and got back into the car. Through
plate glass windows what looked like members of a seminar
or conference, all men, were dining. Freddie saw them too.
'We can have something sent up,' he said, already disappointed. It was his fourth hotel of the evening, and none had
corresponded to his original, his ideal hotel, in which, somehow, he would be the only guest, honoured and prized by the
proprietor, who would be a discreetly attractive woman of a
certain age, perfectly silent unless he wished to talk. He saw
a younger slimmer version of himself; he saw appreciative
glances from villagers who knew their place. He did not want

chandeliers, in which, inevitably, the bulbs, although numerous, were too weak, and long airless corridors, and waiters whipping silver domes off plates of unfamiliar fish. He wanted to feel at home, and wondered how he could ever manage to do so again. At that point he felt unwell, and put his hand to his heart. Harriet was at his side, vigilant.

'It's been a long, tiring day,' she warned. 'Tomorrow we take it easy.'

'Tomorrow,' he said, in a voice that wheezed slightly, 'we look for a flat. Furnished. Rent it by the month.'

She did not have the heart to argue with him.

Both slept badly. Harriet woke early, worrying about Freddie, worrying about Immy, who, she thought, had not been given sufficient warning of their departure. When would they get back, to reassure her? More important, how long were they to be away? She had not taken seriously Freddie's suggestion that they look for a flat. This was not their home, nor was it ever likely to be; she had in mind a visit to this Lecoudray, and then a swift return to London, where they were, or would be, safe. She thought that this might be accomplished in the space of a week, but intended to keep her thoughts to herself. She saw Freddie stirring, watched him carefully as he made his way to the bathroom, and ordered breakfast. She had to admit that he looked better, acted more like a man. This adventure, or initiative, had served the purpose of reviving him, of reminding him that he could make certain choices, could pay effortlessly for certain mistakes. The rejection of all those hotel rooms, which, though doleful, had not been entirely impossible, had stimulated him; he would now bend the country to his will until he was satisfied that it met his requirements. The sun rose magnificently and imperviously outside the window; inside, all was discreet luxury, infinitely depressing. Both the discretion and the luxury annoyed Freddie, as did the noise of trolleys in the corridor, and the cars starting up in the car park. It was already hot. Suddenly, Harriet herself wanted air, and silence. She would have liked to be alone, but suppressed this thought. She watched him pick up the telephone, order a taxi. If I let him have his own way in this adventure, she thought, then maybe it will be my turn to have mine, one day, when we are home again.

Their driver, this time, was a younger man, placid and relatively cheerful. He seemed to understand instinctively that Freddie was both rich and unwell, yet did not take undue advantage of the fact. Instead he drove them carefully along the lake shore, from which they could see small yachts, like tidy children, bobbing at anchor in minuscule boat basins, and municipal flowers, gravely chosen with an eye to maximum contrast of colours, blooming obediently in equally small flower beds. Yet as the sun rose high in the sky and flooded the lake, without in any way piercing its opacity, they began to see a more benign landscape, bushes and trees of lilac and wistaria cascading over low stone walls, a glimpse of snow on distant peaks, and, spreading outwards and upwards, green hills dotted with peaceable houses, each with its own view of life below, in the valley, and its own sloping meadow to isolate it from its neighbours.

It was absurdly scenic, and yet it was properly domesticated. It would, Harriet saw, be possible to live here, to take an evening walk along the lake shore, watching a great red sun sink into those grey waters; it would be possible, and even desirable, to turn, eventually, towards home, and to sit on a balcony until the light had finally faded. The bed, ultimately reached, would be white, austere. This life would be possible with a lover, with whom in fact it would be idyllic. She imagined the silence, like the silence at the end of the world, which would unite two lovers after the long disparate journeys which had eventually brought them together. How they

would turn, from the balcony, in the fading light to that white
bed! Even now, in the hot car, with Freddie's heavy body
beside her, she saw the rightness of that conclusion, after
which she would be indifferent to death, or punishment. If
only, she thought, circumstances and her own nature had
favoured a more decisive way of life. Yet she could see that
somehow her own unconsummated longings had derived an
odd beauty from the very fact of being unconsummated. In
whatever dreams and desires she had entertained she had
always seen herself as free and unencumbered, neither wife,
nor mother, nor daughter, whereas her very real situation had
militated against her taking any definitive steps to free herself.
Outwardly conventional, she could now see that she was
inwardly conventional as well. And now there was the additional worry of Freddie's health, for if he were to die she
would be faced with the very real dilemma of choosing her
own life, of acting on her desires, of abandoning Immy to her
young fate, and becoming what she had never been, a vaga-
bond, a fugitive, an escapee. She did not doubt her capacity
to become all or any of these things. But that, she thought,
with a flash of realism, is because I have never tried to be
independent. It is all in the mind, magical thinking. Whereas
reality is the heat from Freddie's body, the bristling blonde
hairs on the back of the driver's neck, and the shafts of sun
dazzling on the waters of the lake.

They drove on, inexorably. Lutry was passed, Saint Sapho-
rin, Vevey. On the outskirts of Vevey the car stopped and the
driver courteously suggested that they might like to lunch. He
himself, it was clear, was dying for a beer. He indicated the
terraces of two hotels and said that if they agreed he would
pick them up again in two hours' time. Had they, he enquired, any particular destination in mind? Montreux, said
Freddie, but they were in no hurry. In fact he himself was
agreeably impressed by the quiet of the place, a sort of suburb,

he supposed, populated by a sparse and docile citizenry, with the great silence of the lake on one side and the spreading green hills above. I will lift up my eyes unto the hills, he thought, and felt vaguely comforted. 'What is the name of this place?' he asked the driver. La Tour de Peilz was the answer. The air shimmered; in the boat basin the little craft were motionless on the tideless waters. Tiny brown waves spread over the cobbles below the wall on which they leaned, momentarily dazzled. 'All right, Robert. Come back in a couple of hours,' he said, handing the driver money for his lunch. All was silent in the midday heat. Reluctantly they made their way to yet another hotel, where they ate more fish.

'You should get a little exercise after lunch,' said Harriet. 'It's not good for you to sit in the car all day. Can't we stop here? At least for the night. I'm awfully tired, Freddie. Could we get a little air, do you think? It might be cooler down by the lake.'

Freddie was now gloomy. It no longer seemed to him to matter when he saw Dr Lecoudray, whose address was safely in his wallet. Now that Dr Lecoudray was within reach there seemed to be no particular urgency in reaching him. The impulse of energy which had brought him to this place was ebbing away; he felt the gradual invasion of an immense discouragement.

'Have you got my pills?' he asked fretfully.

Harriet suppressed a sigh. 'You know I have. Come on, Freddie, let's walk.'

They strolled past the notice which proudly proclaimed that they were on the *voie fleurie,* raised their eyes towards the impalpable cloud that clothed the mountains on the far side of the lake, and lowered them again to the careful lawns and flower beds of the municipality. They turned inland, away from the lake, up a little street which lay open and deserted in the sun. Freddie stopped, straightened up, looked about him.

'Some decent building here,' he said. 'Good sensible domestic architecture.'

He saw balconies, shutters, pitched roofs, shadowed entrances, secrecy and order. He was attracted, and saw, with an intimate thrill, that he was about to make a significant personal choice, in which Harriet would have very little to say. The car, and Robert, were waiting by the lakeside.

'Robert,' said Freddie, choosing to make this announcement to his chauffeur rather than to his wife. 'We are looking for a furnished flat. Is there an agency around here?'

Robert brightened. 'My cousin,' he said. 'In Vevey. He is the best. He will find you what you want.'

By the late afternoon they were installed in the Résidence Cécil, a white concrete building in a daring but not outlandish Art Deco style, reassuringly small, promising all modern comforts. Their apartment, which belonged to a wealthy widow, was furnished with an extravagance, a shamelessness which Freddie found immediately reassuring. Harriet opened all the windows, took a deep breath of air, and turned round to view, with stupefaction, the parrot-green sofa, the yellow and white striped armchairs, the black coffee table complete with large Japanese ashtray and a flowering gloxinia in a ceramic pot which might have been left there only that morning. Green garlands studded the cream coloured carpet, and flowered chintz of staggering munificence was looped and draped at the windows. Cushions, in the same chintz, were placed primly in the angles of the cockatoo sofa. Freddie sank into one of the striped chairs, visibly exhausted. That happened nowadays, the sudden expiring of energy. Harriet went into the bedroom, which was less dramatic, was in fact rather prim, with *toile de Jouy* wallpaper and a plain carpet. She turned back the *toile de Jouy* counterpane, revealing a heavy white duvet. Then, abandoning the still unpacked suitcases, she went and stood at the window. After a few minutes of reflection she walked back into the sitting-room.

'How long did you take this place for, Freddie?' she asked.

He looked shifty but resolute. 'Five years, actually,' he said.

'Five *years*?'

'Be sensible, Harriet. If I'm to have any treatment I'll have to come back for check-ups, won't I? It all takes time, you know. And I'm sick of hotels. Cheer up, old girl. We don't have to live here all the time, just spend part of the year here.'

'I can't leave Immy on her own.'

'Miss Wetherby is there, isn't she?'

'But she might want me, need me.'

He looked at her coldly. 'Don't be a fool, Harriet.'

She was obscurely aware that he would have his way whatever she said, that he was exacting his revenge on her. It was as if he had divined all her secret thoughts, had known for ever that it was for love of her daughter that she endured all the rest. And yet he knew her to be blameless. He resented her technical innocence, which meant that he could not punish her more directly. All this she knew, and knew that he would not forgive her. Time was short for him; he would be ruthless. Goodbye, my life, she thought. Aloud she said, 'There is nothing to eat.'

'I'm not hungry,' he said. 'A sandwich would do. The shops must still be open. Why don't you look around?'

'Of course,' she said. She was anxious to get away from him, out of the oppressively tidy room, out into the air. The evening was beautiful, and she must not let him see her anger.

She found a small supermarket, bought bread, coffee, and mortadella. To buy more would be to acknowledge that she was putting down roots in this place, for which, nevertheless, she felt a bewildered sympathy. Dogs were now being walked by the lake, along the *voie fleurie;* passing cars signified the end

of the working day, the beginning of the long benign evening. If we find the clinic tomorrow, she thought, and make
an appointment for a consultation, there is no reason why I
should not go home immediately afterwards. There are things
to do, clothes to pack. And yet she knew that she would not
leave Freddie. She did not know how ill he was, had chosen
to trust Mordaunt's optimism. This uncharacteristic behaviour must have tired him mentally, as well as physically. She
did not know how long he could last, was unwilling to make
demands. What he had done—and she was uncertain as to
how deliberate his actions were—was to remove them from
a life in which she might have made an independent decision.
She respected his desire for health, for safety. She respected
his instinctive urge towards a longevity which might, even
now, be fatally compromised: she could not help but respect
this. At the same time she permitted herself a glance beyond
his life, beyond his death. I shall not weaken this time, she
thought, and so thinking walked back to the Résidence Cécil,
where she found Freddie, still in the yellow and white striped
chair, and now fast asleep.

    She telephoned Immy, at the flat, but got no reply. She
dialled Miss Wetherby's number: again no reply. She glanced
at her watch and calculated that it was the time at which Miss
Wetherby habitually took the dog out. Perturbed that nobody knew where she was, she sent a telegram, giving their
address and telephone number. Then she woke Freddie, gave
him his pills, and shepherded him into the bedroom, now
shadowy in the grey light of the declining evening. Freddie
slept again, at once. She herself stayed awake a little longer,
then fell abruptly into blackness.

    They awoke, bewildered. A scarlet sun was already creep-
ing over the horizon, although the bedroom was still in
shadow. They had both slept so deeply that it took them
several minutes to understand where they were. After a mo-

ment of panic they settled down to a cautious contemplation of their new situation.

'There's no need to get up yet,' said Harriet. 'How do you feel?'

'All right,' he answered. It was always an anxious moment for both of them. Early morning brought a state of alertness which somehow contained the germ of an emergency. In a flash she knew that if anything further were to happen to Freddie it would be at this hour of the morning, when they were both tousled, unlovely, in an atmosphere of disordered bedclothes, with the rank taste of the night's saliva in their mouths. She got up, put on water for the coffee, ran a bath. While Freddie sank back into a further doze she went to the telephone and dialled Immy's number: still no reply. This strengthened her resolve to return home as soon as possible.

'Come on, Freddie,' she said. 'Breakfast is ready, what there is of it. Then I think you might ring up this clinic. There is a telephone directory under that table, the one on which two volumes of the works of Voltaire are so carefully placed, between the ceramic plate on the ebony stand and the lamp shaped like a candlestick. With the peach parchment shade,' she added.

'You seem to have recovered from your fatigue,' he remarked. 'By the way you forgot the butter. And there is no jam.'

'No jam at all,' she agreed. 'Have you taken your pills? Then I think you should make that call. Then you can come shopping with me, and remind me what I might be likely to forget. That way there can be no mistakes.'

She walked into the bathroom, surveyed her face in the mirror, put a comb through her hair, and sprayed cologne on her wrists. She was becoming angrier by the minute. She saw that her face was flushed, and willed herself to remain calm.

'Ready?' she enquired, in a heightened but agreeable tone.

'Wear your linen jacket. It will get very hot later, if yesterday is anything to go by.'

They clattered down the stairs, not yet accustomed to the silence of their surroundings. There were no children in this building, that much was certain. Who lived here, besides themselves? She felt coarse, intrusive, saw, yet again, that Freddie was too big, too old, saw also that he was a bad colour. She took his arm, but he moved away from her.

It was with a certain feeling of relief that she saw another human figure by the glass door of the entrance, a small man, who swept off a broad-brimmed panama hat to reveal a head of flowing grey hair.

'*Bonjour!*' said this person. '*Soyez les bienvenus! La propriétaire m'a dit qu'il y avait un nouveau voisinage.* Papineau,' he added. 'Joseph Papineau. *A votre service.*'

'Good morning,' said Freddie repressively, and strode on ahead.

Joseph Papineau expressed radiant delight.

'But you are English! But this is wonderful! I lived in London for thirty years. I was at our embassy there. I came home, well, back, when I retired. May I enquire . . . ?'

'Our name is Lytton,' said Harriet, taking the proffered hand. 'We came here for my husband's health. That is, we are only passing through. We have taken the flat on a temporary basis. My name is Harriet,' she said. 'And my husband is Freddie. At the moment we are looking for the Clinique Lecoudray. Could you direct us?' She consulted the paper in her hand. 'Rue du Bois-Gentil,' she added.

'But my dear lady, you are only five minutes away! I know it very well. Allow me to accompany you. Which one of you is ill?' he enquired sympathetically. Harriet decided that Monsieur Papineau was no fool.

'My husband has had a very slight stroke,' she told him. 'Oh, he had made a complete recovery, but he needs a certain amount of care. And Professor Lecoudray is, I believe, warmly recommended. Our doctor in London spoke highly of him.'

His hand under her arm steered her to the pavement, where Freddie was waiting. Why did he have to be so truculent? she wondered. This man was harmless, welcoming. Of course, he was a diplomat; he was bound to have excellent manners. He made Freddie seem crude. At the same time she warned herself not to become too expansive. It would be easy to lean on this man, with his childlike smile and his shrewd eyes. As if aware of her difficulty he returned her to Freddie, who was standing morosely in the sun.

'My dear sir,' said Monsieur Papineau. 'My dear Monsieur Freddie. You could do no better than consult Professor Lecoudray. The man is a magician! People come from far and wide to see him. And the clinic is very fine. Of course, we are famous for our clinics. If you can walk a little way?' he enquired of Freddie. 'Or, if you wish, my car is at your disposal.'

Freddie brightened. He brightened still more when, after half an hour—Monsieur Papineau's five minutes—they came to a sumptuous villa set in a sweeping, gently terraced garden. White awnings and blinds protected various balconies from the sun. Utter silence prevailed. *Et voilà la Clinique Lecoudray,*' said Monsieur Papineau gently, as if he feared that they might be overwhelmed. It was clear that he had no intention of leaving them, a fact for which Harriet was grateful. They entered a reception hall, their footfalls heavy on the marble floor. Only Monsieur Papineau made no noise, as if noiselessness proclaimed him as a native of the place more surely than any card of identity. A handsome woman of about forty, with blonde streaked hair, dressed in an immaculate white suit, emerged equally noiselessly from a glass-doored office.

'Mr Lytton?' Her English was unaccented. 'Professor

Lecoudray will see you in fifteen minutes. Would you like to wait in my office?'

Her office was clinically pure, yet luxurious, grey and white, extremely feminine. Her desk appeared to be a Louis XV table. She wore gold bracelets on both wrists.

'I am Denise Schumacher,' she said. 'Professor Lecoudray is my father. As this is your first visit perhaps I should explain what we do here. We have a full range of services,' she went on fluently. 'Cell revitalization, examination and treatment of sexual impotence, treatment of varicose veins, plastic and aesthetic surgery, weight reducing programmes . . .'

'My husband has had a stroke,' said Harriet.

'Of course, your husband will have a full medical check-up,' said Mme Schumacher with a touch of sharpness. 'All our patients have a twenty-four-hour investigation before we undertake any treatment. Professor Lecoudray will probably suggest that he come in tomorrow.' Her telephone purred discreetly. 'Ah, I think he is ready for you now. We take all major credit cards,' she added. In all this, Monsieur Papineau had sat there like a relation, or a family friend, one hand cupped behind his ear, as if intent on catching every word. Harriet was grateful for his company, as she waited for Freddie in the marble tiled hall. Occasionally a woman in a white overall, bearing a pile of spotless white towels, emerged from a door and pressed the button for the lift. Otherwise there was no sign of human activity.

'Don't you think I might have been allowed to see him, the professor, I mean? After all, I am Freddie's wife. I have to know what is going to happen to him.'

Monsieur Papineau smiled gently, as if he knew exactly what was going to happen to Freddie.

'He will want to see you afterwards, I dare say,' he told her, but idly, as if it made no difference what she was told. 'He

usually recommends a week's stay every few months. That is
what generally happens.'

'And how long does this last?' asked Harriet.

Monsieur Papineau turned to her with his sweet shrewd
face. 'For ever, my dear. For ever.'

He took her hand, patted it, and gave it back into her
keeping. She felt the tears rising.

'I must get home,' she said. 'My daughter will be wondering where I am. I must go back to London, to my daughter.'

Monsieur Papineau turned his head towards her. 'Of
course you will go home,' he said. 'But you will come back
from time to time. After all, this is a delightful place. It will
not be so bad, you will see. You will get used to it.'

At this point Freddie appeared, looking flushed and gratified. 'He wants me to come in tomorrow,' he said. 'For tests.'
He seemed excited by the prospect. 'Marvellous fellow, very
handsome. Speaks perfect English. Of course, they're all dip-
lomats here. I thought the daughter rather charming too,
didn't you?'

'No, I didn't,' said Harriet. 'And now I suggest we have
lunch. Won't you join us?' she asked, or perhaps begged of
Monsieur Papineau. Freddie said nothing. Monsieur Papineau studied them both for a fraction of a second. 'I should
be delighted,' he said. 'La Ruche is highly recommended.
Won't you be my guests?'

'No, no, wouldn't hear of it,' said Freddie, now restored to
good humour. 'You must be our guest. You've been very
kind, looking after my wife. Appreciate it. And perhaps after
lunch you could tell me where to buy a hat like yours. He told
me to keep my head covered.'

'It was rather a long way to come to get that sort of advice,'
remarked Harriet, as they made their way down the hot stone
steps of the terrace. 'I could have told you that for nothing.'
Freddie took no notice. 'I'll leave you after lunch,' she went

on. 'You can go and buy your hat with Monsieur Papineau. As you noticed this morning, I had forgotten the butter. A mistake like that must be rectified as soon as possible.'

'*Mais oui, sous peine d'amende*,' said Monsieur Papineau gaily, taking them both by the arm. Under his influence a civilized atmosphere was restored, was sustained throughout lunch in the dark little restaurant, with the fan turning lazily on the ceiling, and the geraniums brilliant through the window. Stirring her coffee, Harriet said, 'You have been so kind. When shall we see you again?'

'I am here every day,' he said. 'Here is my card. Perhaps you will let me call on you tomorrow, when Monsieur Freddie is in the clinic?'

'I should like that,' she said. 'And now, if you'll excuse me . . .'

They both stood up to watch her go, a slender woman in a navy blue linen dress. The birthmark, thought Monsieur Papineau. I thought she was here for the birthmark. The husband, of course, is in ruins. That heat, that colour. He offered his wallet, but politely accepted Freddie's refusal. 'If you could walk into Vevey,' he suggested. 'Delahaye will have a suitable hat.' He usually shopped in Geneva, but forbore to say so. He felt a sympathy for the man, whom he saw buoyed up by false hopes. He must not offer advice, he warned himself, although it was in his nature to do so, having held a position at the Swiss Embassy in London for this very purpose.

Harriet found a bookshop, which made her feel better. She bought some paperbacks, then went back to the flat, where she telephoned Immy. Again there was no reply. But it did not matter; she would be home within the week. She willed the time to pass, had almost forgotten why they were here in this place, but was forcibly reminded when Freddie returned, looking congested.

'I think I'll lie down for a bit,' he said.

'Yes, lie down,' she agreed. 'I'll bring you a cup of tea.'

She sat at the window quietly, her books in her lap. At six o'clock Freddie woke, took a bath, and eased himself back into bed again. She spent the evening sitting on the parrot-green sofa, trying to read, her gaze straying to the window. When the light faded, and the grey shadows she was beginning to know so well invaded the room, she laid aside her book and silently joined Freddie. There was nothing else to do.

'Your daughter is very young?' enquired Monsieur Papineau the following morning, walking her beside the lake. They had delivered Freddie, who was rather silent, to the clinic in his car.

'My daughter is nearly twenty-one,' she replied.

'That is not very young,' he said gently.

'But you see, I love her so much.'

'Ah, yes.'

They walked on.

'Forgive me,' she said. 'I must seem very silly to you.'

'No, no. I know about love. I had a governess whom I loved very much. She was with me all her life. I still miss her.'

'You must tell me about her,' she said.

Across the lake she could see, or thought she could see, a village, perhaps a little town, at the foot of the mountains. The sun lay hot on her shoulders. The village, or the town, lay veiled in a grey mist.

'If I were allowed to pick the flowers I would give you one,' said Monsieur Papineau. 'But one is not allowed to pick the flowers here. Not like England.'

She smiled. 'You are so kind.'

'Not kind,' he said. 'I am like you. Lonely.'

19

'YOU'RE SURE you'll be all right, darling?'

'Oh, Mother,' said Immy, with elaborate patience. 'What can happen to me? You'll only be away a month. We went through all this last year, if you remember.'

'It's just that I don't like to think of you alone in this house.'

'Wetherby's downstairs, isn't she?'

'Miss Wetherby, darling. And I hardly think she'd be much good at defending you.'

'There's the dog. And anyway I'm out most of the time.'

Where do you go? She longed to ask, but said nothing.

They were in Imogen's flat, tidying up. Harriet's presence was allowed on such occasions, even welcomed, although Imogen's general mood was one of disaffection. She had not asked about her father's treatment, for which Harriet could hardly blame her: she thought it farcical herself. The prospect of sitting in that elaborate little room while Freddie solemnly booked into the clinic for his vitamin injections filled her with despair. Yet she was intent on behaving well, went along with his obsessions, his little manias, which were becoming more pronounced, resigned herself to the company of Monsieur Papineau, who remained devoted but who now wished to talk about himself and his memories of London, an ideal city, as he saw it, and one which did indeed seem ideal to Harriet as she sat obediently on a public seat overlooking the lake, improving her French from the book in her lap. A terrible calm had fallen on her life, as if the lake were indeed an inland sea in more ways than one and she herself adrift on it. Three times a year she and Freddie went to Switzerland, where Freddie, looking complacent, received his injections. The mere touch of Professor Lecoudray's hand was apparently enough to restore him; she had to admit that he was better, was even rather well. But she distrusted Lecoudray, suspected him of advising Freddie on the desirability of sexual activity, for several times his hands had fumbled over her, in a way which was now repugnant to her, and he took to watching her when she was bathing, sometimes hitched himself up in the bed to pull at the straps of her nightdress. She regarded this as a form of senility, although it seemed to put Freddie into a genial mood. She thought that he must have conversations with Lecoudray of which no woman would approve. Certainly he came back to the Résidence Cécil rejuvenated, with stories about his nurses—Colette, Irène— which were supposed to excite her. She knew that the younger girl, Colette, was superbly attractive, as he repeatedly told her. Irène, a middle-aged woman, was handsome and stern, and was thus another source of anecdotes. Harriet had found Irène sensible: the sternness seemed to proceed from a certain disgust with several of her wealthy patients, for whom she was obliged to perform services which they should have performed for themselves. She regarded Harriet with a sympathy she did not bother to disguise. Yet Freddie continued to flourish, and Harriet saw them condemned to spend longer and longer abroad, while Immy became more and more unknowable. For she had to admit that she knew nothing of her daughter's life beyond the fact, the rather surprising fact, that she continued to work at her advertising agency, that she the nearness of such disgrace, which somehow, she knew, Imogen sensed and condemned.

She could not blame her. Both she and Freddie were graceless now, as if he had passed the affliction on to her, jovially recruiting her in his own deterioration. In between his newly confident gestures and Monsieur Papineau's reminiscences she felt amazed, astounded, as if this fate were worse than any infidelity could have been. And yet she had brought it on herself, was alone to blame, and all that she could do now was to protect Imogen from any suspicion of what her life had become, although she thought she knew that Imogen had sensed it and was properly disgusted.

She was allowed into Imogen's domain on a Saturday morning, for a cup of coffee, in return for general services. Such moments were precious to her, although Immy never said much. A week's confusion awaited her loving hands: Imogen's immaculate appearance was not reflected in the disorder of garments lying over the backs of chairs, the tights and stockings soaking in a basinful of water, the muddle of underwear, all of it expensive, in the laundry basket. Once the washing machine was in operation she was awarded her treat, her cup of coffee, although this was somehow a disappointment, always short of what she desired. She longed to give advice, but what advice could she usefully give, apart from timid and anodyne suggestions that too much coffee dulled the complexion. But Immy's complexion was faultless, always had been. There were the recommendations to lock up properly, to eat sensibly, that she invariably made before going away, but these were routine, and no notice was taken of them. Then, on her last Saturday before her renewed exile, she cast around desperately for something to detain her, and, folding the clothes taken from the washing machine, said, 'Oh, how silly. I forgot that cardigan. Have I seen it before? Navy is not generally your colour.'

was increasingly beautiful, and that she had an extensive social life which was somehow a secret.

Imogen did not enquire after her father's health, or take even a polite interest in his progress. She found him, if anything, pathetic, but had done so for a long time. Harriet could not bear her to know of her father's intimate behaviour, felt indeed that her daughter must be protected from all suggestions of stain, of soil, although she knew, but knew without the support of any fact, that Imogen was no longer innocent. So long as it is only Julian, she thought, waiting in vain for Imogen to confide in her, as she thought other women's daughters must do, although she had never confided in her own mother when she was young. On the contrary: there had been between them that electrically charged sense of things unsaid, and the mute appeal that she should free them all from their difficulties by marrying Freddie. As she had done. But these were old thoughts, which she usually suppressed. What she could not suppress was her yearning, her longing that her daughter would somehow emerge from her silence, her offended silence, it sometimes seemed, and express joy, anticipation, fervour. Instead of which there was this curious indifference, which she suspected was only assumed for the benefit of her parents, as if it were essential that they should be kept at arm's length.

Harriet feared that she had somehow lost her daughter's love, and blamed herself for it, as if she knew herself to be too dull and uninteresting to be attractive to a girl like Imogen. If she had had that secret life which she had promised herself, she thought the girl would have looked on her with more respect. But she had not had it. Instead she was rewarded by Freddie and his rejuvenated advances, abortive as they were. She could not help but feel that the only tactful thing to do was go away, taking her unregenerate husband with her, so that her daughter should not be contaminated by the sight,

Immy flushed, that very faint flush of hers, which proceeded from annoyance rather than embarrassment, and
snatched the cardigan, which smelt damp, away from her.

'It's Lizzie's. I borrowed it.'

'Oh, have you seen Lizzie? I'm so glad. Well, you'd better
get it back to her. No,' she said suddenly. 'I'll take it back
myself. I'll go to Judd Street myself. Will she be there if I go
one evening?'

Imogen shrugged. 'No idea. I shouldn't think she goes out
much. She's got this job now, walked straight into it when
she came down. Something to do with publishing.'

'How clever of her. She was always a sensible girl. I'm so
glad you've kept in touch, darling.'

'Actually, that cardigan could be thrown away,' said Imogen. 'She said it was an old one.'

'It's certainly not something you'd normally wear,' agreed
her mother. 'And it smells musty. Oh well, poor Lizzie. Does
she like living in Judd Street?'

'Couldn't say.'

The telephone ended the conversation: Imogen's face was
immediately absorbed, remote, though she answered in
monosyllables. Harriet waited, with a look of not waiting on
her face, until Imogen waggled her fingers at her, and she was
reluctantly forced to get up and make for the door. She blew
a kiss, was rewarded with another waggle of the fingers, and
went down the stairs.

Very well, she thought. I will go to Judd Street and see
Lizzie. I will find out from her where her father is: after all,
the query is quite in order. She is not to know of my interest;
she will not be involved. I shall comb my hair and put on
lipstick as if at any minute I might run into Jack, for who
knows? If he is not there now he will be there one day, as I
shall. For now it was important to her to make contact before
she was taken away to that silent room, with the parrot-green

sofa and the volumes of Voltaire, before she had to undergo
Freddie's advances and Monsieur Papineau's family photographs: she must go to where Jack had been, and might be
again.

On the following Monday she left the house at six. She
hesitated as to whether or not she should take the car, but felt
such a renewal of energy that before she knew it she had left
the car behind and swung on to a bus. It was a damp mild
evening with an indeterminate sky, the beginning of a spring
that would not declare itself. All day she had longed for the
sun; now she longed for it to be dark, as if darkness were more
conducive to her secrecy. Only in the unlovely street did she
feel a touch of fear. It was deserted, silent, all the normal
passers-by gone home, and now real darkness, or rather dimness, discoloration, was coming down, signalling that the day
was over, and that different activities would now be expected
to take place. Her hand to her throat, she entered the building, took the wheezing lift, stood before Jack's door, and rang
the bell.

The door opened on to Lizzie's inscrutable face. In a great
wave of disappointment, but somehow still buoyed up by the
fact that she was in this place, Harriet greeted her, was allowed in, saw distractedly how plain the room was, how
brown, how cold, felt momentarily sorry for the girl, who had
presumably been eating her supper, if that yoghourt carton
was her supper, in these disheartening surroundings.

'I hope I didn't disturb you, Lizzie,' she said.

'I was working,' was the uncompromising answer.

Harriet saw, with a sharpening of her attention, the volume
of Vuillard reproductions, the intense checked and striped
material of Vuillard's mother's dress.

'So clever of you to get that job, Lizzie,' she said. 'You
must come and tell us all about it sometime.'

But Lizzie was no longer in a mood to be patronized. Her

present independence was hard won, and less enjoyable than she had foreseen. She had tried to harden herself, with some success. It was difficult for her to deal with feelings, her own and other people's. Eagerness, avidity made her shudder. She was more than ever determined to keep this foolish woman at bay.

'I brought your cardigan,' said Harriet helplessly. 'The one you so kindly lent to Immy.'

'You needn't have bothered.'

'It's no bother.' She wondered why the girl was so unresponsive, as if she were annoyed at the visitor, or maybe just indifferent, as she always had been.

'You're keeping well, Lizzie?'

'Very well, thank you.'

'Quite happy here? You still keep in touch with Elspeth?'

'I see her from time to time.'

'And your father?' Her voice was light. 'Still in Washington?'

'Yes.'

That was all. She supposed she had got the answer she had come for, and yet she was oddly disconcerted by Lizzie's face, which she saw as stern and unforgiving, as if all were known to her. But that was ridiculous: the girl was practically a stranger these days. Nevertheless, she felt chilled, crestfallen. The cardigan had been thrown on to a chair, in a corner, although Lizzie was always so neat. The whole encounter had been odd. Out in the street she shivered, saw a taxi, which she hailed as if it were a lifeboat and she wrecked at sea. Huddled in the back (and now it was quite dark) she felt she had come near to making a fool of herself, and had a sense of danger. For once she would be glad to get home, just as she would be glad to leave that home in a few days' time. It seemed only realistic now to see her life as a series of escapes, which she must somehow, expressionlessly, manage.

In the same fretful damp they took the taxi, the plane, the other taxi, and came to rest in the absolute silence of the Résidence Cécil. As usual, Monsieur Papineau, hearing their steps on the stairs, came up with the milk, on his face the same look of fearful joy at the resumption of the conversation which had been interrupted by their last departure. Now that they were regular visitors, practically residents, he had lost something of his original authority, looked to them more to repair the loneliness which sprang into relief only when company was available, and captive. Freddie more or less ignored him, looked on him as a sort of concierge: with a sigh Harriet set to to make good the omission. Without him she would have felt desperate, although she now had to endure family reminiscences. Yet she knew that on the following morning he would drive Freddie to the clinic and return to walk her along the lake, urging her to activity, to exercise, or, alternatively, to relaxation, as if he had only her good at heart. She settled down to a month of this, desired only to be left alone, to sit in the silent room and will herself to peace. Her life, though intolerable, was calm, prosperous. All she had to do was endure it. She took up her book and persevered. At night, with relief, she plunged into sleep, all the more precious when Freddie was not there. She woke each morning with surprise, as if she had not expected to do so.

Each day she underwent a peaceful eclipse, becalmed by her walk along the lake shore, by Monsieur Papineau's conversation, to which she listened with half an ear. His role in her life was now indispensable: without him she might have sat all day. Instead, they walked. 'Our constitutional, Harriet,' he would say, presenting himself at the door with a beaming face. They lunched together, walked again in the deep calm of the afternoon. Then she gave him a cup of tea, assured him that she had things to do, saw him go down the stairs with the slight look of disappointment that she knew so well, and settled down with her book. Her life was so healthy that she thought she must last for a hundred years. As the light faded she stood at the window, watching the few cars of the evening speeding away to their unknown destinations. Time passed in this way, each day like the last. When Freddie came home she was surprised to see that three, nearly four weeks had gone by in this fashion.

One day the nurse, Irène, called on her way home: Professor Lecoudray would like to see Freddie in a month's time, instead of the usual three.

'He's not worse, is he?' asked Harriet, alarmed.

The woman shrugged. 'His blood pressure is bad. One must remember his age.'

She looked curiously round the room.

'Et vous? Vous avez tout ce qu'il vous faut? Vous n'avez besoin de rien?'

They spoke in both French and English. Thanks to her reading Harriet was now fluent. But she deduced that she was an object of pity, and that the visit was for her benefit more than for Freddie's.

She no longer desired to be at home, felt in fact as if home were a fiction, less real than the fictions she read. Yet she packed up, locked up, said goodbye to Monsieur Papineau, told him that she would see him in a month's time.

'Ah,' he said, momentarily alert. Then his gaze slid off into the distance, and his usual smile took its place.

The journey home was tinged with staleness, anticlimax. Of the two of them only Freddie was alert: she viewed his high colour and his good spirits with equal misgivings. Arriving in London she was aware of the chary light, the low-banked clouds, the endless stream of cars. After her silent month she felt jolted by the noise, almost frightened. Her heart beat faster than usual; in her mouth she tasted blood. She was relieved when the taxi drew up in Wellington Square, yet the same heavy-heartedness made her stumble on the steps. What is wrong with me? she thought. I do not usually react like this. She dragged the suitcases into the hall, dropped the keys into her bag, and straightened up, alert, aware that something was out of joint.

'Harriet, I've told you, I won't have that dog in the house. What is it doing here?'

'It must have got out,' she said. 'Or Miss Wetherby had something to do up here.' But she hurried into the drawing-room, where the barking had come from, to find Miss Wetherby seated in Freddie's chair, her hand on the dog's collar, trying to restrain him.

'Miss Wetherby! Are you all right? Has there been a break-in? There's nothing wrong, is there?'

Miss Wetherby, with an obvious effort, stood up and came forward.

'Mrs Lytton, Mr Lytton, I'm afraid there's been an accident.'

'Imogen,' said Harriet, turning sick and faint.

'You must be very brave . . .'

'Where is she? Where is my daughter?'

Miss Wetherby shook her head at Freddie. 'The police came round last night,' she said, in a low voice, as if Harriet must not hear. 'A car accident. One of those open cars. She was killed instantly.'

'Where is she?' cried Harriet.

Miss Wetherby shook her head again. The policeman had told her that Imogen's body had been badly damaged. This she had decided to keep to herself, although the decision weighed on her: both looked so dreadfully ill, and she feared a heart attack, a collapse of some kind, which she would not be able to endure. She took an anxious look at Freddie, whose high colour had faded to nothing. She longed to get downstairs, to her own bed. She felt sick, tired out; she had vomited the night before, after the policeman had gone, but she knew that for them the ordeal was just beginning.

'Harriet!' cried Freddie, clutching at his heart.

She looked up from the drooping thoughtful position into which she had fallen, on the chair which Miss Wetherby had helped her to. She gazed at him in silence for a few seconds, before reaching for the telephone and dialling the doctor's number. 'My husband is unwell,' she remembered saying, and then blackness came down, and all she could hear, very faintly, was the dog barking again, in alarm, as Miss Wetherby stumbled forward to catch her.

There followed a period of semi-consciousness, prolonged by the doctor's sedatives, so that for several days she was not completely sure where she was. She remembered someone telling her that Immy was dead, although she only intermittently believed this. At her side Freddie sighed and groaned and wept all the tears she was unable to shed. She ardently wished that he would go away; she needed all her concentration for the task in hand, which was to endure, to stay alive, when death was all she craved. She was dry-eyed, dry-mouthed. Miss Wetherby brought cups of tea, which she sometimes drank. When Freddie at last got up she fell asleep immediately. It was only the condition of the crumpled bed, where she had lain for six days, that finally goaded her to some kind of activity. With a deep sigh she pulled off her nightdress and saw that some wasting had taken place, some loss of substance. It will not be long, she thought gratefully. Bathed and dressed, she felt alarmingly light-headed. Carefully she made her way down to the drawing-room; carefully she sat down. There was nothing to be done. She sat all day, waiting for thoughts of Immy to come back to her, to battle their way, as they must do, through the confusion in her mind. Inclining her head she appeared to be listening for that elusive voice. But nothing came through, and only the remnants of her

usual discipline kept her in her chair, that and the knowledge
that Freddie was out somewhere and was perhaps unwell. Left
to herself she would have gone back to bed.

Every day she made her way down to the drawing-room
and sat politely in her chair. People came and went; many she
did not recognize. She was aware of her parents, their
shocked concern, her father's uninhibited weeping. The sight
of him, as always, made her resolute. She got up, went down
into the kitchen, made coffee, found cake and biscuits. Her
father ate gratefully, the tears drying on his face. Her mother,
suddenly old, smoked, eased a throbbing vein in her leg, took
aspirins from her bag. It was only by resuming some sort of
control (but she had at no point felt out of control: that was
the curious thing) that she could persuade them to leave.

Freddie wept from time to time, Miss Wetherby, exhausted, asked if she might visit her sister in Somerset. 'Just for
a week,' she said.

'Of course,' she replied. 'There is nothing more to do
here.'

After a fortnight, with the house silent and empty, she sat
in her chair, and by succumbing to a half-sleep succeeded in
seeing Immy's face as it had been when she was sixteen or
seventeen. 'Ah,' she breathed, nodding in gratitude, as if after
a visitation. It was then that she realized that all she had to do
was wait for this to happen again. She knew that sometimes
Immy might be too far away to come to her, but she was
prepared to wait. She would spend the rest of her life, what
was left of it, waiting, and then she would go to join her.
There was only the matter of Freddie to be settled. It hardly
mattered now which of them went first. She had sent him off
to his club, seeing with pity his bowed shoulders, his shrivel-
led neck. She felt for him, but could not console him. There
was no consolation.

All the time she remained calm, so that he frequently

accused her of being unfeeling. Only once did she falter, when, one silent afternoon, the doorbell rang, and she had answered it: on the doorstep Mary and Pamela, looking awkward, pale, embarrassed, as they had done when they were girls at school, taken to task for some misdemeanour. They stood close together, as if in fear. She saw Pamela's hair, greying now, her reddened complexion, was aware of Mary's scent, their outstretched hands. She leaned her head against the jamb of the door until the tears were under control, then embraced them both.

'And you've come so far,' she said. 'You will never know . . .' But gratitude was too affecting, so she hastened down to the kitchen, and busied herself. They followed slowly.

'I've brought some eggs,' said Pamela. 'From the farm.'

'Here's a cake,' said Mary. 'Don't worry, I didn't make it. Harrods. Give me a knife, Hattie, we'll eat it now. You're terribly thin.'

'How did you know?' she finally asked them.

'We saw it in *The Times*,' said Mary.

'How strange,' she said. 'Freddie must have put it in. I've hardly known where he was these past few days. I made him go out this afternoon. He's not well, you know. He'll be so sorry to have missed you. The girls, he used to call you. And Tessa, of course. It has all been a heartbreak, hasn't it?'

Mary exchanged a look with Pamela. 'We'd better go,' she said. 'We only came to bring you our love. Any time you want a break away from here you're always welcome, you know.'

Pamela took her hand. 'David joins me,' she started awkwardly. 'Oh, hell. You know what I mean. Take care of yourself, Hattie. That's all I can say.'

She saw them off, waving until the car was out of sight. Then she saw Freddie, on his way home, and waved again. At this sign of returning vitality he brightened, but his moods were now unstable and he was soon inert again. That evening she managed to cook Pamela's eggs; they ate them carelessly, vacantly, on a corner of the kitchen table, not talking to each other. Even the chairs on which they sat were askew, as if they were both strangers in a public place. There followed the hour they both dreaded, when the silence of the evening came down. Freddie would have liked to watch the news, but his wife's gaze was so remote that he feared to disturb her. When the doorbell rang she gave a great leap, as if brought forcibly back to life. 'I'll go,' he said. He was anxious to get away from her.

When he came back it was with Lizzie, who strolled in cautiously, her hands in the pockets of her denim jacket. Harriet stared at the sight of one so young, when her other visitors had been her own age, or older. Her resistance she immediately converted into a semblance of her usual good manners.

'Lizzie!' she managed to say. 'How good of you to come. Sit down. I'll make some coffee.' She in her turn was anxious to get away, feeling revulsion for this burdensome visitor. When she went back into the drawing-room she was aware that Freddie had been questioning the girl.

'It wasn't Julian,' she heard Lizzie say, and then she immediately started talking about Lizzie's work, in a high social voice. Freddie looked at her as though she were mad. She did not care. She did not want their interruptions.

Lizzie saw them both in the unshaded light, as separate as if they were political prisoners in the same cell. She saw the birthmark flaring on Harriet's white face, saw the tremor that agitated Freddie's hands. Of the two of them he seemed more anxious for her company. Harriet, she thought, had almost entirely removed herself, although she sat there, apparently attentive, but as if she had some trouble hearing what was being said. Imogen's death was shocking to Lizzie, but not particularly moving. She needed to think about it. This visit was premature; she was not ready for it. There was little she could say, much that she could not.

Harriet kissed her when she stood up to leave. That much she was able to manage. She let Freddie see her out.

'Good of her to come,' he said, as they prepared for bed. He sighed. 'I shan't be sorry to leave.'

'No,' she agreed. 'It hardly matters where we are now.' She knew, as she suspected he did, that they would not come back.

'You'll leave Miss Wetherby here?' he asked her.

'Of course. I must go down to Brighton tomorrow, to say goodbye to my parents.'

It was the last time, she thought, that she would make such a journey. She sat in the tightly shut room with her mother, who was unusually silent. 'I sent Hughie out,' she said. 'This has all been too much for him.'

Harriet realized that her visit was not entirely welcome. I must look a sight, she thought vaguely, aware of the looseness of her dress. 'Don't worry,' she said.

They sat in silence until it was time for her to go. 'Go before he gets back,' said her mother.

They stood up, embraced. Merle was shockingly aware of her daughter's changed appearance.

'Poor child, poor child,' she said.

'But she was a young woman,' protested Harriet. 'A beautiful young woman.'

'No, dear,' said her mother sadly. 'I meant you.'

20

THE WEATHER that year was magnificent. Each morning the scarlet globe of the sun rose calmly above the grey waters of the lake: each evening Harriet strolled down the rue du Château to watch the light fade and the sun finally disappear. Walking back to the Résidence Cécil she wrapped her arms round herself; she now felt permanently cold. Her state of mind reflected a perpetual absence, as if all her emotions had been laid aside, deferred, until she should have the time and the courage to consult and examine them. She dreaded the chill of the evening, dreaded going back to the flat where Freddie awaited her care. She felt pity for him, but knew that the distance between them was now so wide that it could never be bridged. By maintaining a rigid politeness she dealt with his needs. He on the other hand was given to fits of temper, bursts of weeping, as if some essential control were gone. She wondered whether there had been additional damage to his brain, or whether he were merely allowing his growing resentment of her a free rein. He accused her of heartlessness and it was true that she had never shed a tear; rather she had retreated into herself, as if she had become deaf. She prepared their evening meal while Freddie watched television. When the melodramatic tones of the French weather forecaster had subsided she went in to him, helped him up from his chair, then led the way back to the kitchen. They ate in silence. Then he watched more television until he fell asleep, when she would wake him and put him to bed.

Little was said between them. They had become strangers to one another, each retaining some impression of a former part to be played. Of the two of them Harriet was the more proficient, although in reality she was a sleep-walker. Her duties were now automatic, and were automatically carried out: the marketing in the early morning, the preparation of lunch, and then Freddie's afternoon rest, when she sat trying to read, although the book was frequently laid aside. Monsieur Papineau usually joined them for a cup of tea, yet the balance of their friendship had very slightly shifted. Harriet sensed that he was fearful now of her polite reserve, as if the terrible reality of what had happened had estranged him. He felt for her, but could not express his feelings, which were confused. The tragedy had impinged upon his own comfortable nostalgia; his stories of life in London, nights at the opera, Sundays taking his governess, Missy, to tea at the Hyde Park Hotel, fell on deaf ears. His own dead love, that same Missy, had died in her late seventies, when Monsieur Papineau was already a mature man; how could this death be compared with the other? And his love for Missy, which was real enough, had in it something of the love of a boy for an older woman. It was as a boy that Monsieur Papineau had grown old; beneath the polished manners were the innocence and eagerness of childhood, but also its revulsions. Harriet now seemed to him cold. He preferred the company of Freddie, with whom he was able to shake his head over Harriet's tearless state. He even felt a slight thrill of disloyalty when Freddie told him that Harriet had always been an unfeeling woman. 'I'm sure I don't have to spell it out for you,' said Freddie, with heavy emphasis. Monsieur Papineau felt horror and fascination. Freddie's decline put him more within Monsieur Papineau's reach. Together they played the occasional game of chess, while Harriet put on a sweater and walked down by the lake.

And Monsieur Papineau was indispensable when Freddie felt unwell. *'Allons-y, avançons,'* he would call out gaily as he guided the bent figure into the bedroom. This gaiety was well within his capabilities, for he liked the sensation of virtue, was in fact enlivened by it. What he could not tolerate was Harriet's remoteness, which made him uneasy. He had no resource against the encroachment of fear: it made him fretful, uncomfortable. He admired Harriet, felt affection for her, but these days she inspired a melancholy which was unwelcome. On Freddie's better days he took him out in the car. That way he could honestly feel that he was helping them both. At such times he greeted the return of his habitual good conscience with relief, as if it were an old friend. On Sundays he went to church. It was important to him to behave decently. Therefore he devoted himself to Freddie, leaving Harriet to the solitude she now seemed to crave.

Freddie's treatment became intermittent, and then finally ceased, when, by common consent, he was recognized to be too frail to benefit from further visits to the clinic. Instead, one of his nurses, Irène, was seconded to the Résidence Cécil to look after him, a fact for which Harriet was profoundly grateful. Irène was given the spare room, the small white room which had been left untouched by the interior decorator, who had deemed it appropriate, in its unadorned state, for the servant who would occupy it. The presence of this unsmiling, even severe woman relieved Harriet, although she no longer looked for the pleasures of company. Nevertheless, to see Irène's head bent over her sewing by the light of one of the elaborate lamps gave her a timid feeling of normality partially restored.

'You're sure you don't mind being here?' she asked.

Irène snorted. 'It's what I trained for. What do you think I do there, most of the time? Pedicures, for rich women! At least this is serious.' She meant *sérieux*, respectable. She forbore to add that she needed the extra money, merely telling Harriet that her daughter was expecting again. She sighed, then held up the beautiful nightdress she was stitching for Harriet's approval.

'How ill is he?' asked Harriet.

'He is being well looked after,' temporized the nurse. 'Don't worry. He is not suffering.'

'How long?' pursued Harriet.

'Who can say?'

With Freddie gone, she thought, they would all leave, Irène, Monsieur Papineau. She would be left alone, with no further duties. There would be a relief in the cessation of her normal activities, although she was tired when she contemplated the duty of living the rest of her life. It did not occur to her to end it by violent means; she rather thought that she would let it slip away. Yet even this idea was curiously repugnant to her. Her heart still beat strongly, her eyes still saw the sun going down into the lake, her legs still carried her effortlessly on her morning walk. What she craved was not so much death as silence. These days the flat seemed crowded, overpopulated, with Freddie and Monsieur Papineau in the bedroom and herself and Irène in the drawing-room. The smell of Irène's carnation scent bothered her, until she got used to it. And all the encroachments—Irène's sewing basket, Monsieur Papineau's chess board—she regarded with something like bewilderment until she shrugged her shoulders and accepted them. But she was not at home. That was her principal feeling. She was not at home anywhere. She might have come to terms with her present surroundings if she had been left alone, but there were three strangers to contend with, for Freddie was now more comfortable with Irène and Monsieur

Papineau than he was with her. She did not actively imagine how life would be when he died, did not in fact believe that he would die, for he cheered up in company, and seemed relatively comfortable. Only with Harriet was he largely wordless. At night they settled down for sleep in the big bed, earlier and earlier. Sometimes his hand felt for her breast, then fell away. 'No good, no good,' he would groan, and shed a tear. She waited, in silence, until he fell asleep. These times were the most difficult, for try as she might she could think of nothing to say to him.

He got better, was livelier, even went out in the car one day with Monsieur Papineau, although he had to be helped up the stairs when he returned. He had a bad night after that, and on the following morning half fell as she took him through to the kitchen for breakfast. She noticed that he ate carelessly, could not locate his plate, let his coffee drip down his chin. 'Freddie,' she warned. 'Wipe your mouth.' In reply he put his head down on the table and began to sob. 'Irène, Irène,' she cried. The nurse came running in, took one look at Freddie's face, with the smear of butter on the forehead, and said, 'Ah.' Together they lifted him from his chair, and took him back to the bedroom. He said nothing while they put him to bed, eventually lay back on the pillows, a final tear drying on his cheek. They sat with him all day. At five o'clock Monsieur Papineau put his head round the door, saw them at the bedside, and exchanged nods with the nurse. Harriet was aware of his frightened face slowly disappearing, of the door slowly shutting. An hour later Freddie fell asleep, peacefully, it seemed. Harriet and Irène withdrew to the kitchen, ate swiftly, smoked a cigarette.

'What will happen now?' asked Harriet.

'*Ma pauvre petite dame,* only one thing can happen.'

'Then I must be with him,' she said.

'Freddie,' she said, into his sleeping ear. 'Forgive me. Forgive me for not loving you, as a wife should love a husband. Forgive me for disappointing you, for not coming up to expectations. You are a good man; the faults were all mine.'

She took his hand. 'Freddie, can you hear me? Don't be afraid. I will never leave you. I never left you, did I? We managed, somehow. But then it all changed, didn't it? After that there was nothing more to say. How could we even pretend that we were the same people? If I have seemed unsympathetic it was not because I didn't feel for you; it was because I had run out of emotional disguises. The truth of the matter is that we gave up in different ways. You managed to grieve for her, while I have not yet started. I perceive every-thing as a distraction from the main business of my life now, which is trying to recapture Imogen. Even your illness is a distraction, because when I am attending to you I am trying to see her face, which is puzzlingly out of reach. I know that it will come back to me one day, but in the meantime I am hemmed in by circumstance. I need a great absence. I even need your absence, although my life will be strange without you. What shall I do when you are no longer there? And yet I know that I will manage, just as I know that you will be glad to shed this body which torments you. Perhaps death is not the punishment I always thought it must be. Simply one must greet it when it comes, so that there is no time for fear. I can't join you yet. But I shall stay with you until then.'

So many years, she thought. Turning to him in the bed, she said again, 'Don't be afraid.'

They thought he must have died in the night, or in the very early morning. They thought that Harriet must have been asleep when it happened. When she awoke it was to a great silence. She looked at him, saw that he was colourless, felt his cheek. For a few minutes she lay there beside him. Then she got up, still anxious not to disturb him, bathed and dressed. In the kitchen she put water on to boil, as she always had done. When the coffee was made she took a cup in to the nurse, and announced that Freddie was dead. The sun was rising on to another perfect day. She noted this while Irène was making the necessary telephone calls. Then, as she was no longer needed, she walked out and went down to the lake. She sat there, in the beneficent heat, until she judged that she might be needed again. When she rose from her seat her only thought was that now at last she could be alone with Imogen.

Monsieur Papineau wept. He wept throughout the funeral, then, with a great sigh, cheered up again. When Harriet clasped his hands and kissed him in gratitude for being so good a friend he assured her that he would not abandon her. She in her turn assured him that she was all right, that he must not feel that he had to keep her company: he did not see that she craved solitude. Together with the nurse she cleared the bedroom, arranged for Freddie's things to go to the Red Cross. Then she helped Irène to pack up, stripped Irène's bed, and remade it with pristine white sheets. 'You could have a guest,' said Irène. 'You could have someone to stay.' But she knew no one, although she did not say so.

Shortly the weather broke, and rain fell steadily. For days she stayed in the flat, in a state of latency. She thought that she ought to go back to London, knew that she should, but was somehow incapable of summoning the energy to buy her ticket. Gradually the light went, and the days shortened. The lake was now grey from morning to night, and a chill wind blew. In the spring, she thought vaguely. I shall go in the spring. Go home, she corrected herself. But it was no longer home to her.

As the winter closed in she forced herself to go out, to buy food, although she felt no desire to eat. Sometimes Monsieur Papineau came up and had tea with her, partially reassured by her calm demeanour. When the days lightened again it was he who wondered aloud when she would go home, saw her reluctance, did not insist. She was grateful to him for his tact. Throughout the following summer he took her out for walks; sometimes they lunched together. 'Your parents?' he questioned. 'I telephone them every week,' she answered. 'They seem to be all right. But I should see to Miss Wetherby. She is alone too now.' In the end, on a fine September day, it was he who went with her to the travel agent, took her to the station, saw her on to the train. At the airport in Geneva she was surprised to see so many people. She had seen hardly anyone for nearly a year.

England seemed strange, a foreign country. As always, when coming back, the house confused her. When she put her unfamiliar key into the unfamiliar lock the dog started to bark, and she almost turned round and left again. Miss Wetherby's anxious face, appearing at the top of her stairs, forced her to behave normally.

'Mrs Lytton! But I didn't know you were coming! I would have got some food in!'

'Don't worry,' she said. 'I can go out again later.'

'Let me make you a cup of tea, at least.'

'Yes, I should like a cup of tea. I'll come down to you, shall I? I must just take a look upstairs.'

In the drawing-room Miss Wetherby had put dust sheets over the sofa and chairs. Otherwise all was in order. Harriet climbed the stairs to Immy's flat, knowing that this was why she had really come, but, opening the door, was defeated by the silence of the place. She thought she could smell scent, but how was this possible, after two years? Or was it three? She tried hard to remember, but encountered a blank in her mind. It must be three years. The scent came from a cake of lavender soap in the bathroom. She opened the windows, let the evening breeze blow through, then shut them again and went down to Miss Wetherby.

Tea restored her, but now she felt frightened, as if opening

Immy's door had opened doors which she had so far succeeded in keeping closed.

'There is no cake,' fretted Miss Wetherby. 'If I had known
you were coming . . . Perhaps a little toast?'

She smiled. 'My father always used to make me toast for
tea,' she said.

Miss Wetherby too was frightened. 'I suppose you'll be
thinking of selling the house?' she said. 'Unless you decide to
come back.' All this time she had lived in fear that Harriet
would put the house on the market, and then where would
she go? She paid no rent, subsisted on various small pensions,
could not afford to buy anything. A residential home, she
thought, if I could find one. But would a home take the dog?
There was her sister, in Somerset, but her sister lived in a tiny
cottage, and on her last visit they had both been uncomfortable.

Harriet came back to earth with a jolt. 'Oh, no,' she said.
'I shan't sell the house. This is your home. It is yours for as
long as you want it.'

Miss Wetherby's face cleared. 'I'll take care of everything
here,' she said. 'I suppose you'll come back?'

'No,' she replied. 'I don't think I'll come back.'

They sat in silence. Finally Miss Wetherby reached out a
hand, which Harriet took. 'You were so good to Imogen,'
said Harriet, for now the name had been spoken.

'I go up there every day. Just to dust, and keep everything
fresh.'

'Yes. Please do that. I shall leave again tomorrow. I don't
think I can stay here now.'

She slept fitfully, got up early, said goodbye to Miss Wetherby, and was gone. She hardly noticed the return journey.
She was back in the Résidence Cécil just after lunch, which,
as usual, she did not miss. The flat was warm, silent. Again she
thought she caught the ghost of a scent, and then remembered

that Irène had looked in to see her just before she left. She telephoned Monsieur Papineau, to let him know that she was back. Then she went out again, to get in some provisions, called in at the bookshop and bought more books, for how else was she to get through the coming months if not by reading? Immy's ghost had receded from her: she could no longer bring her to mind. This tormented her. The long loving communion she had promised herself had not taken place. This was now her grief, as if her original grief had become even more grievous. Sometimes she thought she caught a glimpse of Immy's face, and at such times she started up with a shock of delight. But these were fragments, and Immy's face at such times seemed stern, closed. 'My poor darling,' she said at such times, and heard herself saying the words out loud. The sound of her own voice startled her. This way madness lay.

Other thoughts worried her. I was not nice to Lizzie, she thought. When she came round, on that terrible evening, I was not nice to her. I made social noises, and then escaped to the kitchen. It was not her fault that I found her presence too much to bear. She did her best: I'm sure she always did her best. She was no match for Imogen, of course. Yet they kept in touch, even though Lizzie may have felt a little jealous. She was always such an odd girl, nothing like her parents. Tessa, that other ghost, crept back into her mind. I shall ask her to stay, she thought with surprise. I shall ask Lizzie to stay. It will be easy not to talk about Imogen, or rather it will not be easy, but I shall manage it. I shall warn her not to mention Imogen. For now she could not bear to share Imogen with anyone else. Imogen was too elusive, must be protected until she chose to manifest herself, as one day she surely must.

Immediately, strangely comforted by the thought of something definite to do, she sat down and wrote to Lizzie. She wrote kindly, calmly, feeling stronger in herself now that she had someone young to think about again. Someone young! And she had lived so long among the elderly, her parents, her husband, Miss Wetherby, and now Monsieur Papineau. The sight of an unmarked face was so precious to her; when she saw a child she longed to reach out and touch it. Of course, Lizzie was now a stranger, but she had always felt a sympathy for the girl, looked on with a mixture of admiration and pity as Lizzie made her uncomfortable way in the world. Nothing had been easy for Lizzie, yet she had survived. And it was not kind to take no further interest. She would hate Lizzie to think her unkind, to be left with that impression of haste and withdrawal that she must have taken away with her. In her letter she included a simple warning that Imogen was not to be discussed. It would be exploiting Lizzie to ask her here for purposes of mutual reminiscence. And Lizzie had always had such difficulty expressing herself that it would be unfair to require her to talk when she so clearly preferred not to. A strange girl. She would leave her entirely free, let her come and go as she pleased. She might be lonely: Harriet knew nothing of her friends but imagined that Lizzie led a solitary life. She liked to walk, Harriet remembered. Well, there were beautiful walks to be had. She would cook meals again, invite Monsieur Papineau to dinner. The evenings might be dull for her, but she was a great reader. That Harriet remembered quite clearly. And now that she herself read so much they would have something in common, something to discuss.

She telephoned Monsieur Papineau and invited him for an aperitif. Already she felt more purposeful. 'Joseph,' she said. 'I am having a young friend to stay. You must help me to entertain her.' For she did not doubt that Lizzie would come. They planned a series of events, anxious that the visitor should not be bored. That evening, poring over maps and restaurant guides, they were animated. He noted with relief that she had colour in her cheeks. When he stood up to go

she gave him her letter to post. Then she took up her position
at the window. Oh, Imogen, she thought, come back to me.

But Imogen did not come back. Instead images of closure
came and went. When she caught sight of Imogen's face it
was as if the girl had a finger to her lips, constraining her to
silence, constraining them both to silence. Something was
missing, some knowledge. In the latter part of her life Imogen
had been unknowable: there were secrets which had never
been told. Freddie, she knew, had been suspicious, but she
had indignantly refuted his suspicions, which she had casti-
gated as unworthy. Unless she lived in perfect trust how could
she live at all? Yet she was surprised to note that she was now
impatient for Lizzie's arrival. The spare room was ready. She
made a list of things to buy, noticed at last that she was eating
very little, vowed that this would now change. I could telephone her this evening, she thought. But no, that would be
precipitate. I must be patient and let her make up her own
mind. She always hated to be hurried.

In the end it was Lizzie who telephoned. Solitary, as Harriet suspected, she had had to make hard decisions about
holidays, was always non-committal when they were discussed in the office. She had announced, since it seemed to
her to be expected, that she was going walking in the mountains, as she half supposed she then must do. Harriet's letter
relieved her, since it meant that she need not tell a lie. She still
found this a problem, was so anxious not to fall into error that
she usually kept her mouth shut. At meetings, when asked if
she agreed to something the others had decided, she usually
cleared her throat and said 'No'. 'Thank *you*, Lizzie,' said the
head of her department, amid general laughter. 'Now we
know where we stand. All right, everyone, as we decided.
Begging Lizzie's pardon, of course.' The ensuing scraping of
chairs, as everyone stood up to go, usually brought on the
discussion of holidays. Now at least she would have some-

thing to tell them. She was aware that they thought her odd, a poor mixer. Extremely good at what she did: that was the consensus. They liked her, even liked her intransigence. Some found her attractive, with her straight light-coloured hair and her wide impassive eyes, but no one asked her out for more than a drink. This did not worry her. She had a boyfriend, a man she had met at Oxford, who had stayed on to do his D.Phil. He had hopes of a fellowship. They saw each other rarely, but wrote immensely long letters. This was how she usually spent her evenings. But he was spending the long vacation in America: another reason to accept Harriet Lytton's invitation. On the telephone she asked if she might come the following week. Harriet, surprised, said, 'Of course, dear, come as soon as you can. I will express your ticket to you.' 'There's no need,' said Lizzie firmly. 'I've got plenty of money.' Harriet, with a sigh, reminded herself to expect this. So unlike Imogen, she thought. Yet at the same time came another thought: Lizzie is incorruptible.

Unwelcome, this, as if it cast a different light on Imogen. She closed her mind to it, and went to bed.

Lizzie, emerging from the airport at Geneva, thought that Harriet must have married again, for she was in the company of a small eager-looking man in a curious velvet beret. At the same moment Harriet saw her, a thin slight figure, wearing what looked like, but could not be, the same denim jacket and jeans, a nylon holdall slung over one shoulder. 'But she is a little girl!' exclaimed Monsieur Papineau. 'No, she is the same age as my daughter,' said Harriet absent-mindedly. How curious, she thought. I said that without a qualm. But I must be careful not to burden Lizzie with comparisons. 'Here you are, dear,' she said cheerfully. Monsieur Papineau was surprised at the change in her voice, which had become artificial, he thought, as he relieved Lizzie of her holdall and led the way to the car. Harriet felt indifference creeping over her, as

if the impulse behind her original invitation had died, leaving
behind only the prospect of effort and weariness. She felt her
age, of which she had previously been hardly aware, wanted
only silence and her bed. Yet here was Lizzie, to be entertained for an entire fortnight, and she doubted whether she
had the energy to sustain her presence for another minute.
Everything goes, she thought, tolerance, patience, even
emotivity. I am fond of her, wanted her to come, and now
I wish she had stayed at home, as I half expected her to. How
on earth are we to keep her amused? But Lizzie was looking
with interest and a mild degree of pleasure at the passing
landscape. 'I thought we'd eat at home this evening,' said
Harriet. 'And then we'll take you out and about. I expect you
are out a lot at home?'

'Oh, no,' said Lizzie. 'Anyway, I like to go to bed early.
I've always liked going to bed.'

'How interesting,' said Harriet. 'So have I. And you'll find
the air here will make you sleepy.'

That much agreed on, with some relief on both sides, they
settled down to tolerate each other's company.

Cautiously, in the days that followed, they admitted that
things were not too bad, were even going rather well. Lizzie
departed each morning with a packed lunch, and made her
way by train to Les Pléïades, so that she could at least go home
and report that she had walked in hills, if not in mountains.
This much inaccuracy she could allow herself, but no more.
She arrived back at around teatime, to find Harriet in the
kitchen, consulting cookery books.

'What would you like to eat?' was the usual enquiry, to
which she inevitably replied, 'I usually have some cheese and
an apple.'

'So do I. But we shall have to do better than this tomorrow.
Joseph is threatening to make his crêpes Suzette.'

The evenings were quite companionable. They watched

the news, viewing the weather forecast as if it were a dramatic performance they could not afford to miss. After this they settled down with their books.

'Such a strange novel I'm reading,' Harriet said. 'Stendhal. I don't know if I like it.'

'An acquired taste,' agreed Lizzie, who had acquired it, and was a lifelong convert.

'So glad you've kept up your French.'

'Well, the grandparents,' Lizzie replied.

They conversed in brief telegraphic sentences, as if they had been together for ever.

So far each had been successful in avoiding Imogen's name. It was a relief to both of them that this had been possible. One night, however, Harriet had been woken by a nightmare, in which Imogen had played a prominent part. She struggled to remember it, but on waking felt only shock and disquiet. She thought that the dream had taken place in Wellington Square, that it was evening, that she had been sitting with Freddie in the drawing-room, that Imogen had come in white-faced, as if ill. 'Don't touch me!' she had said in the dream, and had disappeared. So insistent was this image that she thought it might even be a memory, that all this had really happened. Yet casting her mind back she encountered only a closed door, the closed door of Immy's bedroom. All that day she was troubled, vaguely sick. She was grateful for Lizzie's absence, and, when she returned, for her silence. She thought the girl looked stern again, or was this her imagination?

'Are you all right, dear?' she asked.

'Yes, thank you.' Nothing more was said that evening.

They took her out to lunch, to dinner, anxious for her to enjoy her holiday. They went to Lausanne, to Montreux, to Evian. Lizzie was moderately pleased by all this, cautiously allowed that she was enjoying herself. She had turned a delicate pink, even filled out a little. When they looked at her they nodded to each other with satisfaction. They could not bear the prospect of her leaving. Monsieur Papineau was delighted with her. Yet Harriet was aware of something that remained to be done.

On Lizzie's last evening she summoned her courage, and said, 'I know I can trust you, Lizzie. You were always such a fine character. I want you to tell me the truth. Was everything . . . Was Immy happy, do you think?'

Lizzie lost something of her colour.

'Oh, I don't want to upset you, dear. I know I said we wouldn't talk of this. Only she haunts me so, what I can see of her. She never confided in me. And as you were such a good friend . . . Those weekends she spent with you, when you went up to Oxford. I never questioned her, of course, but she spent such a lot of time with you, I wondered . . . "I'll be at Lizzie's", she'd say, if Freddie asked her where she was going. Why, she even came back with one of your cardigans, do you remember?'

Lizzie, willing her face to impassivity, as she had so far managed to do, remembered Imogen's only visit to her, in Judd Street, when she was working at the bookshop, remembered the chattering teeth, the odour of blood, remembered the cardigan she had draped round Imogen's shoulders, remembered, with eternal shame, running to the door in terror. So much blood, which she had cleaned, working half the night. She had vowed never to see Imogen again, and had never done so, had hoped to bury the scene for ever. And now this.

'I know you'll tell me the truth,' said Harriet, the tears rising. 'You always told the truth. Was she happy? Was it a happy friendship? Did you love her?' she asked, breaking down at last.

'Of course,' replied Lizzie, tears of outrage in her own eyes.

But it was herself she despised, not for the lie, but for the difficulty it caused her.

'So silly of me,' wept Harriet. 'But I know how you must miss her.'

'Of course,' said Lizzie.

'Go to bed, dear. I've upset you. I'm so sorry.'

'That's all right,' said Lizzie, clearing her throat.

'I'll bring you a hot drink. Oh, I'm so glad we've had this talk.'

When she went in later to Lizzie's room, with a glass of warm milk and honey, she took her book in with her. She was calm now. 'One more thing,' she said. 'Your French is better than mine. Tell me how you would translate this. It is important to me.'

She opened her book, and read.

' "*Mais Madame la Duchesse, la mort est un mot presque vide de sens pour la plupart des hommes. Ce n'est qu'un instant, et en général on ne le sent pas. On souffre, on est étonné des sensations étranges qui surviennent, et tout à coup on ne souffre plus, l'instant est passé, on est mort . . .*" '

'Death is a meaningless word for most people,' Lizzie translated. 'It is only a moment, and generally one does not feel it. One suffers, one is surprised by the strange sensations that arrive, and all of a sudden, the moment passes, one is dead.'

' "*Ah! Monsieur,*" ' Harriet went on. ' "*C'est le moment de la mort dont je ne puis supporter l'idée.*" '

'It is the moment of death that I dread.'

She remembered the passage. It was one of her favourites.

' "*Mais, Madame,*" ' Harriet went on, with rising conviction. ' "*Ce moment est occupé par une douleur quelquefois bien peu vive. On la sent encore, et par conséquent, l'on vit, on n'est pas mort, on n'est encore que dangereusement malade. Tout à coup, on ne sent plus rien, on est mort. Donc, la mort n'est rien. C'est une porte ouverte ou fermée, if faut qu'elle soit l'un ou l'autre, elle ne peut pas être une troisième chose.*" '

'But Madame,' said Lizzie. 'That moment is taken up with a little pain. One still feels it, and therefore one is alive, one is not dead, only mortally ill. Suddenly one feels nothing, one is dead. Therefore death is nothing. It is a door which is either open or closed, it must be one or the other. There is no third way,' she finished.

Harriet closed the book. 'Thank you, dear. Thank you. No third way,' she repeated, and smiled.

They saw Lizzie off the following day. 'Goodbye,' they said. 'Goodbye. You'll come back?' they enquired ardently.

'Of course,' she said, for a third time. This time it was not a lie. 'My father,' she said. 'I telephoned him to say I was coming. He said to send you his love.'

Jack Peckham. Another lifetime.

That evening Harriet, standing at the window, saw the sun descend majestically into the lake. Turning, she surveyed the empty room. My life, she thought, an empty room. But she felt no pain, felt in fact the cautious onset of some kind of release. Vividly, she caught sight of Immy's face. She drew in a deep breath, laughed. There it was again, Immy's face as it had always been. She laughed again, at the image of Immy's laughing face. Sinking on to the sofa she let the tears rain down. Never to lack for company again. All will be as before, she thought, as she wept in gratitude. When my little girl was young.